Where the dark fish swim

Mark Bishop

ISBN-13: 978-1540878267

ISBN-10: 1540878260

DEDICATION

For my inspiration and my support – my wife, my son, my dad and my mum…

…but that is an entirely different story.

Dear Huck,

Before we get into all of the detail, before we come to the what and the when and, most importantly and probably most terribly of all, the why, I need to start with the simple truth.

I'm sorry and I love you.

This is not going to be easy. I don't know how much of this you will already know when you come to read it, or how much you will remember of the short time we had together. Too short in all truth. But of all the things I am going to say, out of all the noise and the darkness and the pure shit I'm going to bring into your life, out of all our wonderful family secrets, you deserve to know that at least there is something good and something right in this whole mess. And that thing is you, Huck. You're all that really matters in all of this.

I'm sorry and I love you, Huck. Please don't forget it.

Other than that I didn't really know where to start. I mean, what do you say to someone when, by the time you come to read this Huck, we won't have spoken or seen each other for ten years or more? What do you say to someone you barely even knew in the first place and yet, someone you are so much a part of?

Your mum said that I should start simple. That I should start by telling you about me and something about my life and how I got where we are right now. She said if I just start with what I know and let it all out then eventually I'll find it all just pours out of me. Like an avalanche, she said. Maybe that's what I'm worried about, worried I'll start an avalanche and I won't be able to stop it. I'm not so sure that's such a good idea. Not so sure this is going to be that easy to write and not so sure that starting off by telling you all about me is going to make you want to hear the rest of what I need to say.

So why don't I start by telling you what started off this little trip we're on? Why it is that, while I'm writing this, you and I are sat in the back of a second hand campervan I bought just two weeks ago. A VW Campervan that is exactly the same make, model and colour as the one me my mum and my father used to go on holiday in when I was a child. Explain why your mother is driving and why she has a look on her face that is half joy and half fear. Why we are together for the first time in our lives and why it will be the last time we are together. Why I've done all the things I've had to do over the last week and why I'm going to do what I need to do in the next few days.

And the start of all of this was the last time I saw my best friend, Jack Lawrence. Of course it was Jack. Who else could have started something like this?

Just say his name out loud to yourself for a second, Huck.

Jack Lawrence.

It sounds like a strong name doesn't it? Like something out of a great movie. Jack Lawrence – Action Hero. Jack Lawrence – International Super Spy. Jack Lawrence – Ladies Man. Jesus. A far more interesting name than mine ever was. Jack Lawrence versus Michael Brighton. Christ, I never stood a chance. It's a strong name isn't it? Strong and yet, there was something about it that drew you to him at the same time. Jack Lawrence – The Nice Guy Who Always Finished First. Jack Lawrence – The True Friend. I was always envious of that name. So much more exciting than my own. I wonder if it made him a more interesting person than me? I wonder if just a name could have that kind of an impact? Do you like your name, Huck, I wonder? When your mother and I were first together she said she always wanted a boy and wanted to call him Huckleberry. I wasn't sure. It sounded like a dog's name if I'm honest but it definitely grew on me the more times I heard her say it. And she was always going to get her way. I like it now and like Huck more than Huckleberry. She told me that when she was a girl her mum had read her Tom Sawyer and she had begged her mum to start reading it all over again as soon as she finished because she had fallen in love with Huckleberry Finn. She wanted to name you after him. She said it reminded her of how fun and innocent and exciting life can be, especially when you're a kid. I wanted you to have an interesting name, just like Jack did and I guess that worked. Huck has a certain something about it doesn't it? Now I see you I am sure she was right about your name, as she was about so many things. Has she read those books to you? You should get her to read them to you if she hasn't. I see a lot of that wonderful boy in you already, even though I hardly know you.

Anyway, I'm babbling. My childhood was, well, was mixed to say the least. I grew up as the only child to a mother who loved me and a father who didn't want me, but we'll come to that later. Being an only child, when I was home, I spent a lot of time on my own, which in some ways was good but mostly wasn't. It was good to be alone away from my father. I didn't have that many friends growing up but I was lucky in the one that I did have. Luckier than most. Lucky that I had my one, only and best friend in the whole world, which was Jack. Just thinking about him puts a giant grin on my face. He lights me up in a way that, now, only compares to the way your mother does and the way my mother used to. The way you do too, Huck. When I think about him I can already feel the mood in my mind shifting, can feel the darkness lifting and the muscles in my cheeks aching with a smile. The truth is though Jack didn't really need a name to define who he was – he was a winner in everything he ever did. I mean that literally. He never did anything wrong. Never lost a single thing he tried to win.

The last time I saw Jack was about two months ago. I was living in London then, with Natalie, and I was living a life that I hadn't expected. Doing things I should never have been doing. But we'll come to that shortly, Huck. He came to see me because I needed to see him and because I had asked him to. I needed to see a friendly face and, let's be honest, I've never had many of them to call on. Even less at that point in my life.

He met me at a Costa Coffee shop just a little away from Euston Station. I had a plain black coffee and he had nothing. I was waiting for someone else to come and meet me so I could get on with my work and I had some time to kill. I didn't think he would come, but he did. It was a long way for him to come and we hadn't seen each other for a long time. For years in fact. I had honestly expected him to say no but of course he didn't. Not Jack.

"It's been a long time," he said, smiling at me across the table.

"I know," I said, "but I needed you."

"I thought you'd forgotten about me," Jack said without a hint of doubt in his smile. He knew it wasn't true. How would I ever have forgotten about Jack? I shook my head and he nodded back at me.

"So why now?" he carried on, but he already knew the answer to that too. Still, I had to show him. I pulled a piece of paper out of my pocket, flattened it out and put it on the table between us. I didn't look up at him then, just stared at a spot on the table just to the side of the piece of paper. I didn't want to focus on it. He stood up and leaned over the table, reading the piece of paper upside down but without touching it.

"Oh," he said, sitting back down and laughing a little, "is that all?"

Is that all? I thought. Jesus.

"Well", he said, the smile back on his face, "what are you going to do?"

"I don't know," I said. And I didn't, I honestly didn't. I just kept staring at that piece of paper and thinking about them.

"Well, if you want my advice, and I know that you do, I suggest you quit all this," he said, waving his arms around the coffee shop, "forget what's on that piece of paper and just come home instead." The smile was gone then. He was just staring at me across the table.

"Hey Buddy," a voice said from behind me. I turned around and saw a guy, my guy, stood near the counter of Costa with a large sports bag in his hand. "I brought back your stuff," he said.

I stood up from my table and walked over to where he was stood. We talked briefly and he gave me the bag, but when I turned back to the table we had been sitting at Jack was already gone. Just the sheet of paper was sat there on the table waiting for me.

And that's how it started. That's how I finally got started on this whole crazy thing.

And now your mum has just asked me if we're ready to start on this leg of our journey. Ready as I'll ever be I guess and so I nodded. She gave me the thumbs up and that beaming smile I'm sure you love. I'm sure you love it already, how could you not? She does look tired though, your mother, and yet she still somehow manages to look as radiant as she always has. Full of life and yet completely spent of it. She has turned back around now and started the engine. The van rattled nervously before it coughed and spluttered and then suddenly roared into life. I saw your mother's shoulders relax when she realised it was going to work and we are on our way.

And that means I need to be on my way writing this otherwise I'm just going to piss about and do nothing and then I'll have wasted my chance.

I've asked your mother to type this up when she gets home but to keep the original copy. I apologise in advance for my language Huck, I'm sure a few bad words will slip in every now and again. Christ, I'm sure they already have. I'm also sure it won't be anything you haven't heard before. If you're anything like me by the time you read this you'll have heard them all. And if I spend time choosing my words I'll never get anything written down. My handwriting isn't great either – it never really has been and it's worse now – but I want you to be able to see how I wrote so you have something genuinely from me, if that makes sense? They say you can tell a lot about someone from their handwriting. I don't know if that's true. A mess is what I guess you would take from mine. Still, it's something from me to you. You could keep the Campervan but I guess it won't be of much use by the time you are old enough to drive it. It's barely much use now. And the strain I will have put on it over the last couple of weeks driving up and down the country probably hasn't helped. I imagine this will be its last trip. It's not mine anyway is it? Not really. Better that your mum sell it and use the money for something honest and useful. A holiday maybe.

I've also asked your mother not to change anything I've written and I've promised to write everything as it comes into my head and not to try and second guess anything I'm writing. I might ramble a little, but to understand everything you need to know as much of it as I can tell you. And nothing is ever straight forward I'm afraid. Your mum wants to give it to you on your fourteenth birthday but I think that might be a little young. She will know you better though and I trust her. She thinks you'll be old enough to understand by then and at the same time not too old as to have formed a view of me that can't be reversed, or at least altered slightly. How could you not form a view of the man who walked out before you were born. Jesus.

Anyway, Huck, although I've said a little I haven't really explained where we are, you, your mum and I, or why the three of us are travelling together to the north coast of Scotland. It'll take a while to get there, especially to the bit where you and your mother come into it but it's important you know the whole thing.

Up until about two weeks ago I was living in Ealing in West London. I never expected to end up in London at all. I certainly never had any great desire to be there, not when I was young and certainly not when I left you and your mother. How I came to be in London isn't a particularly exciting story – I just kind of drifted here really. When I left your mother I moved further south, not very far but far enough that I wouldn't see anyone who knew either of us. I went looking for work which isn't easy when you're a young, University drop out with no real skill, no reference and no place to call home. I ended up taking pretty much the first job I could find, which was day work on a farm – I got paid by the hour but I got to live and eat on the farm. The pay wasn't exactly great but it was cash in hand, which was OK with me. However, by the time I paid for food and a bed I didn't have much left. Certainly not enough to be sending you money home, Huck. But it was work and I needed something to live off.

I didn't last long there though. My boss and I had a disagreement, nothing much, but it was enough and I couldn't stay there anymore. He was a drunk and that didn't sit well with me. I didn't say anything, I just left one night and didn't go back. I got a lift further south and found something similar on another farm but that didn't end well either and so I moved on again. And on, and on. Every job I had either ended up with me leaving because I didn't fit in or because the work eventually ran out or because they found someone who would do it better than me and I became surplus to requirements. I didn't care. It was enough to get by on and even though the work was hard and the pay awful, it took my mind off leaving and what I had done. Eventually I was close enough to London and needed to find something more permanent, and something so that maybe I could send some money back to you and your mum. So I thought I'd try it. I didn't expect to end up finding a job in the first hour I was there. Luck I guess. Or not.

I arrived in London on a miserable autumn morning – cold and wet and windy. I'd never been to London before and I didn't really know what to expect. You hear things about how noisy it is and how unfriendly everyone there is and you get a picture in your mind, you know? An idea of what it will be like. But it wasn't much like that. It seemed much like anywhere else to me, just a lot bigger and dirtier and everyone in a rush to get somewhere. It was about seven in the morning when I arrived, still slightly dark. I expected it to be warm in the city, I don't know why. I grabbed my bag out of the bus and asked the driver if he knew somewhere I could look for a job. He told me there was a job center close by but that it wouldn't open for a couple of hours. I thanked him and made my way to the nearest warm place that was already open, a Starbucks. I was tired as I hadn't slept and I wanted to sit down and just rest somewhere a little more comfortable than the bus had been. And I wanted coffee, so the Starbucks would have been about perfect.

Typically though, as I would later find out was pretty common for a London coffee house, it was already busy. Commuters, early risers and shift workers filled up the place and there were no empty seats left. I waited patiently in line for my coffee and stood awkwardly for a while, not quite quick enough to find myself a seat. I stood and looked outside, watching the rain streaming down the window, dark and cold. And then in the corner of my eye I saw a darker shadow moving across the window. I turned my head to look at it but as I did it moved away. One of *them*.

I shook my head and it was gone.

I looked around and managed to find a single lonely and, crucially, empty chair opposite a large black woman who sat engrossed in a newspaper. I moved over to it and she didn't even look at me when I gestured to sit down, which I took to mean the seat was free. I muttered something to her but she didn't take any notice so I sat down. However, no sooner had I got settled when a thirty-something in a pinstripe suit marched over to me.

"Excuse me mate but I was sitting there," has said.

He held his coffee in one hand and a leather bag in the other. He had a copy of the Financial Times stuffed under his coffee arm and was gently tapping his brown leather shoe on the floor, waiting for me to move for him.

"Oh I… I'm sorry," I mumbled and started to get up. I knew he hadn't been sitting there before me. I'd watched him walk in the door after me. I'd noticed him specifically because of the way he was dressed and wondered what kind of job warranted dressing that well on such a miserable day. Banker, I had guessed. Or maybe the Financial Times was just a part of the look. Either way he looked exactly the way I would imagine a banker from the eighties would have, right down to the slicked back hair. Maybe that's what bankers still look like these days, I don't know.

"Yeah, I just went to get a copy of the paper, so if you don't mind," he said, putting his bag down ready to take his rightful place and wafting the paper toward me as some sort of sign of proof. He knew he was lying but clearly he didn't care. He was obviously someone used to getting what he wanted. I decided it would be easier just to move and let him have the seat, and I had started to get up until a voice stopped me half way up and left me perched there.

"Go away," it said, not loud but forcefully. It took me a while to realise where it was coming from until I realised it was being spoken from behind the newspaper opposite me.

"I'm just going," I said.

"Not you," said the newspaper, "Him." She didn't make any indication as to who she was speaking to. No movement of the newspaper, no pointing at who she really meant, but both the Banker and I knew exactly who she was referring to.

"Look love," said the Banker, "I'm not sure this is really anything to do with you is it? So if you could just go back to your paper."

The newspaper moved down slowly and purposefully and I caught a glimpse of the woman's face for the first time. She was black, as I said, and maybe in her mid-forties, although it was hard to tell. Her skin was smooth and it shined, which made her look younger and her eyes were so bright. She wore big, gold hooped earrings, which stood out as the only colour she wore. Everything else was black and her hair was shaved close to her head. And she was big, but not out of shape. She was big in a solid way. Big in a way that made you think she looked after herself. Big in exactly the way I never was. And she was powerful. But despite how strong she looked her face remained emotionless. She never once looked at me and yet something in the way she looked told me she was on my side, told me that she was going to help me. It also told me she despised the Banker and wasn't about to put up with any of his attitude, no matter how important he thought he was. And all this time, all the while I knew she was looking out for me, she still terrified me. It was clear whose side you wanted her on in a fight. As she started to talk again she turned her face to look at me, but again it wasn't me she was talking to.

"Go away," she repeated. "You haven't been sat here. The last person sat opposite me left three minutes ago and was a Spanish woman breastfeeding her beautiful new born baby boy. Now I may be mistaken, love, but are you a Spanish woman breastfeeding her son? Because your titties don't look big enough for a meal to me."

It wasn't until the word titties that she looked at him, but even then it was an expressionless face. There was nothing aggressive about the way she asked this. It was a genuine question, as if he might well confirm indeed he was a Spanish mother and it would be her mistake after all. All the while I remained half standing, half sitting and not knowing what to do with myself. The Banker didn't answer, even though she gave him plenty of time. He just stood there and shuffled from foot to foot. If I hadn't been so shocked I would have fallen over.

"Thought not," she added. "Now fuck off."

All of this, even the final insult, was said without her voice raising even once. Without any hint of emotion. Nobody around us was even aware a confrontation had taken place. And yet everything about it was threatening. The Banker muttered something under his breath, something that could easily have been either an apology or an insult, I didn't hear it, and he left. Despite all the things I would later come to think about this woman, she certainly had a way of making people understand her point of view.

"Thank you," I muttered and tried to look around the Starbucks for something to distract me or for somewhere else to move to, but she hadn't finished with me yet.

"You need to stand up for yourself more, young man," she said. If only she knew.

"Well, yeah I suppose," I said.

"I mean it, otherwise people are going to be walking over you your whole life," she replied, suddenly paying more attention to me. How right she was. "Tell me something, what brings you to London? I assume from the bag with your pants hanging out the corner that you've either just arrived or you're just leaving, and you don't seem like you're waiting for anyone. And it's too early in the day to be leaving London. Plus you look like you don't belong here."

I looked down at the open zip on my bag and indeed a pair of my boxers were clearly on show. I embarrassedly stuffed them back inside and zipped up the bag, all the while trying to look away from her but not quite being able to. There was no escape.

"Yeah I've just arrived. Just now. I'm looking for work, I guess and maybe somewhere to live," My voice trailed off as I realised I was saying too much.

She kept looking at me, almost urging me to be more confident. And it worked. I spoke again with more authority in my voice. "I'm trying to find a job and definitely somewhere to live."

"Interesting," she nodded to herself and smiled. "And what's your name?"

"Peter," I lied. To this day I don't know why I lied. She had been nothing but nice to me but I was still unsure of her and more than a little afraid. As it turned out it was a lie that might well have saved my life. Well, maybe. But we'll get to that.

"Peter", I said again, "Peter Cricklow.".

Peter Cricklow was the name of a man I had worked for a few months previously and not a particularly nice one. The first one I had a falling out with. The drunk. It seemed fitting that if I was going to lie about my name I'd use the name of someone like him.

"Well Peter Cricklow," she said, still smiling and pronouncing every syllable of my name carefully, like she was committing it to memory. "If you don't have anything better to do and you think we could get along then I have the perfect job for you. How would you like to work for me?"

"Are you serious?" I asked, unsure if I could really be that lucky. She nodded her head.

"What do I have to do?" I asked.

"Let's meet somewhere tomorrow and we can sort out the details then," she said. "Where would be good for you?"

"Well, so far this is the only place in London I know. So, here?"

"Ok," she said, getting up. "Be here tomorrow at eight thirty am, Peter Cricklow."

And with that she left. I sat there for a while not really knowing what to do with myself. I had expected to spend the day at the job center, answering difficult questions about my recent past and then perhaps going from shop to shop trying to find someone who would give me some work. I hadn't expected to find something in the first fifteen minutes of being in the city, and possibly somewhere to live too. I didn't know what it was going to be, of course, but equally it didn't really matter. Whatever it turned out to be it couldn't be any worse than what I'd done before and whilst she might scare me she did seem straight forward and honest. And she had stood up for me. Nobody else had done that in a while. So I thought I would chance it and if I never saw her again I could always start looking for a job tomorrow. It was only a day.

Being at a loose end, I then decided I would rest for a while like I had originally planned. I would just sit and watch everyone else in the coffee shop. I've always been a people-watcher, always enjoyed just sitting and seeing everyone else go on with their lives. I've never fit in that well I guess Huck, never quite connected with that many people if you know what I mean? Enjoyed being on the edge of the room rather than in it. Your mum always enjoyed it too. Sometimes we would just sit and watch people, the two of sharing a single cup of coffee and watching the people around us, not speaking to each other, just enjoying being there and being a part of the world together.

After a while I closed my eyes and drifted off. Then I was back there in the boat. Cold and wet. The water moving swiftly all around me. The dark shadows drifting under the boat and I shook myself awake again and got another coffee.

I stayed in the coffee shop for another two hours and had another two cups of coffee. It was less busy by then and nobody minded me just sitting there doing nothing. I don't think anyone even noticed I was there. After a while I decided I ought to go and look for somewhere to stay that night. I didn't need to go too far from the Starbucks to find somewhere and I didn't want to either in case I couldn't find it again. I walked down a couple of streets before I found a cheap chain hotel and booked myself in for that night. It cost me more than I had expected but I didn't care. I needed somewhere to stay and I wasn't sure I wanted to sleep out on the street in London. And anyway, I had a job waiting for me tomorrow, assuming she kept her promise and came back. The hotel let me store my bag and I spent most of the day wondering round the area a couple of streets around the Starbucks, not really doing anything. I sat in a pub for a while, nursing a single pint of orange juice and lemonade and just listening to the other people talk. Eventually they let me into my hotel room at four and I sat and watched TV for a couple of hours before eventually falling asleep for a while at least.

I didn't sleep much that night, just like I didn't sleep much the night I was born. The night Jack was born too actually. We were born on the same day in the same ward of the same hospital – the John Radcliffe in Oxford – and he won that race too. He was born before I was by about fifteen minutes and that was despite the fact my mother went into labour first by a good few hours. He was just raring to get out into the world I suppose, eager to get on with life and start winning. Being born first he was of course the elder, and that carried great kudos when we were kids. He was also three ounces heavier than me and, although we looked quite similar until the age of about four, he was always slightly bigger than me as well as being faster, stronger, better looking and smarter – all the things that matter to a boy as I'm sure you know. Plus he could talk to girls, something I could never do. I didn't care though, not back then. I was never jealous, I just adored being around him.

The fact we ever met was a coincidence. I know this because my mum has told me the story of my birth a thousand times over and every time she did I would revel in the story. Something about the first time I met Jack was hugely important to me and I wanted to be able to remember every detail of those first few days. Jack's mother, so my mum told me, was never meant to be giving birth at the Radcliffe but was instead meant to be treated in a private hospital a little further away. However, the two of us were born in the autumn and big winds had brought a tree down on the Lawrence's car and they couldn't drive it to the hospital. The taxi driver that eventually came to pick them up was new and got lost trying to drive to the private hospital and so had driven his way back to the Radcliffe to get his bearings. By then it was too late to go somewhere else. They thought there was a complication with Jack and Mrs Lawrence, which it turned out there wasn't, and so instead she was brought in and set up next to my mother. They never complained about a thing though, the Lawrence's. Didn't complain about a single thing my mum said. Just smiled and oh-well'ed and got on with it. They were like that. My father always told me you got rich by never being satisfied unless you got the best of everything. The Lawrence's weren't like that and they did OK. More than OK.

I don't know if this still happens but back then you stayed in the hospital overnight after you gave birth and my mum and Jack's mother were in beds next to one another. Despite being a healthy weight and despite the long labour, when I eventually did come out I came out a little too quickly and it meant the bones in my skull didn't quite form properly and I was left with a headache or something and I wouldn't stop crying. I still have a soft patch right in the middle of my skull that your mum thinks is adorable. Apparently I screamed from the moment I was born and wouldn't stop. I had to be taken away from my mum because she was so exhausted from the labour and they wanted her to be able to rest. She worried about me though, laying in her bed fretting about whether or not I was OK and it was Jack's mum who calmed her down in the end.

The two of them were sat together side by side in their beds after giving birth. Mrs Lawrence was smiling all the time and enjoying being a mother again. My mother worried endlessly. They didn't know each other and my mother wasn't great with small talk. She just sat there watching Mrs Lawrence with Jack, his mother cooing over him and cuddling him non-stop. My mother sat there just staring and fidgeting with her hands, wishing she had someone to hold and fuss over. Jack's mum could see that my mum was upset and worrying about me and she asked my mum if she wanted to hold Jack. My mum said she nearly cried. She took Jack and just held him for a while giving her first cuddle since becoming a mother. Something else Jack beat me to.

Mr Lawrence came to visit and brought three bunches of flowers – one of which he gave to the midwife, one to his own wife and one he gave to my mother. He then got both the mothers tea and sat talking with them for a good couple of hours before he went home to look after Jack's older brother and sister.

"Look at the little chap," he said, beaming down at his new son. "He's got his mother's eyes for sure. And her smile. My God he's beautiful."

"And his father's hair," Mrs Lawrence said, beaming right back across at her husband and ruffling his head. Mr Lawrence lifted Jack up and held him into the light.

"I think you're right," he said, kissing the top of Jack's head.

"Would you like me to go and check on your son?" he said turning back to my mother. My mum smiled and said it would make her feel much better if he didn't mind, which of course he didn't. She was worried there was something wrong with me and the nurses were just being kind. He nodded and wandered off down the ward, still clutching his new born son. He was gone for fifteen minutes or so before he came back, still smiling and rocking Jack to sleep.

"He's fine," he said smiling down at my mother. "He's just getting used to his new surroundings. Our first born cried for a while too, didn't he," he said smiling at his wife. "And we were worried out of our skins but he'll be fine. I've already introduced these two to one another and they gave each other a little wave. I'm sure they're going to be best of friends." My mother sighed and thanked him and rolled over to get some sleep. Mr Lawrence stood in the window holding his son in his arms, looking out across the world and whispering something into Jack's ear. What it was he said none of us will ever know but them.

"Look after that lad, he's going to need it." That's what I imagine he said.

My dad eventually returned having gone back to work after my birth. He spent all of about five minutes with my mother, came to look for me, presumably was disappointed I was the one that wouldn't stop crying and went back home again. The next day my mother and Mrs Lawrence were both to be sent home. I had stopped crying for the time being at least and had finally agreed it was time I ate. Jack had barely made a peep all through his first night and had taken to breast feeding instantly. Both mothers were discharged at the same time and taken out by their respective husbands, one more lovingly and carefully than the other. They swapped addresses and telephone numbers and agreed to meet up in a few weeks when both were settled in.

"I doubt we'll ever hear from them again, fucking toffs," my Dad said. But he was wrong. The Lawrence's weren't like that. They weren't like that at all. They have always been a huge part of my life.

I'll tell you more about my parents later, we're just stopping for a break.

So like I said, I barely slept that first night in London. I had been used to staying in busy houses on the farms and had gotten used to the paper thin walls and people moving about at all hours. The late night comers and goers living out their lives. People up at all hours talking and drinking and arguing. But somehow this was different. This was my first night in London. The noises felt stranger, more aggressive even though they were just the same. The lights were different too. A constant stream of blue flashing lights illuminating and conjuring up images of accidents and robberies and stabbings and gangs and God knows what else. Someone stopped and stood outside my room for what seemed like a very long time, not moving, just standing there and breathing. I could hear the creak as they moved their weight from one foot to the other. I thought about opening the door and looking to see what was happening outside but I didn't. I rolled over again and pulled the thin duvet over my head. I thought back to when I was a kid.

There used to be a lot of noise in our house at night too. The constant back and forth of my father shouting and my mother drunkenly trying to pacify him. Nobody bothered to try and protect me from what I heard. Sometimes it was just raised voices, other times blazing rows that went on for hours and made the neighbours bang on the walls and shout at them to shut the hell up. Sometimes the police came but not often. Not often enough. All the while I would lay in my bed and stare at the ceiling, trying to sleep, but never being able to. Not really wanting to. Stuck between the nightmare of my reality and the reality of my nightmares. I'd lay there for hours sometimes and listen to the snippets of the barely muffled back and forth I could hear through the walls.

".....don't know why I put up with you, don't even know why I lower myself to this shit...."

"....end up like this? Huh? Explain that to me. What the fuck happened?...."

".... even mine? That's a serious question, because he sure seems like..."

"...How could you even ask....."

Sometimes the arguments would burn out quickly and they would go to their separate beds. Sometimes I would hear the door slam and the familiar stomp of my dad's footsteps away from the house. Other times my mother would creep into my room and wrap herself around me and I'd feel safe and terrified at the same time. She would hold me and sob into the back of my head as we both drifted off to a peaceful sleep, safe with each other. Those nights I dreamt happy dreams and I woke up happy in the mornings. Other nights she would creep in and curl herself around and I would have to hold her, hold her while she shuddered and wept and my dreams would be broken and dark.

The nights when I was alone my dreams were the worst. Those dreams weren't safe. My thoughts were haunted by the dark fish.

I wish she'd been there that first night in London.

I met Natalie again at the Starbucks the following morning, just as she had said she would. I was surprised she had turned up. She even bought me a coffee.

"Right then, Peter" she said. "Here's how it works."

The job she had for me, as I had guessed, wasn't exactly a legitimate one. Not that many of my jobs had been completely legal. Truth be told, whilst I was never entirely sure what I did for her I had a pretty good idea. She gave me a cheap mobile phone, a simple pay as you go one, and a single key on plain black key-ring. Every so often, she said, sometimes more than once a day, sometimes not for a week, I would receive a text from a random phone number which would give me the names of two places and two times. I was to go to the first place at the allotted time and someone would give me a bag and I was to take it to the second place at the second time. Always the same type of bag – a dark blue Nike one with a distinct orange ribbon tied on the handle and a thick number lock holding it closed. I would arrive first and someone would come in, say hi to me and give me the bag that I'd forgotten the last time I'd seen them – left it in their car or at their house or whatever. I would never recognise the person, always someone different, but I'd recognise the bag. The other person would know who I was. The person I would deliver the bag to was always different as well, but they'd recognise the bag as well. I was never to look in the bags. I was pretty sure it was drugs but I never found out. I didn't care. It was simple and, while it was all a little odd, it couldn't have sounded like an easier job. Curiosity got the better of me initially though.

"What's in the bags?" I asked even though I didn't really want to know.

"I don't know what's in them," she said. "And I don't want to know. That's the point. You don't know where they are going, you don't know where they have come from and you don't know what's in them. And everyone involved knows that's how it works. That way nobody can ever accuse you of having done anything. All I do is run the delivery service"

I never found out if she actually was lying or not. Part of me thought she knew what was in them and didn't want to say. But I never found out.

"What if I get caught then?" I asked.

"Nobody has ever been caught," she replied. "Plus the chain is too long. If anyone did ever get caught it would just lead to a dead end anyways – a line of faceless nobody's just like you and me. You don't know who the person is you got the bag from and you don't know who you gave it to. You'd just say you were doing a friend a favour and you didn't realise you were doing anything wrong. It just works, so don't question it. Plus you don't know what's in them anyway and you don't have the number to open to the lock, so it wouldn't matter if you did. So don't ever ask what's in them again. OK?"

"And what do I get in return?" I asked.

"Room and board with me," she said. "I have a nice house in a quiet street where the people who work for me all stay. People just like you – nice guys. I give you a bed, all your meals and anything else you need. Anything. No money though, other than a bit of pocket money. That's how it works. But you won't need any anyway, you can just come to me and I'll get you what you need."

And so that's how I ended up becoming what I'm pretty sure was a drug runner. Writing that down looks pretty strange now I think about it but it is what it is. We picked up my stuff and we got a taxi to a big Victorian house not far from the station in Ealing. As we drew up I couldn't believe what I was looking at. It would have cost a fortune to have bought a place like that in any town, never mind being in the middle of that part of London. It was in a good state too, freshly painted and well kept. Nothing suspicious about it at all. Looking back I guess that was the point. It would have a cost a fortune to rent, even more to have owned it but I'm not sure she had the mortgage on it. Not sure she even paid the rent. Just a part of the chain I guessed.

I knew what I was doing was wrong Huck but frankly I didn't care at that point in my life. I wasn't exactly happy with the way my life had turned out and I certainly didn't think I had much right to anything better. I'm not proud of it, that I spent part of my life doing something like that. But what choice did I have? I really couldn't do much else and I couldn't go back to you and your mum. I was lucky I had anything at all and if I hadn't taken that job I'm fairly sure I wouldn't be here now. So there you go. The money situation didn't worry me other than that I didn't have anything to send to you and your mum, but I figured you would be OK. I figured your grandparents would look after the both of you. I was used to living off pretty much nothing and in the two years in between leaving your mother and arriving in London I had managed to scrape together a little bit of money, stashed away in my bag. Nothing much but when it was time to go it would still be there to get me on my feet if I needed it. I always assumed I'd be allowed to leave at some point. Just give the phone back and disappear. Looking back maybe that was naïve. I'll never know if that would have worked out.

The other people who lived in the house were quiet and most of us kept to ourselves. They didn't really look like drug runners but then again neither did I, not really. Just a regular bunch of people who needed something to do. No-one special. Maybe that was the point. A bunch of unnoticeable nobodies. We worked during the day and it was always at sociable hours, which I guess was part of the point to keep things inconspicuous as well. I don't know what the other people did. Like me their phones would go at random times and they'd be off. They'd disappear with nothing, come back with nothing. Nobody ever mentioned the work. They were all nice guys, just like Natalie said, and they kept themselves pretty much to themselves, which suited me fine. We were all friendly, but none of us were friends. We knew names but not much more than that. Nobody really talked about their pasts, especially me. Everyone lived hand to mouth but nobody wanted for anything. We didn't live an extravagant lifestyle – not what you might associate with a drug lord and her minions - but it was comfortable. I don't think Natalie was a drug lord if I'm honest. I think she was just like us. But there was always food on the table and beer in the fridge for the rest of them. We had Sky TV, little comforts like that.

The only person who had any money was Natalie and it was the only really strange thing about the whole set up. Once a week, every Friday night, she would sit at the table in the dining room with a bag full of cash – the only thing of note that ever came into the house. I have no idea where it came from and no idea where most of it went. I never saw it arrive and only occasionally saw it go out. She would sit and count it into piles, working one of those old accountants calculators with a paper roll in the top and she would tut and click her tongue as she counted out the money. She would talk to us as she did that, complaining about whatever was on the TV and giving her view on the world. When she was finished she would pack all the money into the bag, carefully placing each stack into it, and then she made a phone call. It was the only time I ever saw her on the phone and it was always the same conversation. The person on the other end seemed to do most of the talking, not that I could hear them, and she would just read numbers off the paper and then say "yes" and "down, yes, down" and then eventually hang up. They didn't sound like good phone calls. Then she would take the bag upstairs and later that night, sometimes other days I supposed, someone would come and pick it up, would give her our spending money and then would disappear again.

Only once did I see where she kept our money. I was coming upstairs one night, just after the guy had come to collect the bag, and her door was open. I watched her take the bundle of cash the guy had given her and then I saw her open the drawer in her chest of drawers and take out another, bigger bundle. She weighed the two piles up for what seemed like an eternity, smiled nervously and put the two piles together in one. Then she bent down, pulled the rug aside and lifted a floorboard, taking a tin out from underneath it. She opened the tin and put all the cash in and then stuffed it back underneath the floorboard and patted the rug back into place. She didn't see me and I never said I thing. Why would I?

And that's how it worked for five years of my life, everything ticking along without so much as a hiccup. My nine to five was literally going from coffee shop to coffee shop, from Costa to Starbucks, from a Burger King to a McDonalds. I must have done them all in my time. Every chain shop in London. There was never even a hint of trouble. At least, not until the last time.

We've just stopped off for a break so your mother could get out and stretch her legs and go to "powder her nose". It was a good point to stop anyway. While we were waiting for your mum we were looking at the toys they sell in the service station. Nothing very exciting. You had your heart set on a pretty lethal looking gun that shoots tennis ball sized bits of plastic around – not really ideal for the back of the Campervan I don't think, particularly when we're driving up the motorway. We want to get there in one piece. I was looking at a plastic farm set – I used to have one just like it when I was a kid. Like I said, the first place I worked after I left you and your mother was a farm. It was nice there and mostly peaceful. I felt like I belonged there, if only for a little while but the farmer couldn't afford to keep me on past the lambing season so I had to move on. It's strange, don't you think, the different jobs people end up in and how they get there. I wonder what you'll end up doing. Maybe by the time you read this you'll already have your heart set on something.

As a boy I had always wanted to be an astronomer, which was a pretty farfetched idea looking back at it but you obviously don't think of it at the time. That dream had followed me all the way up until I was about 15 though, at which point my career advisor at school informed me I'd need to get much better grades in my GCSE's and A-levels than I could reasonably expect to get and I would need to go to University to do a pretty intense degree – something like Astrophysics or Applied Mathematics or something else beyond someone like me. I did OK at school but not that well. Certainly not well enough to be able to get into a decent university to do something like that. Now I look back I don't even know if I liked science all that much. I think I just liked the idea of space, the beauty of it. I loved looking at the night sky and thinking about things that were far away from where I was. I had this huge fascination with the Northern Lights – I'd seen them on TV sometime as a kid, maybe eight or nine, and did a big project on them when I was at school – all the science behind it and that kind of stuff. But it wasn't the science I really liked. I thought they were beautiful and magical and something not of this world. I guess it was hardly enough to base a career on though.

The one person who unsurprisingly did achieve his childhood dream though was Jack. Most kids grow up at some point wanting to be a fireman, a policeman, a farmer or something like that. It's weird how those are the dreams that kids have. Why as kids do we want such simple jobs and then feel like we have to go and do something complex and stressful - lawyer, doctor, banker – all of that kind of stuff? Why can't we just keep with the simple jobs like Jack did? Most children seem to flit from one to another every week – I know I did and I guess nobody really knows what they want to be until they grow up. Sometimes even then. But not Jack. No, Jack stuck to what he wanted. Despite all his talents and all the great things he could have gone on to be, Jack had a single, unwavering belief he was destined to become a fireman. It was the first serious ambition he had at what must have been around nine and he never swerved away from it. The local fire brigade came into his primary school to give a talk about fire safety and shock the children with videos of unwatched chip pans bursting into flames and smokers falling asleep and setting fire to their sofas and other careless faults that scared every other kid in the room. Not Jack though. He'd been fascinated with how heroic the fire fighters were. I remember him going on and on about how that was what he wanted to be and how he was going to get there and how proud his mum and dad would be when he did. His eyes would light up and he'd walk taller just thinking about it.

It seems like a waste, sometimes, him wanting to be a fireman given everything else. Jack was bright. Incredibly bright actually – he got all A*s at GCSE and four A's at A-level, including maths and physics. He was good at all the things I wasn't, which was virtually everything. Had he wanted to, Jack certainly could have gotten a place doing Astrophysics at Oxford or Cambridge. But it wasn't what he wanted and, true to his word, as soon as he received his A-level results he marched straight down to the local fire station and signed up. It wasn't a waste. His parents couldn't have been more proud of him. Nor could I.

"Imagine our Jack, doing what he had always wanted," they said to me, tears welling up in their eyes. When I'd told my father I'd gone through clearing to get my place at university and was off to Leeds Met to do psychology he'd laughed at me.

"Fucking psychology," he'd said, "what the hell are you going to do with that?"

"I don't know," I said, "I thought it might be interesting."

"It's a lot of mumbo jumbo bollocks is what it is," he snorted back at me, looking somewhere over my shoulder. "They just fill your head up with all these pathetic experiments they've done on rats and monkeys – as if somehow we're the same as them. Why don't you do something useful with your life?"

"Like you have?" That's what I wanted to say. Is what I should have said. I didn't though. I just stared at the floor and mumbled something about how I was going to go anyway and it was my life.

"You'll never last the first year," he said and went back to eating his dinner. As it turned out that was one of the last meaningful conversations we ever had.

He was right, of course, but he didn't know that for a long time. If you have kids, Huck, be supportive of them. Challenge them, of course Huck, want them to be the best they can be, but be supportive of them as well. Promise me that?

Anyway, back to Jack. Not only did Jack achieve his dream, but he was unbelievably brilliant at it as well. Or maybe not so unbelievable, this is Jack we're talking about after all. He passed the fitness tests first time round, which is apparently incredibly hard to do, but then again he'd always been a bit of a superstar athlete at school. He'd captained the athletics team, the swimming team and the football team at his school and he was the school tennis champion. Then he flew through the actual training and was putting out fires across the county in record time. No looking back, no fear. Apparently the chief had never seen anyone so enthusiastic and so naturally gifted. It was so typical of Jack.

There were countless times he'd appeared in the papers, mainly just the local newspaper, the Gazette, but still. He was personally responsible for saving the lives of four people on three separate occasions, including once when he went back into a burning building to save a young girl despite his oxygen tank suggesting he didn't have enough air for him to make it there and back, never mind having to share some with the child. Once he'd got back out, carried the girl over to the ambulance and checked she was ok, he got straight back onto the main hose to carry on putting the fire out. He was a hero. Not just a hero. He was a God. That makes it sound like the rest of the team stood back watching him, which they didn't, but Jack was something special. The reporter from the paper asked him about the oxygen levels in his tanks and whether he knew he had enough left. I'd read that report over and over a thousand times.

"I wasn't sure. I took a real big breath before I went in," Jack had said in the report. "I've always been a strong swimmer, I guess the practice helped." He cracked me up. He still does whenever I think about him.

"Yeah but to last that long," the reporter asked "is practically a miracle. You must have the lungs of a giant!"

"It's all down to the training," Jack replied. "Any of the lads could have done it. I was just the lucky one who happened to be in the right place at the right time."

Humble to the last was Jack even though he had every right not to be. And the other firemen loved him for it. Made them feel as big as he was whenever he spoke about them all.

My life during the time I spent with Natalie, those five or so years, wasn't anything like that exciting Huck. Jesus, five years. How did I ever last that long? You would have thought living in a drug den for five years something exciting would have happened, but it really didn't. The truth is that, while it was simple enough, it was pretty monotonous. I spent most of the time sitting around the house, waiting for my phone to go. Going out of the house wasn't strictly forbidden but you knew it wasn't really allowed for anything other than going out on jobs. You knew from the way Natalie looked at people when they mentioned they were going to go out, knew from the conversations that happened behind closed doors when people did. Some of the guys were allowed to go out for a run but they didn't really even want the exercise. I think it was more to stave off the boredom and get out of the house than anything else. Natalie always asked how long they were going for and when she got back she would question them for what seemed like hours. Where had they run? How fast did they go? Was it busy out? You could see her doing the mental math in her head, trying to work out if the time and the route made sense. The interrogation was more exhausting than the run. I genuinely think they just wanted to be outside and do something normal. They weren't doing anything wrong. Well, nothing more so than the wrong we were all doing in that house. So some kept fit, others played computer games. I read. The most exciting thing that happened for me in the house was when Natalie occasionally bought me a book back from wherever she went when she went out. An unread Stephen King was the highpoint of my month and if that doesn't sum up my life there I don't know what does.

So I read. I Read and I thought. Thought about what I was doing. Thought about what your mum was doing. Thought about you. I didn't know anything about you of course. No idea what you looked like, no idea what you were doing or where you were living. I didn't even know if you were a boy or a girl then, not to begin with. So I would sit in that house and make things up, make up stories about what you looked like and what you would doing. Imaging first days at school, you playing in the park, you getting out with your mum. None of that lived up to the real you.

And everything was calm and peaceful and simple. And then one night I had the dream, Huck. I had the dream and the dark fish were all around me and your mum was in the boat with me. And at first I couldn't work out what was happening. She had never been there before, it had always just been me and Jack in the boat with the dark fish swimming all around us. And it had always been quiet. But not now. Now there was a terrible noise everywhere and it was coming from your mother. She was screaming. Screaming louder than I had ever heard anyone scream, including my own mother. I could see her staring wide-eyed into the water, looking at the dark fish and I could see her belly. Her great big, round pregnant belly and I knew it was a dream, right? I knew it had to be because she must have given birth to you years ago but I also knew what they wanted. I knew what the dark fish wanted was inside her. Was you. But I couldn't move. No matter how hard I tried I couldn't move myself from my end of the boat and the boat got longer and longer and Jack just sat next to your mum and looked at her as she screamed and screamed and he just stared at her with a stupid blank look on his face and I couldn't move and I screwed up my eyes and I screamed.

And then I was awake in my bed and the guy in the room next to me was banging on the wall and telling me to shut up.

That was the first night I started calling. I wasn't meant to. Natalie had given strict instructions that the phone was only to be used for work. But I needed to know your mum was OK. Needed to know that my dream was just a dream, even though it couldn't have been anything else. And so I dialed the number and it rang and rang and she answered even though it was late and I said nothing. She asked if someone was there a couple of times and I couldn't speak so after a while she hung up. She barely said anything but it was her, unmistakably her.

I started calling a lot after that, risking it even though I knew what trouble I would get into. I would top up the pay as you go mobile out of my savings and kept track of it to ensure Natalie wouldn't notice. Sometimes when I was on my way home I would try calling. I would call up your mum's house or your grandfather's. Sometimes somebody would answer, sometimes the answer machine would click in. It didn't matter, I would never speak anyway. Mostly your mother would answer and after a while, I don't know how, she knew it was me. Maybe she recognised the breathing, maybe she just figured there was nobody else that would keep calling like that. The first time she said my name I hung up immediately in a panic and I guess that confirmed it. Sometimes she would be angry and shout at me, other times she would plead with me to come home, to come home to both of you. Sometimes she would say nothing and we'd both just sit there in silence until she sighed and hung up.

And then something different happened. You answered, Huck. It was the first time I heard your voice. The first time I knew you were really alive. The first time I knew your name. The first time I knew you were a boy. The first time I could put anything to make sense of the thousand images I had in my head.

"Hi," you said.

I didn't speak. I couldn't.

"Hello?" you said again. I could hear your mum calling in the background, asking who it was.

"I don't know" you called out, shouting at your mother but directly into the mouthpiece of the phone. I heard your mother call back to tell you to ask.

"Who is it?" you asked.

"Who is that?" I managed to say. You laughed.

"It's Huck," you giggled

I hung up the phone and I sat and wept the whole train ride home.

We just stopped to fill up again Huck – both us and the van. The man behind the counter asked where we were going and I told him we were heading up to the north coast.

"Tough roads up there this time of year," he said, nodding at me knowingly. "It's been good so far this winter but it's going to get bad, you mark my words. Take it slow and steady is my advice."

It's funny how everyone is always so eager to pass on their advice, like everyone is some great fountain of knowledge. Your mum said one of the things I should do is to give you some advice in this letter, or whatever it is. She said it would be my opportunity to pass on some of my wisdom to the world. Tell you all of the things you'll need to know to help you grow up to be a man. Her dad, your granddad, the Cap as I always knew him as, was always full of advice, most of it useful and only a little of it mad. He's a good man your grandfather. If you don't have a new dad by the time you're reading this, Huck, I'm sure the Cap will be doing a good job as a replacement. I wish I had had someone like that in my life when I was growing up. But my father wasn't like that. Wasn't exactly a source of inspiration to me, Huck. He's left an impression on me, that's for sure, but not the one you'd want your father to leave on you. Not sure he did anything to help me grow up to be a man. Not that he didn't try, in his own special shitty way. He was a constant source of encouragement and ideas for self-improvement, often bawled at me the second I did something wrong.

"Don't fucking do it like that."

"Why don't you think before you act you useless fuck?"

"Why can't you be more of a man? You're so fucking weak."

And on and on and on. Always shouted at me, straight into my face, his teeth dark and yellow, the muscles in his neck straining, the spit flying into my face, the emphasis always on the *fuck*, never using my name. I remember the first time he shouted at me like that. He had wanted me to pass him a screwdriver while he was trying to fix the fridge. I passed a wrench and he shouted at me. I was six. I would try and apologise every time, try and understand what it was he wanted from me. And yet, for all his wise words none of it made any difference to the way I turned out. Didn't help me to become what he wanted me to become anyway. Maybe I wasn't listening properly. Maybe he didn't explain it right. Maybe I was just too stupid, just didn't understand it. Maybe I just didn't want to be what he wanted.

Anyway, whatever the reason I've never really given anyone else advice.

But I guess there is one thing I can say to you. It's not really advice so much as it is an observation. Jack was brave, Huck, I already told you that, but there are lots of brave people in the world. Lots of people can be brave at times, brave in different ways for different reasons. Brave for doing and saying heroic things and for being strong and defiant against all the odds. All those things great films are based on. And what I've realised Huck is there are really two types of brave in this world. There are those people who are brave in a split second – people with brave jobs like soldiers and fireman and people who are brave without a moment's notice like the guy who runs out in front of a car to stop a child from being hit, and the man who chases after a mugger or steps in to stop a fight to protect someone else. These are people who are brave without having the opportunity to think about it. They don't really know they're being brave because they don't have the chance to think about it. That's not to belittle the type of bravery they have. Far from it in fact. They do some of the bravest things you or I could ever imagine and they do it without even thinking about it. I just mean they are people to whom bravery comes naturally without them even needing to try. It's in their DNA I guess, they can't help but act on it.

Then there is the type of bravery when they know the thing is coming, where they can see it coming for minutes, hours, days, years, however long, and yet they do what they need to do anyway despite how hard and painful it is going to be. Sometimes they do it even in spite of knowing how hard and painful it's going to be because it's the right thing to do. People who protest against things even though they know other people will look down on them and fight against them, shout at them and hurt them or lock them up. People who go to war zones or places where's there's disease and death, even though they know everything will be dirty and hard and far away from their families and their simple lives. That is a bravery that requires a huge amount of strength, inner strength, because you have to think about what is going to happen and then do what you don't want to do anyway. That's what your mother is doing now I think.

Some people have both types of bravery within them. Jack has both. Jack's truly the bravest person I have ever met and later I'll tell you why. If I can give you one piece of advice Huck, it is to be brave and to be brave whenever you can, whether you want to or not. I know you have it in you, that you have something deep inside you that you just have to pull out of yourself. It will be hard but you have to try.

I am not a brave man Huck, not in either sense of the word. In fact, I am a coward. I always have been, ever since I can remember. I wasn't brave enough to stand up to my father no matter what he did to me and my mother. I had so many chances to stand up to him and I never did. Wasn't brave enough to stand up to anyone my entire life. Wasn't brave enough to love your mother. Wasn't brave enough to stay with you.

I wasn't even brave enough to leave Natalie's house like I should have done a long time before I eventually did. I ended up running away, which is where my story, where all of this, really begins I suppose.

I had just been to the doctor – one of the few trips I took out of the house alone when I wasn't working. I'd had to get permission from Natalie of course but she was OK about it, so long as I told her exactly where I was going and when I was going to be back. I had been for some tests at the hospital the week before and the doctor had called me in to give me my results. As I stepped out of the surgery my phone buzzed. I pulled it out of my pocket and looked at the message.

"Starbucks, Marylebone 11:30, Costa, Liverpool Street, 3pm," it read, nothing else. Just another job.

I looked at the time on my phone. It was only 10:30 and I had plenty of time to get there. I looked at the pamphlets I held in my other hand that the doctor had given me. I wasn't allowed to give anyone my mobile number and so he'd scrawled his office number on one of them as well as his personal mobile number and his home phone number. I'm sure he wasn't meant to do that. He'd also scrawled the words *call me* in capital letters across the top of it. He was a nice man and I knew he was only doing his job. I'd sat there and let him finish his speech and write down all the numbers before he finally gave up trying to talk to me and I left.

I thought about calling your mother and then didn't.

I sighed and let the pamphlets fall into the bin outside the door to his office.

Marylebone, as it happened, was the Starbucks I'd first met Natalie in and was a fitting place for it all to end. I walked in, straight to the back of the queue as I always did, bang on time. There were a couple of people in front of me but the place was pretty calm for that time of day. I waited patiently in line until I got to the front and ordered my coffee. When I finished giving my order I turned round and a saw skinny guy I'd never seen before was stood in the door way holding the usual bag and staring at me. When he saw that I saw him he waved, and walked over with a big smile on his face.

"Hi buddy!" he beamed, "I think you left this in my car the other day after football."

He said it loud enough for everyone to hear but casually, to ensure nobody would in any way think the meeting was anything other than someone handing back a casually forgotten kit bag to their friend. Two buddies just meeting up. He moved toward me and as he did he pushed the bag into my chest with both hands, a little more forcefully than I was expecting, and I fell back into the counter a little. He moved his head so his mouth was briefly uncomfortably close to my ear.

"When you get out of here, fucking run mate," he said. "Sorry buddy, it's your fucking problem now."

And with that he pulled away, gave a sympathetic smile and was gone. He was out of the door before I even had time to think about what was happening and I saw him walking quickly off down the street. At first it hadn't dawned on me what he had said and then it hit me. This was different. Something was wrong. I looked around in panic. Suddenly everyone seemed to be looking at me, everyone seemed to be eyeing me up. Maybe it was just me being paranoid but I don't know – this had never happened to me before. I needed time before I left. I picked up my coffee and almost dropped it I was shaking so much and went and sat on the nearest chair I could find. I couldn't think about anything other than what was going to happen when I stepped out of the coffee shop. Presumably they wouldn't do anything in here – it would make too much of a scene and there was too much that could get in their way. It was hard enough walking round the place as it was without tripping over something. But would the police care about making a scene? What if it wasn't the police? They'd have arrested me by now wouldn't they? OK. So I had to get out quickly and then run, presumably. But was that drawing attention to myself? Maybe I should casually walk out. Maybe I should stay here all day and wait for someone to come and find me. Natalie maybe? But I couldn't miss the drop. Natalie had always said that – don't miss the drop, never miss the drop, you don't want to know what will happen if you miss the drop.

Fuck.

I took a sip of my coffee but it turned my stomach. I felt sick. I looked down into my black coffee and I saw it. I swear to God I saw it, moving under the surface of my coffee. The coffee was jet black and somehow the dark fish was darker still against it. I shook my head and it was gone again. But I had seen it, it was there and it wasn't a good sign. Maybe I'd just been thinking too much about what the doctor had said. Either way it wasn't good. Something bad was about to happen. I didn't know what but someway or other I was going to be in trouble. They only came when I was in trouble.

A thought went through my head. I should keep the coffee. If someone attacked me I could throw it in their face. Couldn't I? Could I do that to someone? Yes, I could. I could throw the coffee, dark fish and all, at them. Right in their fucking face.

Maybe they just wanted the bag, maybe I should just give it to them, maybe just leave it on the floor here and walk off. Although, that would still mean missing the drop. I couldn't do it. I needed to either get the bag out of there or let whatever was going to happen, happen.

I quickly flicked my gaze between the different people in the coffee shop, eyeing up who it was waiting for me to leave. Nobody looked particularly thug-like, but then neither did the guy who made the drop. Neither did I. Neither did Natalie for that matter. A guy in a suit kept looking at me, a cop maybe? There were two of them together, not talking but just sat there looking around. Could they be cops? There were also two young men in jeans and t-shirts who kept looking around, but they might just be ordinary kids, kids are always edgy. Pumped up on too much caffeine. Maybe I'd had too much. Maybe the other guy had. Maybe he was just paranoid. There were two casually dressed black guys in the corner. Stop stereotyping, I thought. Plus they looked way too relaxed and were joking around, too much to be paying attention to anything other than their own conversation. Whoever it was that was after me, they must be outside.

Or the suits, the suits were still my best bet. Could be someone inside and someone else on the outside. Maybe they tracked my phone and read my messages and they knew where I was going to be. I'm trapped. Shit. Maybe I should just leave without the bag. Can't. I'd miss the drop.

I stood up and quickly looked around. Nobody else moved. I picked up my coffee and the bag and then looked around, as if making sure I hadn't left anything behind. Really I just wanted to see if anyone else started to pack up, but they didn't. I moved slowly towards the door and still the rest of the coffee shop carried on with their everyday lives, completely ignoring me. As I tried to open it the door stuck in my hand and it took a couple of pulls to get it to open. The adrenaline in my body meant when I finally managed to loosen it up the door swung open way too quickly and I almost hit myself in the face with it. I pulled myself together, stepped out and stood in the street, the door closing itself behind me.

I don't really know what happened then. One minute I was stood holding the bag, the next I wasn't. There was no struggle. No attack or anything like that. Nothing. Some kid ran past me and kind of bumped in to me and then I just didn't have it anymore. It took me a couple of seconds to realise what had happened and by the time I shouted "Hey!" the kid was gone. A few passers-by stood, gawking at me, open mouthed, but nobody did anything. I simply stood there, watching the kid run down the street and disappear into the street full of people.

"That kid just stole your bag," a woman pointed out to me, as if I didn't know.

But it was too late. He was gone. The door to Starbucks behind me suddenly flew open and I span round on my heels to see the two suits rushing hurriedly out. Our eyes met for a second and they suddenly stopped in their tracks and stared at me. I pointed down the street in the general direction the kid had run.

"Someone just stole my bag," I explained, looking round at the gawkers for confirmation.

The woman nodded at the two suits in agreement. The two suits looked at each other, one inhaled a deeply frustrated sigh and then the two of them walked off in the opposite direction to the one the kid had gone in, as did the passers-by. The woman tutted at me and walked off too. I was left alone and it was as if nothing had happened at all. Is that what happened if you got mugged in London? A few looks of consolation and a smattering of sympathy and then off you go? Even the plain clothes police officers, assuming that's what they were, couldn't be bothered to help you. I couldn't decide if I was fortunate not to have the bag when the two of them came out or whether my problems would be increasingly worse when I went back to Natalie's house. Either way, I concluded, it wasn't going to work out well.

It took me about an hour to get back to the house in Ealing. The whole tube ride home I simply sat and thought about what was going to happen to me, running different scenarios through my head. The dark fish stared at me from my mind the whole time. None of the scenarios I thought up ended well for me. I worked out a best case in my head. I figured the guy who dropped off the bag knew he was being followed, or at least that I was, and he would have to let someone know what was happening. The kid who stole the bag, I assumed, was therefore part of the plan to make sure the bag didn't fall into the wrong hands. Maybe I should have been thankful of him. He had been sent to take the bag and do the drop instead of me. It would look like a simple mugging, which probably happened a hundred times a day in London, and therefore nothing to pick me up for. It made me feel better knowing that was a possibility. That it could be true. But it didn't really dispel the sense I had inside my head that this was going to end up badly. The dark fish stared at me.

What if he wasn't part of the plan? What if it was him I was meant to be looking out for? What if the suits were really the people who were supposed to be looking after me?

When I got back to the house Natalie was stood in the door waiting. She clearly already knew what had happened and she was visibly angry. Furious even but trying to keep her cool. I'd only ever seen her angry once before, and it hadn't been at me, thank God. A kid had used his phone to text someone, a girl he had started seeing somehow, and arranged to go on a date with her without telling Natalie. He had picked her up in a coffee shop was the rumour and had already met her twice before he got found out. Natalie went ballistic at him. She exploded at him for about forty-five minutes before his phone went again for a pick up. He didn't come back. I don't know what had happened to him but he didn't come back. But that had been his fault. He had gone against the rules. Mind you, so had I. But that had nothing to do with this. What happened that day, that wasn't my fault, couldn't have been. Could it? Had I been careless somehow? No. Still, she didn't look happy. Nobody else was in the house – all coincidentally out on errands.

"What happened?" she asked as soon as I reached the door step.

She moved aside briefly to let me into the hallway but couldn't wait any more for answers and so we talked there. I told her exactly what happened, embellishing nothing and giving her every detail I could. Just the facts. She listened intently, the whole time stretching her fingers. She did it whenever she was tense – I'd seen her doing it when we were watching something dramatic on TV, or when someone was back from a drop off or a run later than she had anticipated. She asked me question after question, sometimes interrupting the answers to her own questions before I had time to finish so she could ask another. She asked a lot about the kid and about the drop off guy but mostly she wanted to know about the two suits. What they had looked like, how they acted, how they spoke. I had to describe them about five times before she was happy with what they looked like.

"Did you follow the kid?" she asked.

"No," I said, "You told me never to draw attention to myself. Plus he was too quick, he was gone before I even noticed he had taken it."

She nodded but carried on staring at me. I couldn't tell if she was disappointed in me or not. No sign I'd either done the right thing or the wrong one. Either way she was mad. And scared.

"What did the suits do?" she asked.

"I told you, they just walked off," I replied. "They didn't even say anything to me. They looked pretty disappointed with what had happened to tell the truth."

She nodded again. Suddenly her phone buzzed in her pocket. She pulled it out and stared at the screen. I'd never seen her being summoned by text before and I assumed it wasn't a good sign. She confirmed it.

"Fuck."

"Who is it?" I asked, but she didn't respond. "Do you have to go?" She carried on staring at the screen, not moving. "I'm sorry I let the kid get away," I added. "I genuinely am. Natalie?" I pressed too much.

"Natalie? What's in the bags, Natalie?"

I knew as soon as the words left my mouth it was a mistake, but I didn't think it would get the reaction it did. I'd barely finished the last syllable of her name before her balled fist connected with my left temple. I've been punched before, plenty of times, but not since I was a kid and never by someone with that much weight to put behind it. I stumbled back into the front door and then sat down hard on the floor. The pain shot through my temple and the hurt from landing on the floor went the full length of my body. A second later I felt the blood start to tickle down the side of my face. Definitely a black eye, possibly a decent scar to go with it, not that that really mattered, and my back would hurt for a few days at least. She stood over me, looking down at me, breathing heavily and quickly, her hands still balled by her sides and the muscles in her arms tense. She reminded me of someone I'd seen stood in that position a hundred times before. A monster, stood over someone I loved. A bully stood over me.

"I told you never to fucking ask me that," she screamed. "If you ever fucking ask me that again I will kill you, you understand me?"

I barely managed to nod. I could feel the blood draining from my face much faster than it was dripping down my cheek. Her phone buzzed again and she pulled it out of her pocket. Another curse slipped out of her lips and she turned and walked upstairs. She returned a minute later with her coat on. She didn't say anything to me, didn't even look at me. She just walked past and slammed the door after her.

In that minute, sat on the floor, my head pounding and my heart racing I decided I was done. I had to be done. I didn't want to, couldn't, spend a minute more in that house, doing that work. Time was suddenly so short and I realised it now. Realised that the things I needed to do, that I had been putting off ever since my first trip to the hospital two months ago, needed to be done otherwise there was a chance I wasn't going to get to do them at all. If I stayed here a moment longer they might not let me leave again. I might not be able to. And I needed to see you, Huck. Time to go.

I stood up, gingerly at first, and then realised I wasn't in as much pain as I thought I might have been. I went to the bathroom to clean myself up – it didn't look as bad as I had thought it would. I'd seen worse, a lot worse. Maybe a bruise around the eye but the cut had already stopped bleeding. I'd have a headache for sure, I could already feel it coming, and I'd get stared at for a few days but it was nothing serious. Next I went to my room and pulled my bag from under the bed. Even though I'd lived there for five years I'd never really unpacked the few important possessions I had and it took less than a minute to throw my clothes in the bag and zip it shut. I picked it up, went out into the hall and almost down the stairs before I doubled back and went into Natalie's room. It took me a couple of times to find the floorboard that was loose but when I did it came up easily. There was the large biscuit tin wedged underneath. I didn't open it, I just shoved it into my bag, walked down the stairs and out the front door. I half expected Natalie to be stood there, waiting for me to run out exactly as I had, but she wasn't there. A little bit of luck.

I ran to the tube station as quickly as I could, which took me about ten minutes. My back was killing me the whole way but I had to get away. I didn't want to be there when she came back, maybe when they came back. I didn't know who she would bring with her. I no longer worried about drawing attention to myself though, I just needed to get out of there. On my way I deleted everything from my phone – messages, call history, the lot – and threw my mobile phone, turned to silent, into some bushes on the side of the road. I don't know how easy it is to track a mobile phone, particularly one that wasn't "smart" like most of them are these days, but I decided I didn't want to take the chance. It wasn't as if I had anyone to call anyway. Without my phone the only link they had to me was the name Peter Cricklow and they could follow that trail all they wanted, I didn't care. I felt a sudden sense of relief.

I got the tube to King's Cross station. It had never been near any of the previously agreed drop off points and I thought it might be a safe place to go. They might have people everywhere, they might not. Maybe they didn't even know I was gone yet. Not necessarily solid logic, but I needed to go somewhere. On the underground I pulled out a piece of paper I had in my pocket and looked at it. It was a raggedy piece of old yellow note paper, written a long time ago, and one I knew well. I'd stared at that piece of paper a thousand times before. I knew every crease, every coffee stain. It was torn at one of the edges and the blue ink was smudged on one of the names where I'd touched it too often. There were six names in all, the six people I needed to see before everything would finally be OK. I said them out loud to myself as I sat there, the only person in my carriage.

Paul. Mum. Rebecca. Huckleberry. Him. Jack.

I thought about it for a while and then put the paper back in my pocket and stared at the window opposite me until we arrived at King's Cross, thinking of nothing. No dark fish out there, just the dark of the underground pocketed here and there with the light of the stations. From there I had to wait twenty five minutes before they announced boarding for the train to King's Lynn. While I was waiting I bought some painkillers and some plasters and went and fixed myself up in the toilet. I bought some cheap, dark sunglasses as well to hide the bruises around my eye. Then I sat in the coffee shop – a Starbucks as it happens – only this time I didn't speak to anyone and I didn't buy a coffee. I just sat in the corner and waited. When they announced my train I got up and took my seat in the first class carriage – the first and only time in my life I've ever travelled in such style.

The names on that list Huck, they're all I've really thought about night and day for the past six months. Ever since I found out. And that list, those people, they're the reason I'm doing this. They're the reason I bought this stupid Campervan, the reason I've spent the last few days traveling around the country, the reason we're going to Scotland now. Not a long list but an important one, to me anyway. So, you ought to know a little about the people on there before I can really explain this whole thing. Each of them is important to me, Huck, important in the whole stupid journey that is my life. Just, not as important as you.

Rebecca is your mum, which I'm guessing you know already. Of course I think you are familiar with a certain young Huckleberry. Jack I've mentioned a couple of times now and I'll come back to him at some point. More than one point, I think.

The first name on the list, Paul, is the first I went to see, not long after I left London and Natalie and everything. We'll get to him shortly so I'll not say too much about him now. Let's just say he wasn't a friend of mine, Huck. Not a friend of mine at all and he never was. He was someone I hadn't seen for a very long time.

So that just leaves my mum and Him. My father. My dear old fucking dad. I'm sorry, I swear too much in this but, well, you'll understand. Maybe that's how you describe me now. You'd have every right. But let's start with something better.

My mother. Mum. What can I say about her that any man wouldn't ever say about his own mother? She wasn't perfect, I will say that. It takes a lot for me to say that and for a long time I thought that she was, but she wasn't. But she was close, Huck, she was so close to being perfect that I cannot describe how much I loved her. She had imperfections, yes, but they were small and they came from Him. Everything that was wrong with her stemmed from his shit. At least, I think they did. They must have. My mother was beautiful Huck, beautiful, loving and kind. Loving and kind for the most part. There were times, of course, when the drinking hid her true self and that could make her different. It confused her. Could make her cold and mean at times, but it was only the drink talking. Not the real her. And it was him that drove her to the drink and even then she tried to fight it, tried so hard. And she was beautiful. Even with the cuts and the bruises and the scars she was more beautiful than any woman I ever saw until I met your mother. But even in spite of her faults you couldn't image a more perfect woman. Your own mum is the only woman I have ever met to rival her, Huck. I love them both so much.

But my mother Huck, she was like something from a Disney film. She always looked perfect. Well, other than when he had been at her or when she was drunk but mostly perfect. And she was so light, so natural. I remember once we were in our kitchen at home, a summer afternoon when I was about seven or eight, when a bird flew in the window and sat on the kitchen table. She didn't panic or flit at it like some people might. She just stared at it for a while, then she laughed and whistled a tune at it and even offered it some of her wine. It was beautiful. The bird just sat and stared right back at her and then it eventually flew away. I thought for a second it was going to sing right back at her but of course it didn't. She was like that Huck, when it was just the two of us, so full of life. So happy. When it was just the two of us.

She loved to read and tell stories too. Most nights, when it was time for bed and before she went back down to him, she would come to tuck me in and instead of reading me Roald Dahl or Narnia or anything like that she would make up her own stories. She has a wonderful imagination and her stories would go all over the place. She would make up and tell me adventures about me and Jack and I'd lay there, sometimes laughing, sometimes scared, but always so, so happy that I was listening to her voice. Imagining what she imagined. Just the two of us. She was perfect when he let her be. She would stay up with me for hours sometimes and when she eventually said she ought to go back down I would tighten my grip on her hand and she would stay with me until I fell asleep.

She would have loved you. I wish you could have met her. I wish that almost as much as I wish I'd spent more time with you myself. She would have doted on you, Huck. She would have showered you with love and you'd have adored her stories too. She would have made a wonderful grandmother – as wonderful a grandmother to you as she was a mother to me.

I love her, Huck. Love my mother as much as I have ever loved anyone in my life. I loved her.

I wish I could say the same for my father.

I hate my father Huck. I know that is an awful thing to say and I do not use this word lightly, Huck, but I hate him. Loved her and hate him. I hope you won't ever feel like this about anyone, I truly do. Maybe it's what you already feel about me, I don't know. I wouldn't blame you. But I hate him. I think, when I look back, I have always hated him from the moment I was born. I cannot remember a time in my life when I was happy to be around him. Cannot even remember a time when I wanted to be around him. I don't know why he didn't love me, Huck. I don't know what made him hate us both so much. I wish I did. I wish I could have understood him. I wish I could have known and changed it and made it all better. But I never did and I never will. He was a shadow on our house, Huck, a creeping shadow neither of us could escape from until the end.

And yet, after all that, I went to see him. Went to see them all. Or at least I will have done when this is all said and done. I went to come and find you.

We just stopped for another coffee and a quick trip to the bathroom and now we're parked up in the car park. Your mother has decided she wants to take a quick nap before we start on the road again and I can't blame her. We've only been driving for a few hours or so but driving on the motorway can be pretty dull. You have to concentrate on these kinds of roads – other people too eager to get where they're going can be dangerous. We've made good progress on our way, but not as much as your mum would like. I like the drive though. It gives the three of us some time to talk together. I know when we get to Scotland your mum is going to want me and her to talk things through, that she is going to want to understand things the way I'm telling them to you now. I'm not sure I'm ready to tell her. Not quite yet. Not everything.

Still, as I said before we're not in that much of a rush. You're sat now on the sofa opposite me leafing through some comic I bought from the newsagents. You seem to have the same thirst for reading as I always had. I hope it's something you continue to love. Do you have a favourite book? I always liked Moby Dick, all those guys chasing down that White Whale. I wonder if you've read it by now, or if you ever will. You should. You'll like it.

I read loads of comics when I was a kid too. The Beano was always a favourite. I wonder if they still make it, when you're reading this I mean? I would have thought kids found it a bit old fashioned now. Jack used to love the Beano as well. We would spend hours, me and him, in my room reading through old copies, going back over our favourite stories, howling with laughter at the antics of the Bashstreet Kids and Dennis and Gnasher and doing all the voices we imagined they had in our heads. Jack always did the voice for Dennis, I was Walter the Softy. My favourite stories were always the one about the Artful Dodge – I loved how good he was at getting himself out of scrapes. Jack's favourite was Minnie the Minx because she was so feisty. When Jack turned five his mum and dad bought him a dog and we called him Gnipper after the puppy in the Beano. Jack had had a dog before Gnipper called Gnasher, but my dad ran it over. Not on purpose, I don't think, an accident but something I never really forgave my father for. My father never once apologised for doing it.

Gnipper didn't look anything like his namesake. I was never really sure what type of dog the fictional Gnipper and Gnasher were meant to be. Jack's Gnipper was a beagle and a young one, small but with plenty of room to grow.

It was the real life Gnipper that was the source of the first real piece of bravery I ever saw from Jack. We were out walking him on the common near the river, not far from my house. It was a stretch of land that sat like an island in between the two forks of the river. It was January the fifth, just before we were about to go back to school and, whilst the river was high from the winter rains and flowing quickly, the common hadn't flooded like it sometimes did even if it was pretty wet underfoot. We walked along side by side, stopping every now and again to pick up the ball to throw it again, all the while chatting away at a thousand words a minute as kids do.

As we were heading back home Gnipper brought back the ball and Jack picked it up. An idea popped into my head. We'd always been competitive about who could throw it the furthest and, typically, Jack usually beat me without a huge amount of effort. We were walking back to the bridge over the river towards my house.

"Bet you can't get it all the way over the bridge," I challenged. Jack turned and looked at me, the flickering of a smile that always meant the same thing.

"Betcha I can," he said.

He turned to look at the bridge, looked down at the ball and tossed it up and down in his hand a couple of times, sizing it up. He spat on the ground, something we had just learned to do, and threw it with all the might his young arm would allow. It looked good, initially at least, sailing through the air in a perfect arc. Gnipper took off after it as soon as it had left Jack's hand, he knew what game we were playing. But Jack's aim was a little off, as was his confidence in his strength. The ball hit the bridge and bounced a giant loop before landing in the river below. Gnipper wasted no time in diving in to the water after it.

"Shit," Jack shouted. Swearing was another thing we had recently learned to do and so we did it as often as we could, away from adults anyway.

"Shit," I agreed and we ran after Gnipper.

We ran over to the bridge and looked over the edge into the dirty water. Gnipper was gone and the ball was nowhere to be seen. We ran to the other side, following the flow of the river, and looked down and still saw nothing. I was panicking, no idea what to do, my eyes darting from one part of the grey water to another. Jack however, didn't wait. He clambered up onto the side of the bridge and plunged into the water. It was stupid and I knew it, but it was also the bravest thing I've ever seen. I thought about diving in after him but I couldn't. I was too scared, too weak, my feet frozen to the bridge. It would have been a crazy thing to do but I wanted to and I couldn't.

Jack disappeared into the grey swell and the ripple he had made on entering was soon swallowed up by the pace of the river. I waited for him to come up. One Mississippi, two Mississippi.... when I got to ten I was really worried. I left the bridge and went to the bank, running up and down the same stretch of ten yards repeatedly. He didn't appear. I started shouting his name, hoping he could hear me under the water but nothing happened. There was nobody around to ask for help. It must have been at least thirty Mississippi by that point and he wasn't out. I looked back towards the bridge, thinking maybe he was further that way, that he hadn't drifted as far as I had thought, but nothing.

Suddenly, a hundred yards down the river and close to the bank the water exploded and Jack's upper half popped out, Gnipper's head held close to his own. He grabbed the bank with his free hand and tried to pull himself up. I scrambled down to the edge, being careful not to fall in myself. I grabbed Gnipper from him and threw him down on the bank. The dog shook himself free of water, dropped the ball at my feet and then ran off to get his circulation going again.

I turned back to the river bank and pulled Jack out with all my force. He landed on top of me, shivering and spluttering but still breathing, even though it was sporadic. His skin was a deeply disturbing shade of blue and he kept coughing up water for a minute or so. He was shivering so much I hugged him and rubbed my arms up and down him, the whole time him staring into my eyes, trying to speak but not being able to because his body was convulsing and his teeth were chattering too much. I took my coat off and wrapped it round him. He slowly started to stop shivering quite as much, but was clearly still freezing. He managed a brief smile.

"Shit," he stammered, "that was scary!"

Soon he had caught his breath but was still struggling to speak properly. I remember him looking so pale and blue. We started walking back to my house. It wasn't far and it took us less than five minutes to get there and Jack was already starting to look a little better by the time we got home. We walked through the back door into my kitchen and my mum, seeing Jack shivering and pale, dropped the plate she was drying up. I remember watching it fall, can still see it now, tumbling in slow motion and it shattered into a thousand pieces.

I thought we would be in trouble, but we weren't. My mum just pulled Jack to her and hugged him and I just stood there staring at the broken china on the floor. I think Jack's parents were more relieved he was alive than anything else. They both arrived at our house and took him home in the bundled duvet my mum had wrapped him in after she had taken him out of the bath. They smothered him with kisses and he had to fight them because he didn't want to look like a baby, embarrassed with all the affection he was getting. I was jealous. Despite the fact that he must have been freezing cold and feeling like death I wished my dad would have fussed over me like that. I wished it had been me.

Gnipper was fine, not even so much as a doggy-cough. Jack was off school for two weeks with a cold, but nothing more than that. My father was convinced he would get pneumonia and die and he repeatedly shouted at me for being such a coward. A coward! Can you believe that? I had been the sensible one. I hadn't nearly drowned or died of shock or whatever. I had actually been the rational, sensible one. The intelligent one. But he was right. I hadn't done it through calm reason. I'd done it because I was afraid. And that's what pissed him off the most, Huck. The fact I hadn't been the hero.

"Why didn't you jump in?" he would say to me over and over again, sometimes looking at the floor, sometimes looking over my shoulder, never looking me in the face. I said nothing, just carried on looking at the floor too. Sometimes I wished that I had jumped in, that I had had the courage to jump in, but I didn't and it was too late then.

"Why didn't you do it?"

Is that what I should have done, Huck? Jumped in too? I've thought about it over and over and over. A thousand times. Should I have jumped? Should I have tried to be the hero? I don't know. I would have drowned, I know that. I would have drowned and it would have been for nothing. I would have been dead but my father might have been proud of me. Might have thought at least I tried. Might have thought at least I did one useful, brave thing during my time on this shitty earth.

You are so brave Jack. I wish it had been me.

Jack, where are you? I could really use you right now.

We're back on the road again. I offered to drive for a while again and your mum said "no" again. She's stubborn that one. But still, I don't really want to drive. I'm in full flow now. You seem to have noticed that too. You've taken the seat up front, next to your mum, so you can spot cars with new registration plates. It's funny how times change but we always end up playing the same games. Not much else to do in a car I guess. We used to do exactly the same things with the letters on the number plates when I was younger. Back then you knew how old a car was by a letter, not the number, but it was the same thing. Each year a new registration came out in order from A to Z and then it started again.

My mum and I would play it on long car journeys just like you are now with your mum. We'd play on trips to see my aunt or on our holidays to Cornwall and Devon. We'd start by looking for whatever the latest registration was and then, when we found one, we'd move back one letter for an older car and so on and so on. It got more difficult as you went back, looking for older and older cars. We'd play until either I fell asleep, or, as happened more often, my father told us to give it a rest so he could concentrate on driving, or to stop a headache coming on or whatever excuse he had. We usually got to about five letters in before something stopped us.

"Do you have to play that fucking childish ridiculous game?" He would snap, never taking his eyes off the road.

"It's just a bit of fun," my mum would plead with him. "Why can't you ever let us enjoy ourselves?"

He would sigh and tighten his grip on the steering wheel.

"I get enough of this useless shit at work," he would say. "Difficult enough to concentrate there with all this crap going on. This is meant to be a holiday for me."

Mum would turn and stare out of the side window, trying to hide her face from his and mine and thinking, I don't know what.

"Let's leave it a while Michael," she would sigh.

A while would mean for the rest of the trip. The rest of the holiday. The rest of forever. Our holidays were mostly spent trudging through fields on walks or trips to the beach where the three of us would sit and watch the waves crashing on the beach, seeing the other kids having fun. Sometimes mum and I would walk off by ourselves and for a while she would break out of it and be her usual self. But it wouldn't last. Eventually we would have to go back to him.

I remember once we were staying in Cornwall in the Campervan and they had a massive row. A huge one. Bigger than usual. I was made to sit outside of the van while they argued, even though I could hear every word of what they said they were shouting so loud. I sat with my fingers in my ears and my eyes screwed up as much as I could but it didn't help. At least it meant I couldn't see the other kids staring at me. Mum had wanted us to go out for dinner at the hotel she had seen on the drive down and dad had said they couldn't afford it. They'd broken into a screaming match, not about the money or the dinner at all. Then he hit her. I heard it. Half of the caravan site probably heard it and the screaming stopped. Discussion over.

She came out of the Campervan in a slow but defiant way. I'd never seen her look like that. She looked down at me, her eye already swelling up, red around the edges where he had hit her.

"Come on Michael," she said.

It was the only thing she said to me. She took me by the hand and we walked off the campsite, through the village and up the hill just outside of town. When we got to the top of the hill we walked off the road and onto the coastal path at the edge of the cliffs for maybe half an hour until we came to a point that looked out over the sea. There was nothing in front of us but the rolling grey of the ocean as it crashed into the rocks below us. We stood there, the two of us, looking out to sea for what seemed like hours, her holding my hand and crying silently into the wind. I kept asking her what was wrong but she wouldn't speak, just kept holding my hand tighter and tighter. Finally she grabbed my hand tighter than before and smiled.

"I love you Michael," she said. I looked up at her. I didn't understand.

"I love you too mum," I said. She stood looking out into the grey that swept from the beach to the horizon. She never took her eyes off it.

"Do you see them, Michael?" she asked. I looked back out to the sea. I didn't see anything, just the waves. I said nothing, didn't know what to say, she shook her head and smiled at me. And with that we turned and walked home.

We went back there, mum and me, about a year later.

We walked back down to the caravan site and it was dark when we got back to the Campervan. Dad was sat on the step outside looking at his fingernails. When he heard us coming he stood up, his hands balled into fists at his side.

"Don't you ever," he hissed as mum pushed me into the Campervan. Her eyes met with his as she stepped up in after me.

"I can do it whenever I want to," she whispered back, thinking I couldn't hear it. "I hope I don't ever have to, but I can."

Dad sat outside a long time before he came back in. Mum and I slept in the double bed while he slept sat upright in the front seat.

Anyway, I am rambling and you've just shaken me out of it. You just spotted a 2013 plate and shouted about as loud as you can, which made your mum jump. She's beaming though, not angry like my father would have been. She turned her head to look at you for a second, flashed you a smile and laughed.

"Well done kiddo!"

She has an incredibly warm voice, so calm and reassuring and loving, don't you think? I've only ever really seen her angry a couple of times and those have both been in the last few days. Although the fact her voice is so tender and loving means when she is angry it cuts all the deeper. And she was incredibly angry with me. She had every right to be too. But we'll get there in good time.

Try not to make her angry, Huck. I know it'll be hard, especially when you're a moody teenager and going through all the trouble that comes with it. I guess that's probably how you feel now, reading this. She loves you, you know. Loves you more than you'll ever understand until you have kids of your own and then you'll wonder how anyone could ever love their own child any less. I guess you would have to ask my father how anyone could be like that. If you have to be angry at someone you should be angry at me. After all, if there's something wrong in your life you can probably trace it back to me. I'm sorry. I know it won't help you now, but I'm sorry.

And listen to me, I'm still going on. I should do what your mother wants and carry on with my story.

After leaving London I travelled on the train to King's Lynn. I hadn't particularly decided that was where I wanted to go when I left the house in Ealing in my panic, but as soon as I got to the station and saw the name on the departure board I knew that's where I had to go. My mum's sister, my aunt Sarah, and her husband lived in a town on the east coast, which wasn't far from King's Lynn. We'd spent a huge amount of time there when I was a kid. My aunt was fun, just pure fun to be around. She always made me think of what my mother would have been like if she didn't have my father and me around. A loving husband and no children to mess things up. My mum always told stories about them as kids, how they had always been close. Her and my uncle had never been able to have kids and I think that made her even more welcoming when we came to visit. My uncle, Chris, was nice too and he was fun but a little awkward around me, I guess from not having his own kids. I loved my aunt the most though. Perhaps because she was so much like my own mum and because the two of them had so much fun together. When her and my mother were together they both seemed so alive. So happy. Life was so simple that way I think. I think the happiest moments of my childhood were spent with the two of them.

As I've said, my aunt and uncle also happened to live by the sea, which I loved. The three of us, my mother, my aunt and I, would spend hours walking on the beach, me slightly ahead of them as I went off exploring, my mother and her sister talking, laughing and sometimes, not that they knew that I knew, crying together. The laughter could have stemmed from a thousand things. The crying always stemmed from two things; my father and aunt Sarah's inability to have children. My father never came when we went to visit them. He hated to be around the two of them together and my uncle wouldn't have him in the house. I think my aunt understood why my mother stayed with him and tried to make it as easy as she could but my uncle refused to understand. I didn't understand either. I was very young when I first realised my mother and father didn't love one another.

But back to the more recent past.

Once I'd taken the hour coach ride from Kings Lynn train station to the coast I checked into the Bed and Breakfast that stood on the cliff top looking out across the sea. The place had fascinated me as a child and at least once every visit I would stand outside staring up at the place. I had always wondered what it was like inside but had never gone in there. It wasn't the sort of place we would ever have stayed. It was too grand and I wasn't the kind of child to go wondering into places like that. It was one of those old Victorian guest houses that you see dotted up and down the English coast – once it had been a glorious building, and it had been glorious still when I was a child, but now it was weather beaten, with faded and flaking paint on the windows and door frames. When I was child the house itself was white and the window ledges and door frames a light green colour, and always immaculately painted. My uncle told me the combination of the wind and the sand meant it got a good blasting as soon as it was freshly painted and so they had to re-do it every year. When I got there I was pleased to see nothing much had changed and that it was still a B&B. Yes, it was faded and a little tattered. I guessed they had stopped painting as often. The sign on the front was different but the whole place still looked like the image I had in my head. The name was the same too even if the actual sign was different. It simply read "The Dunes", a reference to the great piles of sand that sat between the mainland and the beach itself, and that seemed like a good name to me. I'd spent many a happy day as a child running up and down those sand mountains, tiring myself out while my mother and her sister sat in deckchairs by the beach hut and watched me. My aunt and uncle had bought the beach hut the first time my aunt was pregnant as somewhere they could take the baby during the hot summer days and had never had the heart to sell it afterwards. It too was freshly painted every summer, fresh and new, always ready for us. Always ready for the baby that never came.

The B&B was empty when I arrived and so despite my appearance, which they never asked me about, the were happy to see me. It was so close to Christmas, the couple that ran it told me, and nobody ever stayed. They were surprised to see someone coming in at all, especially as I hadn't booked and it took them a while to get a room ready for me. They were kind and hospitable people though and the old man made me a coffee while I waited. I was given the top room, which was the one that I wanted. I wanted it partly for the privacy and the quiet but also to be able to look out of the large bay windows that hung over the garden that ran to the edge of the cliff. The window in my room had a seat along its length which meant I could sit, leaning against the wall at one end of the window with my legs on the bench, not quite reaching the other end, and look out across the grey sea and sky. I looked down at the garden a couple of floors below me. Once, when I was younger, I had snuck into the garden to sneak an apple from the trees that grew there although the trees were bare now. I looked down on those trees and thought about the last time I had been in that town.

I remember the date we had arrived exactly – April 30th, 1992. It was the day after the day my father lovingly referred to as his "re-birthday". Not his actually birthday but the day of his re-birth, the day his life started again, what little life he had. April 29th, 1992. It was the last day in his life he ever saw my mother. It was also the last day I ever saw my mother. A re-birth of sorts for all of us.

The previous night, the 29th, he had come home from work on time, which didn't happen often, and he was in a terrible mood. You could tell it from the moment he walked in the door – before even. You could almost feel some empty, dark silence coming up the path to our house, the way it feels before a big thunderstorm The way he turned the door handle and shoved the door open was angry. The way it slammed after him even more so. The house shook. The way he hung up his coat – angry. The way he put down his tattered briefcase – angry. The way he moved and talked and just was – angry, angry, angry, For once he looked straight at me, actually looked me in the eye. I can barely remember another time he did that All those years of wishing he would pay attention to me and in that moment I wished he hadn't. Sometimes when he came home he would flick a fake half smile in my direction, or else he would grunt something at me just to remind me he was still alive. Some minor acknowledgement that we were still father and son, by blood if nothing else. But it wasn't very often. He never usually actually made eye contact with me at all and it was difficult to know how he felt. But that night I could see how angry he was as clear as if he had spoken to me. And I could see how much he hated me. He didn't say anything. Normally when he came home looking anything like this it was because there had been trouble at work.

"Got a fucking bollocking for nothing from that hopeless prick of a boss," as he would usually put it. But there was something different about that day. I never knew what. Never. Maybe it didn't even matter. Bad luck I guess.

He walked past me and into the kitchen, where my mother was sat at the table. Not really sitting I guess. I had been in the kitchen not long before my father had come home and she hadn't been sat even then. Slumped would have been a better description. She was having a bad day and when

Mum always

she was having a bad day she slumped a lot. By that time in our lives my mother usually started drinking in the early evening. Sometimes the afternoons if I'm honest. That's a lie. Mostly in the afternoons. Sometimes I wouldn't know when she started, I could already smell it when I got home from school and most of the time when I saw her those days she was either drunk or hungover. When in her life she had actually started drinking so regularly and so heavily I don't really know. When I was about nine would have been my guess, but I don't know for sure. Maybe she had always drunk. Maybe I had only really started to notice it as I got older or maybe it had gotten worse. Either way it quickly became a daily ritual. Hung-over in the morning to see me off to school, if she got up, drunk when I got home, or at least on the edge. Jack's mum would come over sometimes or she would go over there and they would have a drink or two, just something "to take the edge off" as Jack's mum would describe it. But Jack's mum was tame compared to mine. She didn't have the need to take quite as much of the edge off I suppose. Two or three nights a week past eight o'clock she could barely speak. And then there were worse days. I quickly learned how to make it less obvious to my dad, or at least make it less of a problem for him. I had learnt to cook by then and most nights I would make dinner so by the time he came home it would be on the table, the washing up would be done. It wouldn't matter what kind of a state she was in, so long as he was fed and the house was tidy. It's not like he enjoyed her company. I guess he thought she always managed to cook it before she got past the point of not being able to see the recipe book, never mind read it. Maybe he knew the truth. I have no idea. He never asked if it was me. Never thanked me. Barely acknowledged that I was even sat round the table. He would eat in silence, watch TV in silence and the rest of the night would be much the same until I went to bed. That's when the shouting usually started. Sometimes before.

She was having a bad day. He was having a worse day. The perfect match.

That night I hadn't realised how far gone she was. I'd been watching something on the TV and hadn't been paying attention to the time. I'd selfishly been so engrossed in whatever rubbish I was watching that I hadn't realised nothing was cooking and, for once, my father was home from work on time. Bad luck, I guess. Or not. My fault. I hadn't realised the time. It was my fault really.

I don't recall the argument. Not in detail anyway. I think most of the time I tried to blank them out. Most of the time I tried not to listen or would just focus on the television, straining as hard as I could to hear every word the characters on TV said. But I do know what the argument was about - food,

I know that much. A stupid fight about the fact dinner wasn't ready for him when he came home just like it should have been. Like it always should have been. Because he was the man of the house and he'd been working all day and he didn't do all he did for this fucking family so he could come home and not have his fucking dinner ready. It was about food and it wasn't. Wasn't about food at all. It always worked its way back to the state of things. To the state of his life and the way things should have been. To the state of her. To the state of me. Sometimes she took it, apologised for being the mess she was and agreeing it was all her fault and he, angry as he was, would be happy with that response and would sit down in silence or he would storm back out of the house and not come back until the following evening, spending the night God knows where but too disgusted to be around her. Too disgusted and ashamed. Too disgusted and ashamed to be around my mother? I could never understand it. Too disgusted and ashamed to be around me I could understand but how could anyone not want to be around my mother? I admit I didn't like it when she drank, preferred it when she was herself, but she was still my mum. She was still the same wonderful mum she always was. She still loved me. She would have still loved him if he wasn't the way he was.

Other days she didn't take it. Couldn't take it. Had to stand up for herself. Those days were worse. That day was worse. That day was one of the days she wasn't going to take it. The last day she was ever going to not take it as it turned out, although I don't think she knew that when she shouted back at him. I don't think she knew anything much at all that night to be honest but something inside her told her it was a day not to take it. She said something to him, I don't know what. Usually it was a question.

"Why don't you spend more time with him?"

"Why don't you just let him be?"

"What are you doing to make life better for him?"

I've forgotten what she said that night, but I know it was something about me. My fault. I know what she said.

I remember creeping to the door to watch them fight after it had started and I could no longer hear the television. I did that often towards the end. I don't know why I did it. Some perverse curiosity I guess. Maybe I went intending to stop it that night. Planning to intervene just like, in my head, I always planned to. A joke. What would I do? I Always had this great image in my head of me being the hero and never did anything. I always just stood and watched them fight and hated him and hated myself.

It wasn't the worst beating he had ever given her, but it hurt her. Hurt her a lot. Hurt us both. Thinking about it now makes me feel stick my stomach. You can't imagine what it's like until it happens Huck, watching someone you love being beaten like that and knowing there is nothing you can do to stop it. Watching your own mother in so much pain and not being able to do anything about it. I can't imagine anything worse. Nothing I've ever seen in my lifetime anyway. I wanted to stop him Huck, of course I did. I wanted to run in and get between them somehow and push him off her. I wanted to stand up to him like I'd never done before and I didn't care if he hit me or kicked me or spat on me like he did my mum. But I didn't do any of those things. I did what I always did. I stood in the corner of the door, my eyes transfixed on the man hitting my mother repeatedly whilst I felt first my crotch and then my leg grow warm and wet. I told you I am not brave Huck. I never have been. I wasn't a brave kid and I'm not a brave man.

Looking back at it now I could have stopped him. I could have stopped him easily if I had tried. If I'd been brave enough. It would have been so simple. If I'd been man enough Huck. I could have hit him with something. I was ten years old for Christ sake, old enough not to be so fucking useless. I could have grabbed a knife from the kitchen drawer and done something to stop him. I could have just run in and hit him with my fist. I'd seen enough punches thrown to know what a good one looked like. I see kids around today, ten year old kids like I was, and they're mouthy and they fight. Why couldn't I have been like that? There were two of us and just one of him. He wasn't even that big, not really. Just a bully. I could have jumped in whenever I wanted to and ended it. But I never did. I'm a coward. It's my fault he hit my mother and my fault he didn't stop. My fault she left us. My fault because I never stopped him doing it and it would have been so easy. All I could do was stand there gawping and pissing myself like a fucking child.

When he was finished she lay on the floor under him, crying and shaking but conscious. When she cried and shook it wasn't so bad, at least she knew where she was and what was happening to her. It knocked the drink out of her. As he stood there, looking down at her, the anger started to disappear and he looked calmer, just as he always did. But the hatred didn't leave him, that was plain to see. That never left him. Never the hatred or the disgust or the shame. They were always there. And he was never sorry. Even when he was no longer angry with her, he never seemed to feel any regret for what he had done, not even the slightest pity. He would simply turn and walk away, just as he did then, pick up his coat and walk out the door. He walked past me like I wasn't there.

When I heard the door shut behind me I ran over to my mother and wrapped myself around her, trying to soak up as much of the pain as I could with my body. The fact I was wet didn't bother her. I'm not sure she even noticed. Conscious enough to feel her own pain but nothing else. Most of his blows had landed on her stomach, which I guess was a good thing. He wasn't stupid either, not my dear old dad, never hurt her too badly where someone might see unless he was really out of control. A few hits on her face but not too much. Mostly on her stomach. That was where she held herself as she lay curled up into a tiny ball. I just held her.

After about twenty minutes she patted me on the shoulder and I knew it was time for her to get up. Being beaten always sobered her up, at least for a little while. She went upstairs and I heard the sound of the bath running. Once I heard her get in I crept upstairs. I was mostly dry by then but I could still feel the shame and I smelt. I got changed into my pyjamas and put my clothes in the washing basket. I looked in the door to the bathroom and saw that my mother was already asleep in the bathtub. I went and sat on the toilet and watched her and held her hand. Her stomach was red and already turning black. I tried to stay awake, hoping I could keep awake long enough to make sure nothing happened to her in the bath. She had nearly drowned once and I'd had to pull her out. I was so tired. Tired of being there. Tired of him. Tired of myself. After a while she woke up, dried herself off and we got into her bed. Neither of us spoke.

The next morning my mother was up and about before I was. She was hung-over, I could tell she was, and she was in a lot of pain but she was awake and alert. She always managed not to really show the effects of either a beating or a hangover but I could tell. That morning she looked like shit but she was putting a brave face on it. I went into her room to see her packing two big suitcases. She was throwing in everything she owned, pulling out drawers and tipping them in. She handed me a small suitcase – the one I always used when we went away – and told me to go and pack some clothes for a few days.

"Where are we going?" I asked.

"Aunt Sarah's," she replied without looking at me. I guessed my father wasn't coming. I didn't even know where he was. Work I supposed. I was glad he wasn't coming.

She said virtually nothing to me on the way there. We just drove together, side by side in silence. She wore a pair or enormous tortoiseshell sunglasses but they didn't cover up the huge bruises on her face from the one stray punch that had gotten through. It didn't hide her tears either. I didn't understand what was happening.

We had to stop a couple of times on the drive up so she could be sick. I tried more than once to play the registration plate game with her, but every time I asked she simply said "not now Michael" and we would lapse into silence again. No music. Nothing. Just silence and the sound of the road. I think it was the longest time we were together that we didn't speak. The longest drive of my life.

We arrived at my Aunt Sarah's house in the mid afternoon. Uncle Chris was nowhere to be seen. He had gone away for a couple of days or at least that was the story I was told. I guess mum had called ahead. We had been to Sarah's house a couple of times after one of mum's incidents and he was never there. But those trips. I don't know if it was because he was too ashamed to see my mother or my mother was too ashamed to see him. Maybe both. Now I look back I would guess both. My mum and Aunt Sarah hugged and cried for a long time before we went into the house, while I just stood on the porch watching them, scuffing my shoes on the matt and not knowing what to say.

A couple of hours later we walked down to the beach hut and my mum and Aunt took up their usual places on the deckchairs in front. I was told to go and play on the dunes, but I didn't want to go. All I really wanted to do was sit by my mother's legs and listen to them talking, but I wasn't allowed.

"Go and play, Michael," my mother pleaded, "we need to talk about grown up things."

Grown up things. That old excuse. I'd heard it a thousand times before. It was like I was a child. They thought I didn't understand. That I didn't know what was going on. I had been there, I saw what happened. I wasn't stupid. A coward I might be, but I was not stupid. At least give me that. But I couldn't resist doing what my mother wanted and eventually I trudged to the top of the nearest dune, just over the lip and sat myself down. I knew they couldn't see me and I sat there and I tried to listen but the wind was blowing in swirls and I couldn't hear what they were saying properly, only snippets.

"….wouldn't come for me, but he would for him….," I heard my mother say. "…. deep down somewhere he does….would do it to spite me….."

"....safe?" I hear my aunt say and I didn't hear anymore. I can now only guess at what they were saying. I sat there for maybe thirty minutes, not moving, simply staring at the sea in front of me, just like I was doing then in the window of the B&B. The clouds and the sea were a similar grey to that day. When I hadn't heard anything for a while I thought it was time to head back. I stood up and turned to walk back to the hut only to see my aunt sat alone. I ran down the slope of the dune.

"Where's mum?" I asked my aunt. She wrapped her arms around me and started sobbing like I had never seen her do before, not even after the first miscarriage. If I had known that was going to be the last time I ever saw my mother. I probably would have done the same.

Hug your mother Huck. Hug her every day like it's your last. All I wanted was one more hug. Just to say goodbye. Just a chance to say goodbye.

I need to stop for a while.

Happy families, hey Huck? I paint a pretty picture don't I?

Still, I did know one happy family when I was growing up – the Lawrence's. I should probably tell you a little more about them, since they featured so much in my life when I was growing up. Jack has a much bigger family than I ever did. He had an older sister and older brother, which I always thought was amazing and must have been so much fun. I was very jealous. I would have loved an older brother most of all I think. Jack's sister was the eldest though and, in addition to being beautiful, was also incredibly caring and generous, some things she got from her mother. She was four years older than Jack and I and we pretty much saw her as one of the grown-ups. Whenever there was money to be handed out by Jack's mum for sweets or ice cream or whatever, it was always given to Sophie. And she was always good with it, always made sure everyone got their fair share and nobody was ever left without. I admit I was a little bit in love with her growing up. More than a little bit.

Jack's older brother, Tom, on the other hand was very different – he looked after us and he loved us and was great to be around but he wasn't like his sister. He was fearless and full of energy, almost as much as Jack. I idolised him almost as much as I idolised Jack. Jack adored him too. Tom was two years older than us and was bigger, stronger and faster. But he was still a kid at heart and ready for any kind of adventure we wanted to have with him.

When it wasn't just Jack and I it was usually because Tom was with us, and Gnipper of course. Tom taught us how to do everything - climb trees, build forts, fish – everything.

I have a picture of the four of us; me, Jack, Sophie and Tom, that Mrs Lawrence took of us the summer before Jack saved Gnipper from the river. We'd just had a BBQ at their house and we were playing cards outside on the grass. I remember being so happy with them back then, Huck. I've put the picture of it in with this letter so you can see how happy I was with them and so you can see Jack.

Their house was always full of fun. They were also rich. I forget now what Jack's father did, not sure I ever knew to be honest, but it was something important. Always drove a shiny new car – a Mercedes or a Jaguar or something like that, and always in a suit. I can see him now – spotless shoes, a wonderfully fitted grey suit, jet black tie and a white shirt. In good shape too – he was tall and athletic – and when he played with us after work, football or French cricket in the garden, he was always full of so much energy and so confident yet humble. He'd always let us win without it being obvious. Jack's mum was the complete opposite of what my dad turned my mum into. She was the perfect stay at home wife - all dresses and pinnies, flour in her hair and a smell of baking that followed her around. She was clever too, the sort of woman who had clearly made the choice to be at home with her family but could easily have had a glittering career if she had wanted to. The house was always immaculate and there was an endless supply of homemade treats and milk. Their house was a childhood dream.

Given the choice we usually ended up going to Jack's house to play rather mine up until the age of about nine, although after that we tended to hang around at mine. Something happened to his father then. I don't remember exactly what it was. I think he changed his job or something and had to spend much more time at home rather than at the office and he couldn't have us running about the place and making noise. We tended to make a lot of noise, Jack and I. Tom too. It didn't stop us playing together though, we just spent way more time at my house.

Their garden was enormous too and even after we weren't allowed in the house as much anymore Jack and I would still sit in the garden, right at the bottom, away from the house so we could just sit and talk without disturbing anyone. Sometimes when we were down there Tom would come and chat to us and promise not to tell anyone we were there in case we got in trouble, but mostly it was just the two of us. I loved just sitting there and talking.

I remember once, before we were banned from being in the house, we went over there on Christmas Eve. My parents came too, which I remember being both a surprise and awkward. I was terrified my dad would make a scene but he didn't. It's probably my one memory of him being normal. I don't remember how old I was but we were fairly young. It must have been when Jack and I were about seven or eight as it was my first real memory of a Christmas tree. A proper Christmas tree anyway. I remember it being enormous and covered with lights, with an absolutely enormous pile of presents underneath it, all wrapped in reds and greens and gold's. I was in awe. I'd never seen anything so beautiful or so exciting in all my life. A world away from the tree my mum and I would put up. After she left there was nothing.

The Christmas tree downstairs in the B&B looked very similar to the Lawrence's one that I remember but without the pile of presents. The one in the B&B had a few boxes wrapped up underneath but they looked like they had been the same empty boxes put out every year. When the landlady went to sort out my room I picked one up and rattled it. Empty, as I had guessed. But still, the tree was a decent effort given they hadn't been expecting anyone. Later, as I sat on the window ledge in my room and looked down into the garden below me I could see the reflection of the lights twinkling on the grass in the semi-dark. I decided then it was time to see what Santa had brought me.

First, I made sure the door to my room was locked. I didn't think the landlady would be spying on me but I still felt a little uneasy given what I had done. I put my bag on the bed, carefully took the tin out of it and carried it over to the window ledge. When I opened it up I saw exactly what I had expected to be in there – stacks of money. It wasn't a big tin but it was full and the notes were mostly fifties and twenties. I counted it out and was amazed at how much there was of it in such a small space. Just short of sixty thousand pounds. £57,640 to be exact. A lot of money. More money than I had ever seen in my life. More than I had ever expected to see in my life and certainly far more than I had expected to be in the tin but it was perfect. I figured in the next two weeks I'd only need to spend a couple of thousand of that, if that, and the rest would do for what I wanted it for. I took out a few hundred pounds, stuffed it into my pocket, left the rest in the tin and put the tin back in my bag, which I shoved underneath the bed. I thought for a moment about trying to hide the tin somewhere else, somewhere safer, but I didn't. It was fine where it was. The couple who ran the B&B didn't seem like the type who would come snooping around in my

The Plan
key people to see

room. Then I went out and stopped at the local fish and chip shop to buy some dinner and think over my plan.

I decided I would stay in town for a day or so. That would give me time to do a couple of things and really get myself ready for my trip. For this trip. I wanted to rest a little and have my face heal up as much as possible. Then I wanted to mentally prepare myself for what I was about to do over the coming days, which I knew wasn't going to be easy. The more I thought about the list the more I knew I had to do it. But I was scared too. Part of me would have happily stayed in that B&B forever and just waited for it to happen. But I couldn't do that. I needed to find out where everyone on the list was. I knew exactly where Jack was and I knew where my mum was so they weren't going to be the issue. It was the others. I had no reason to believe my dad didn't still live in the house he had moved into when I had gone to University. His factory had closed and moved north to a small town in Yorkshire and he had gone with it. He didn't have a reason not to go I guess. Nothing really to keep him where he was and most of the people he knew were moving with the factory. So he went. I couldn't imagine his life had changed that much. If there was still a job for him at the factory he would still be there and he wasn't the sort of person who would have retired. He wasn't old enough yet and wouldn't have been able to afford it, unless something drastic had changed. I had an address for that house and so I would be able to track him down. He's sent it to me at University with a simple note:

I'm moving, it said, Thought you should know.

Your mother, I assumed, would still live near her parents since she had always been so close to them and, with you around, had probably needed them even more. I had stopped calling the house phone but it hadn't been that long ago that she had still been answering it.

That left Paul.

Paul was going to be the most difficult one since I hadn't seen him since we were at school. I had a plan though. After breakfast the following morning I went into the only electronic shop in town and bought a small laptop. I'd never owned one before. Never even really used one before. The guy in the shop showed me how to load it up, how to get onto the internet and how to connect to Wi-Fi, which I already knew the B&B had. I thanked him and paid for the laptop, giving him a little extra for helping me, before walking back to the B&B and up to my room.

As it turned out finding Paul actually turned out to be far, far simpler than I had ever imagined it was going to be. It just took a bit of time, a lot of clicking around and some mindless chat. I found the internet fascinating, but also surprisingly simple. The guy in the shop had told me I needed an email address before I could do much so I set one up and then a Facebook profile. Ask your mum what Facebook is if they don't have it anymore. I guess they might not even have email anymore by the time you read this. Maybe go to a museum or something. Anyway, then I started to look for people I remembered from school. I started with Paul, obviously, but couldn't find him, so then worked on some of his friends. The trick I learned pretty quickly was to make friends with anyone and everyone he might still be in touch with from school and then I would be able to use them to find him. Maybe. That was my plan anyway. I had expected the first connections to be the difficult part since I hadn't had a huge number of friends at school and so had expected people to ignore me. But they didn't. People actually seemed pretty happy to make friends with me online, and almost as soon as I had sent them the request. Some replies were almost instant, like people were sitting there, staring at their screens and waiting for people to make friends with them. It was strange. I started with a few people I had been vaguely on speaking terms with at school and after I had a few "accepts" I started to become more daring and look for some of the more popular kids from my school who, inevitably, had not been my friends.

Of course, the more people I added the easier it became to find other people I had been to school with simply by scrolling down their lists of friends. Men were easier to find that women as their surnames were still the same. I started to enjoy myself, looking over what had happened since I left school. It was interesting to see who had stayed friends with who, who actually seemed to continue to see one another, who had gotten married to who, which childhood romances had worked and which had crumbled as soon as they went to University or got jobs in the real world. Some people were barely recognisable, others seemed hardly to have changed at all. I found two twins, non-identical admittedly, that we had gone to school with were virtually indistinguishable when I was younger. Now one of them looked like a body builder, tall, and huge with a shaved head while the other looked more like a scrawny, long distance runner with an unkempt beard. I spent an hour or so just scrolling through people's profiles – fascinated with what people were doing with their lives.

The thing that surprised me the most was that a number of Paul's friends, people who had been pretty shitty to me at school, had added me straight away. But when I scrolled down their lists of friends, Paul was nowhere to be seen. They had all been pretty close when we were younger – all went to the same primary school, all lived round the corner from each other. They'd like to think of themselves as "brothers" and, while the rest of them seemed to have remained close, I couldn't see Paul on any of their lists nor in any of their photographs.

Finally I plucked up courage and I sent a message to a bunch of Paul's old friends. It was just a simple "hi, remember me?" The same message to each of them. I thought someone would respond as quickly as they had added me and when they did I could ask them about Paul. But nothing happened. I sat there looking at the screen for about twenty minutes and nothing happened. Eventually I got bored staring at the same screen over and over and decided to go for a walk.

Coastal towns are strange places, especially in the winter. They have a very different feel to a normal town. I remember, even as a kid, driving up there with my mum in early December for my aunt's birthday and thinking how different it was. Everything that is a draw in the summer looks strange and out of place in the winter. The bright colours somehow look less cheerful, look almost like a compensation for the faded place the town is. This town probably thrived once, was probably full of young people all year round. Now it's just full of old people waiting for the end, or at least that's what I saw anyway. It's pretty, in its own bleak way, but you wonder why anyone under the age of sixty would chose to live here. How do they make a living during the winter, or do they just live off the summer and hope the money holds out? There was almost no-one walking the streets when I went out. The cold had made the few people who were out hurry around and wrap themselves up. I love the smell of the place though – the strange mix of wet and sand and fish you get. It's the same in Cornwall and Devon. It's stronger in the winter – maybe that's what brings people here. Maybe they like the smell, the quiet and the bleak landscape. I hope you come here one day Huck, just to see what it's like. You should stay in the old B&B if it's still there.

I wandered around for a while looking for a coffee shop. After spending a few years in London you get used to there being one around every corner, sometimes three or four on the same one. A Starbucks or a Costa or whatever. I didn't find one though, just a small local café run by an old woman who looked and sounded like she'd never left the town and certainly didn't know what a latte was. Despite her age everything in the café looked like it was older than she was. She set me up with my own pot of coffee, a matching set all in fake silver. I guess there was a time when that was what people wanted. Maybe that's what the residents still wanted. I just wanted a latte in a normal cup but I nodded and smiled when she brought it to me. She looked happy to be serving anyone.

As I sat in the café I watched the few people who were out in the street walk past and I thought again about my aunt. The moment I arrived I had thought about trying to find her, going to see her and Uncle Chris and maybe spending some time with them. But I decided not to. If I had gone to see them they would have made me stay too long, would have made me tell them everything that had happened and I didn't want to tell them anything. I didn't want to tell anyone what had happened – only you and your mother. I would have been too ashamed to tell them anything that happened to me after we left a few days after my father's re-birthday. What would I have told her? I dropped out of university, got a girl pregnant, ran out on her and spent the last part of my life ferrying drugs? I'd have had nothing to say. I wondered about her though. I wondered what had happened to her since the last time I had been with her.

When my mum had left me with her my aunt hadn't told me what had happened straight away. I stayed with her for a couple of days and we just did fun things. I later found out she had agreed with my dad to give him time to cool off and decide what he wanted to do before he came to get me. It was just the two of us and we did all the things that she, my mother and I used to do. Except my mother wasn't there. Aunt Sarah was far more generous than she had been before though. Don't get me wrong Huck, she was always generous toward me and tried to spoil me a little on account of the fact that she didn't have anyone to spoil of her own. But those few days she went overboard. We played crazy golf every day, stuffed our faces with ice creams and chips and anything else I wanted. She bought me a Gameboy and about ten games. It was a distraction and I'd have been happy if I hadn't known something was wrong but I didn't let on that I knew.

Eventually my father arrived. Since my mum had taken the car he had come down in the Campervan and it had taken him a long time. I remember he didn't even come in the house, he simply stood on the porch and waited for me to collect my things together so could walk back to the Campervan and he could repeat the journey all over again in reverse. He barely spoke a word to my aunt. I heard them exchange a few heated whispers on the doorstep, clearly not wanting me to hear, most of which seemed to be my aunt begging and pleading with him to do something. Whatever it was he said no. The whole journey back we didn't talk. He just drove.

A couple of years later I found a letter from my aunt pleading with my dad to let me come and live with her and Uncle Chris. I guess that had been what they were talking about when they were stood on the door step and clearly my dad hadn't let me go. She had written it just after my mother had left. It was stuffed in a box inside the bottom of his wardrobe. I was looking for something, I forget what now, and I found it. I wondered why he didn't agree with her and let me go. I still don't understand. I wonder why he didn't take the first chance he could have to get rid of me. He hated having me around, why did he want me to stay? Perhaps he thought at some stage I would have grown out of my difficult phase and become the person he wanted me to be. I never did. I wish I could have at least met him half way. Perhaps he simply did it to spite my aunt. Or my mother. Or me. Maybe he thought that if I went to stay with my aunt that she would someday come back and steal me away and be happy. He couldn't have that. Maybe he just wanted someone to control, the way he had controlled my mother. It wasn't the same though. We didn't fight. We didn't argue or shout or hit each other. We didn't speak. Didn't interact. We did nothing. We simply existed in the same space, neither of us doing much more than that alone or together. Maybe that's what he wanted.

After I found the letter I often wondered what my life would have been like had I gone to live with them. I think I could have liked living there, by the sea. There was plenty of space and time to be alone when you wanted to be in the winter, the grey skies and sea at the time of the year fitted well with my mood in my teenage years. The summer was exciting and full of interesting people to watch and to listen to. Maybe I could have been happier. Happier than I was at home with him. But things happen for a reason Huck and maybe you wouldn't be here if I had gone to live with them. Anyway, if I had moved to live with them I would have had to have left Jack behind and I don't think I could have done that. It was probably for the best anyway. My aunt had enough difficulty with the fact she couldn't have children at all, it probably would have made it even worse if the only child she could have had was me.

Still, a different life might have been nice.

I drank my coffee and thought about that life again while I sat there. I watched the few people I could see walking around the town for an hour and had another pot of coffee, which made the old woman that ran the shop even happier, and then I walked back to the B&B. When I got back to the house I went straight up to my room and sat myself back in front of Facebook. I hadn't expected anyone to write back to me and so I was surprised to see someone had written me a message and even more surprised to see it was a response from one of Paul's best friends at school,

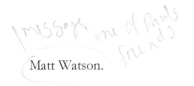

Matt Watson.

"Hey mate – long-time no see," it said and had a smiley face at the end. Nothing more than that. Matt was online. Of all the people I had sent messages to it was strange somehow that he had replied. He had never smiled at me once when we had been at school together. Not a smile I was meant to enjoy anyway. I wasn't sure what to say, worried I'd write something stupid and he'd laugh at me, just like he had at school. I worried it was all a trick and he didn't really want to speak to me at all and suddenly everyone who had "friended" me would suddenly be there, laughing at me. And yet at the same time it didn't matter. It wasn't real.

"Yeah you too." I replied and waited for a response. A couple of seconds later and it pinged up again, like he was waiting for me. Maybe he was.

"What you up to these days, mate?"

It was strange that he was being so friendly. Calling me mate. He had called me that twice now. I don't think anyone had ever called me that, not anyone I knew properly anyway. He was talking to me as if we had been best friends. As though at some point we were great mates and we were just catching up for the first time in a couple of weeks. He'd barely said two words to me in our entire school lives. Well, two nice words anyway. He'd talked at me countless times.

"Living in London," I replied. "Just on holiday. You?" He replied again, almost instantly. And suddenly we were talking. Nothing serious, nothing deep. Just an inane back and forth that went on for maybe twenty minutes, the two of us asking questions we weren't really interested in the answers to. At least, I wasn't anyway. Is this what people use Facebook for? To have pointless conversations they aren't interested in and boasting or moaning about every little thing in their lives?

Eventually we started talking about old times at school. Old teachers, old friends, girls we'd liked. He did most of the talking. I hadn't had many friends at school. Any friends. Just Jack really. I had liked girls but didn't talk to them. There were teachers I liked but I didn't talk much to them either. Just kept to myself. Matt talked me through the lives of pretty much everyone he used to hang out with. Most of them were married with kids, or kids on the way. Some were on their second marriage. Some didn't see their kids anymore. He had been divorced himself and had two kids he only saw at weekends. He was so open. So keen to tell me anything and everything. I didn't talk about you, Huck. Didn't talk about your mum. I

ominous
what happened?

just read and typed back questions. But he didn't seem to want to mention Paul and in the end I had to ask about him.

"After the thing when he changed schools…" Matt started. The thing. He couldn't even say what it was. He paused for a minute, like he was thinking and then he carried on again. "…he got into more trouble and moved away," he carried on. "Not really sure what it was. He just upped and left. He didn't keep in touch with anyone. None of us have really spoken to him since then. A few people are friends with him on here I think. He changed his surname though, changed it to Burrows. I think it's his mum's maiden name or something like that. Not sure why he did it…."

I stopped reading. That's why I hadn't seen him, he'd changed his name. I had seen a couple of Paul's on people's friend's lists but had passed them by looking for Paul Darke. I closed the chat with Matt, I didn't even say goodbye. The chat kept popping up but after a few hello?'s from him he assumed I was gone and he stopped writing. I went back through a couple of Matt's friends profiles and suddenly there Paul was, staring me in the face. Paul Burrows, lives in Nottingham. I don't know why I hadn't spotted him straight away, he had hardly changed at all. He was wearing sunglasses in the picture but it was him alright. I wondered for a minute if he would be able to tell I had looked at his profile and then decided I didn't care. I was going to see him anyway. I clicked through a few of the few photos he had, mainly ones of him with what seemed to be his sisters son. There were hardly any at all but enough to know it was definitely him. There wasn't much detail about him either only to say he now lived in Nottingham and he was chief mechanic and owner of Burrows' Autos. There was no address on the page but it wouldn't be difficult to find. It took me about five minutes on Google to find what I needed.

I hadn't expected it to be all that easy. The truth of it was I was kind of hoping he would be too difficult to find. And if I couldn't find him I couldn't start my list and then it would all be pointless. Might as well not start at all if I couldn't find him. No point in going to see my mum, your mum, him, you or Jack. I'd just have to give up.

I guessed I was going to have to do this after all.

I quickly decided that if I was going to go to Nottingham then I needed a quicker way of getting there. I might as well bite the bullet and get on with it. The ride from London to the coast had been ok, and travelling first class had been strangely fun, even if I had felt out of place, but now things needed to move on. I needed to move quicker. Plus being in my own car would give me time and space to think about whatever I wanted to without being interrupted by ticket collectors or people wanting to share a seat or make small talk. And I had money, plenty of money to do whatever I wanted to do. I thought about buying a car and started searching for local second hand dealers nearby. And then I saw it. Sat there, just waiting for me on the second page I looked at. The exact make, model and colour of VW we used to drive around in when I was a kid. The van I had spent every holiday in from the age of four to the year my mum left us. It had been a present from my mum's parents. "An outrageous waste of money" as my dad had described it, or so my mum told me. My father had sold it as soon as he got back from collecting me from my aunt's house. I'd loved that thing. I don't believe in fate, never have done, but I'm not one to go against the obvious. I used the phone in my room to call the owner and told him I'd be there to pick it up in the morning.

We've stopped to sleep now Huck, parked up in a service station car park. It's raining, huge great droplets hammering against the window. It's not the quietest in the Campervan when the weather's bad outside but somehow the two of you are fast asleep, dozing side by side. I'm sat in the front, staring out of the window into the darkness. Not seeing them, which is a good sign. I listened to the two of you for a while, your mum whispering a story to you until you fell asleep. Another five minutes and your mother joined you. I couldn't get there myself. Too much going on in my head.

I turned around and watched you sleep for a while. You twitch when you sleep, just like I do. The rest of your body lays still but your leg kicks out. I wonder what you're dreaming about?

I don't dream much, Huck, but when I do it's always the same. The same dream over and over again. Not a good dream. I'm sat in a boat on the river. The same river that Jack saved Gnipper from. I'm sat in an old wooden boat on the river and I know it's the same river but I can't see the bank. The river is unimaginably wide but the same river none the less. I know it. No matter which way I'm looking I can't see the bank and I don't know why I'm there. It's hard to tell whether its day or night, the sky is so black. Not black like when there's a storm, not black like at night when its cloudy and there are no stars. Just black and yet somehow I can see. Can see perfectly well. There is a wind, not much of one, but its gentle and doesn't make a sound. It just ruffles my hair and nudges the boat.

It's strange. I have this dream over and over and I know exactly what will happen. I know exactly what I will see everywhere I look and yet I'm scared anyway, even though every time I forget why.

I look down at the water. The water is rushing past the boat quickly, far quicker than it should do. The water is dark and murky and grey. But it isn't the water I'm afraid of. And it's not the blackness either. It's them. They are huge and, though I cannot see them clearly, can only see the shadows they make on the surface of the water, I know what they are. At least, I know what they look like, what they are I cannot say. They look like huge, dark catfish. Dark enough that they cast a shadow on the surface of the water as they swim, a shadow somehow darker than the sky. Their huge mass is larger than the boat I am floating on and their long whiskers trail alongside them as they swim past.

I want to reach out. In my dream I want to reach out and touch them as they swim past and I know I cannot. I daren't even put my hand out to try.

I look down into the boat and at my feet there is an old fashioned fishing rod and a net to land the fish with. Both of them look small and weak, far too weak to be able to catch one of the fish. I don't know what I'm doing there.

I look up and down to the other end of the boat. Jack is there. The boat is long, much longer than it ought to be, and he is a long way from me but I can see him and I know it is him. He is sat with his rod, just like mine, cast over the side of the boat. I can see his red and white float bobbing on the water a little way from the side of the boat. It bobs gently and the line is slack despite the rushing water. Jack has his net between his feet on the floor and flapping around in the net are some of the fish. Only not the same fish, his are small and grey. He is the same age as me but he looks younger. So much younger.

"Jack?" I ask, wanting to make sure it's him. He nods at me and smiles, but says nothing.

"What are we doing here?" I say and his smile turns to confusion.

"The fish," he replies simply. "Always the fish."

I am confused and I look back at the net between his feet.

"Why do you have fish, Jack?" I say. The smile returns to his face.

"We all have our fish, Michael," he said. "You know that."

And with that he picks one of the fish out of the net and holds it out to me in both hands, cradling it as he does so. Twice he offers it to me but I push back in my seat to move further away and I shake my head. The smile is back on his face and it widens and he pulls the fish to his nose, taking a deep breath. Suddenly, one of the dark fish nudges the boat. Not a strong nudge, just a gentle bump, but it is enough to send the boat rocking. I try to look over the side of the boat and see my own knuckles holding on to the edge of the boat. They are white with tension. Another fish nudges the boat and I screw up my eyes.

And then I wake up.

Always the same. I wake up in bed, the blanket held over me and I realise it was only a dream. Only a dream.

Those dreams are over now Huck. Over for the most part anyway.

I hope you dream well Huck.

A quick note before breakfast to keep the story going Huck. I need every second I can get to make sure I get this all down.

First thing the next morning I spoke to the landlady at the B&B and she agreed to take me to the house of the man selling the Campervan. She pulled her car around to the front of the house and I threw my bag into the back and climbed in. I already had the cash in my pocket, which I had taken from the tin. More than he had asked for. It took us a little more than five minutes to get to the house of the Campervan owner and a little less than five minutes for me to agree that I definitely wanted to buy it from him, that yes I did indeed have the cash to be able to pay him. I think at first he thought I was a bit simple, given that I didn't even ask for him to turn the engine over, never mind actually getting in and taking it for a test drive. Still, it had nine months left on the MOT and if that wasn't good enough for me then nothing was. I'd barely be needing the thing for 9 days, let alone nine months. Plus if it didn't start I think he would have had quite a difficult case that he didn't owe me my money back. Then when I pulled the money out of my pocket I think he decided I was a fraudster and he almost wouldn't accept my money until the landlady vouched for me. I paid him an extra few hundred pounds and that seemed to calm him even if he

a relative ?
no time to
know.

wasn't exactly convinced. But the deal was done.

I drove off happy and excited for the first time in a long while. As I was driving back down the main high street I stopped at a crossing to let a woman with her husband and young son cross the street. When they reached the other side the woman turned with her boy to wave thank you and then stopped, her arm stuck in mid-air. Her face turned slowly from a cheerful wave of gratitude to one of confusion. Uncle Chris turned to see what she was looking at but clearly didn't recognise me as he tugged at her coat sleeve to follow him. I put the Campervan in gear and drove. I couldn't stop, not then.

We're back on the road again Huck. Not long now until we'll be turning off the main roads and heading into the highlands. Pretty rough roads, apparently, but I'm sure we'll be fine. This is the first time you'll have been to Scotland your mum said and I said it's the same for me. An adventure for us both. You've already been to more places that I have – all over England and Wales with your mum and your grandparents as well as Spain and Greece. Your granddad spoils you, your mum tells me. I always knew he would. We only ever went on holiday in the Campervan when I was a kid. In fact the only time I stayed somewhere properly was with your mum.

She and I went away to stay in a little hotel not far away from where we lived together. Only for a night. Your granddad had paid for it. "Something special to celebrate," he had said. He didn't say what we were celebrating because it was too early to say it. He didn't want to jinx it. We were celebrating you. It was a beautiful old manor house covered in ivy. It was perfect. Well, almost. Your mother had spent ages looking for the right one for us to stay in. Beautiful location, a quiet little village with a good local pub, a good rating in the guide book. The one thing the guidebook hadn't mentioned was the it was rumoured to haunted, of course they hadn't. Why would they?

"We're not staying," she insisted. "I refuse to stay in this death trap."

"It's just an old story," I said. "It's not really haunted, is it?" I looked at the receptionist and smiled at her hoping she would confirm it but she said nothing and just looked at the desk, hoping for the phone to ring as a distraction. I turned back to your mum.

"Rebecca," I started but she cut me off.

"Do you really want me to stay here in my condition," she said, running her hand over her stomach. The receptionist looked up and a smile shot across her face.

"Oh congratulations!" she said and your mum turned a forced smile to her.

"I can upgrade you to the bridal suite," the receptionist continued, glad to have found an answer. "I'm allowed to upgrade newlyweds and pregnant couples and that room isn't the one with the ghost. It's the old servants ones that are haunted."

It didn't completely get rid of her worries but your mum seemed less tense. We talked it through and agreed we would stay and take the upgrade. It would be nice to stay in a fancy room and we didn't have enough money to stay anywhere else. So it was a choice of either staying here or taking the train back early and just going home. It was the first time we had been away together somewhere nice, somewhere proper. Eventually your mum agreed to stay so long as we left at the first hint of anything unnatural.

We went upstairs and found our room. It was beautiful. The room we were staying in was very elegantly decorated and was far fancier than anything we were used to. There was a deep Victorian bath at the end of the bed. Once your mum had calmed down and we were more settled she actually began to enjoy herself and we spent the afternoon walking through the woods near the house and talking together. Just enjoying being in each other's company.

After that we went for dinner in the pub across the road and I ate probably the best steak I have ever eaten in my life. Your mum had lobster and it came with a bottle of wine. She had one glass, but wouldn't have any more and she offered me the rest. She knew I didn't drink of course but she asked me if I would have a glass, to celebrate and to enjoy myself. I told her I couldn't.

"Please, Michael," she said. "It's just wine and we should celebrate."

"I can't," I said, looking at the bottle and thinking of my mother. She reached across the table and put her hand on top of mine.

"It wasn't the wine, Michael," she said, smiling a soft and loving smile, "and you're not her."

She was right, of course, and she was wrong. And so I poured myself a glass of wine and eventually finished off the bottle while we sat and talked and laughed and thought about our future together. I thought about you, imagining what you might be like. Afterwards, when they called closing time, we walked back to the hotel. Well, she walked and I stumbled a little. We went up to our room and lay together for a while and talked and kissed.

I have no idea how long I had been sleeping but I don't think it was long. I woke up and your mum wasn't next to me anymore. I sat up, a little confused, and looked around. I saw her at the end of the bed, laying in the bathtub and looking at me, smiling.

"Hi sleepy," she said. I smiled back.

"What time is it Rebecca?" I asked, sinking back into the bed and looking at the ceiling.

"You've only been asleep for about an hour," she said. "My back was aching a little so I thought I would have a bath." I nodded and laid my head back on the pillow and closed my eyes again.

"Actually," she said, "before you go back to sleep would you mind getting me a glass of water?"

I swung my legs over the side of the bed and went over to the sink. I let the water run for a while and then filled up the glass. I walked across the room to her and looked down at her in the bath and I stopped. There was no water in the bath. No water at all. Your mother was laying in the bath and all around her, everywhere, were them. The dark fish. She sat up in the bath and they moved around her, swarmed to fill in the gaps where her body had been. Their eyes were blank and they didn't move other than their circular mouths opening and closing as one.

"What's wrong, Michael" she said, sitting further up in the bath tub. But I couldn't move. They were there, they were everywhere. As clear as I can see you now in the van Huck. As clear as I can see the piece of paper I'm writing on. And I know that sounds crazy but it's true.

And then I saw a shadow, a bulge, move across your mothers stomach and I dropped the glass. Less than a month later your mum would announce to everyone we knew that she was pregnant and that night, the night she told everyone that wonderful news, I would leave.

71

We're on the road again young Huckleberry and not far from our final destination now. We're just outside Inverness, which means the main roads are going to stop shortly and we're going to be out in the beautiful Scottish Highlands. I've never been there before but always wanted to go. Apparently the weather is going to be alright for the rest of today and tomorrow so we should be okay getting there. Who knows what it will be like when we do get there – the locals seem to think they've been lucky up on the north coast so far and that winter is about to take hold. I guess we'll see. We stopped off to pick up some more coffee - seriously, don't drink anywhere near as much coffee as I do, it's really not that great for you. Not that it matters anymore. I bought a thicker pad from the services with a hard back so I can write on my lap and all three of us are sat in the front now. We also picked up some travelling music.

There's something about being on the road that means your taste in music completely changes. When you're driving you need something with a good tempo so that you can keep yourself going at a steady speed, but not too quick otherwise you'll end up flying at a hundred miles an hour down the motorway and into the arms of either the police or certain doom . You also need to get some music that isn't too aggressive or you end up driving like a wild thing all over the road and up everyone's exhausts. And ideally it needs to be something you know the words to so you can sing along, but not properly so you don't end up signing so loud you get lost in the music and forget about the traffic.

The one thing, if anything in this world, my father did seem to like was travelling music. Loved Bob Dylan, which was kind of ironic. He didn't have a musical bone in his body, my Dad. He never played anything in the house and would turn whatever my mum was playing either right down or, more often than not, off as soon as he walked in the room. But when we were driving it was a different story all together. He didn't sing but he seemed to like it. Almost smiled a couple of times as he hummed along. My dad and your mum's parents clearly had the same taste in music and we seemed to have been brought up on exactly the same bands – Bonnie Tyler, Tina Turner, ELO, Erasure, all that stuff that you probably think is shit now. But specially Bob Dylan. That's what we are listening to now, A Hard Rain's A-Gonna Fall, by Bob Dylan. He has no idea.

I hadn't bought any music for the trip to see Paul, although I hadn't really wanted any. The journey from the coast to Nottingham was due to take 2 hours and 20 minutes according to the Sat Nav I picked up at a service station just outside of town, but based on the speed of the Campervan, which I was just getting used to, it was bound to take a lot longer. Maybe three and a half hours. That didn't matter to me though because what I really needed was some time to think about what I was going to say to Paul when I met him. This was a guy that I hadn't seen since I was sixteen, almost half my life time ago. And when we had known each other we hadn't exactly seen eye to eye. An understatement if ever there was one.

Paul had been one of the bullies at our school, the typical alpha male type, high on his own emotions and hormones. Actually, that's not a fair description. I'm doing him a disservice. That makes it sound like he was one of a bunch of bullies but he wasn't. He had been the bully at our school and me, out of all of the kids that he had ever picked on, of the hundreds of kids that could have gotten in his way, of all the lives he could have chosen to make miserable, I was the victim. He tortured me for years and years, day after day until he left school shortly before the end of our GCSE year. After that I never saw or heard from him again. Until now that was. For five straight years he made my life a living hell. Or at least, more so than it already was. The only break I got from him was the weekends and the school holidays when I could spend time by myself or with Jack, licking my wounds for a few days or weeks until I had to go back for more. At least during that time I only had my dad to hate me. There weren't many weeks that went by during term time where I wasn't bruised and bloodied at least a little. The holidays were a good chance to repair, so I could go back with a clean canvas for the artist to work on.

It had started on the first day of our second term at secondary school. He and I were sat next to one another in art class, the only class we had together. Mrs Thompson was the teacher, I think. One of the few I had actually liked. Paul had, in fact, actually been pretty friendly to me the previous term. We'd sat next together twice a week for that whole term and talked a lot, laughed sometimes. We didn't have any other classes together but that had been one of the few times a week I had actually enjoyed myself. I stupidly had begun to think I had found a friend in him. But that all changed. That afternoon, the first back after the Christmas break, we had been given the freedom to draw anything we had wanted to. I had decided to draw the view from my window, looking out onto our garden. My family's garden was pretty barren at the best of times. But it was something to draw. It was mostly paved over with a little strip of brown grass in the middle. Mum had done the best she could – potted a few flowers here and there and put in a little bird table.

"Still sober enough to feed the fucking pigeons" my dad would say and laugh at his own joke. She didn't care.

My sketch wasn't great. I wasn't really much of an artist. But Paul's picture was incredible. There was someone with talent. He'd sketched a portrait, from behind, of a young man looking at himself in a full length mirror. You could see the back of the man in the foreground and his reflection in the mirror. It was rough and raw but it was incredible.

"That's amazing Paul, who is it. Is it you?" I asked and I put my hand on his shoulder, an attempt at genuine appreciation.

That was it. That was the thing that I said that would make my next five years at school a living hell. There was no name calling. No snide comment made behind his back. No joke at his expense. No bad tackle in a football game. No girl come between us. Nothing like that at all. I paid him a compliment. I simply asked a straight forward question, one to which I was pretty sure the simple answer ought to have been "thanks" or perhaps "it's just a guy". The man in the picture looked like Paul. Older, but it definitely had his features. But that wasn't the reaction it got.

Paul stopped drawing and turned his head to look at me, brushing my hand off his shoulder. His eyes were wide open and his nostrils flaring. He was breathing heavy and fast, a rage bubbling over inside of him. He was angry. Really angry about what he thought I had just said and I assumed for a minute that he had misheard me.

"What the fuck did you just say?" he snarled through his clenched teeth. I was confused and I tried to answer as best I could.

"Your picture," I stammered, "I…."

I thought he was going to hit me there and then, right in the middle of the class room. Since we spent most of our art classes sat on stools he would have knocked me half way across the room. Instead he sucked a huge amount of phlegm through his nose and his throat and spat right on the middle of my picture. A huge glob of green and yellow splattered across the middle of my page.

"Looks like your shitty garden just got a swamp," he said and turned back to his drawing. I stared first at him and then sat looking at the piece of paper in front of me. I couldn't understand what had just happened. I sat like that for a few minutes and then the bell went to signal the end of class. I continued sitting in disbelief for a for about minute more, just looking at my paper and when I went to turn around and ask what I had done to make him so mad he was already gone. Mrs Thompson snapped me out of my daze and told me to get on to my next class. I screwed up the drawing, being careful to make sure that all of the greenie stayed in the middle of the paper, put it in the bin and then walked out of the door into the hallway.

That's when he hit me.

Now my entire school career might have been a little different had I been a fighter, or at least some sort of a brawler or a scrapper but I was none of these things. Paul was a brawler. Jack was most definitely a fighter. That isn't to say that Jack was the sort of person that went looking for a fight, he has never been that kind of guy. Nor was he the sort of person that wouldn't allow a kid to fight his own battles. He was however the kind of kid that would stick up for someone that was being bullied and he did it on a number of occasions quite spectacularly.

As I think I said before Jack didn't go to the same school as me even though we lived in the same town. He went to a private school a little way out of town, whereas I went to the local state secondary. That meant he was never there to stand up for me when Paul picked on me and Paul wasn't stupid enough to pick on someone on the way home where there were lots of witnesses and mums and dads who might have intervened or put in for a case of GBH rather than a simple playground scrap.

Every school has its bullies though and Jack's school was no exception. There was a gang of older kids at his school, much like our "Band of Brothers" who had been terrorising the playground for a couple of years when Jack arrived. Everyone at his school was afraid of them, including most of the teachers. But not Jack. He was fearless and told me that if they ever came near him, or one of his friends, he would serve them up the beating of their lives. And that's exactly what happened.

The story goes, or so I heard a thousand times over, that one day during break a first year kid had accidentally kicked a football into the back of the head of the leader of this gang. It was an accident, clearly, but he had taken as a massive sign of disrespect. He had even used that phrase apparently – are you disrespecting me? – like he was some kind of teenage mafia don. The punishment would most likely have been dished out there and then had it not been for the whistle going to signal the end of break, accompanied by one of the teachers rounding everyone up. So the kid avoided a beating, at least for a little while, but was told in no uncertain terms that he would "get what was coming to him" at the end of the school day. The news spread like wildfire. There was going to be a fight and it would take place at 3:15pm in the usual "spot". This was two weeks after

Jack had started his second term at the school. The first fight he ever had and he didn't have many more after. The news quickly got round to Jack, who was in the same class as the kid who was about to get a beating. Jack liked the kid and decided that enough was enough. It was time those bullies learned a valuable lesson and got what was coming to them!

After the school bell Jack walked with the kid to the small playground behind the sports hall, where all the fights took place. The kid didn't want to go but Jack talked him into it and instead of being dragged, virtually kicking and screaming to "the ring" where the four bullies stood waiting for him, he walked calmly with Jack by his side. There were around forty or so kids stood waiting for them, the head bully in the middle. Jack walked the kid into the centre of the circle. The kid had been calm up to this point but now the reality of it was starting to settle in and he looked pretty much ready to wet himself. The bully with the dented ego stood cracking his knuckles, balling his fists and generally trying to look menacing. Jack just stood calmly, looking at the bully. It was tense until one boy in the crowd shoved the nervous kid in the back and he moved further into the circle and the bully moved toward him. Things looked like they were ready to properly kick off when all of a sudden Jack casually stepped in between the two of them and spoke into the bully's face.

"Hey guys," he said, "do you mind if I take Luke's place?"

Everyone looked round a little in shock, including all of the bullies and Luke. Not only was this a crazy thing to do in any circumstances but the bullies were two years older than Jack and had a huge height, weight and reach advantage, never mind all the angst of puberty on their side. Why would anyone choose to fight them? Everyone continued to trade glances, a little unsure.

"You haven't done nothing to us, kid," said the main bully.

"True," replied Jack, "but we're all the same us year sevens. Does it really matter which one of us it is?"

The bullies looked at each other and suddenly found the whole thing very amusing. They relaxed and laughed and joked between one another.

"Sure thing," said the main bully, "doesn't matter to us which one of you it is."

The details of the fight itself are vague and varied depending on who you talked to. In some instances Jack took barely a scratch and annihilated all four of the bullies single handed, breaking two limbs and three noses and dishing out a large number of black eyes in the process. Other stories put it as a straight forward fight between Jack and the main bully which, whilst relatively one sided, didn't go all in Jack's favour. One of the versions of it even had Jack at the bottom of a bundle of all four of the bullies only to burst out of the pile, throwing each of the bullies into the air at the same time and managing to get up and drop kick each of them before they hit the ground. I know which story I believe. Jack never really talked about it other than to say he had just helped a kid out of a jam.

However the fight actually went, the result was that the bullies lost and Jack was victorious. After the fight the bullies and Jack shook hands and talked. Jack managed to convince them they would be even more respected if, rather than just beating up and bullying anyone they liked, that they were the protectors of the weaker kids in the school. He said the girls would probably like that too, especially the girl one of the bullies had a huge crush on. Plus, who wanted to be a fighter, he said, and run the risk of damaging their handsome good looks and getting detention. Everyone laughed. Jack was a hero. Girls everywhere swooned and the rest of his time at school was a breeze.

I wish that I could say the story ended similarly with my bullies but the truth is it didn't. When Paul punched me in the face I hit the floor like a ton of bricks. When he kicked me in the stomach I started to cry and I didn't get up. Nobody stepped in to take my place, nobody talked the bullies into helping me and protecting me. Nobody was a hero. I told you I wasn't brave Huck and I meant it. I wish I had been. I wish I'd been a fighter like Jack.

There are some lovely places in the world Huck. Well, I've been told there are some lovely places in the rest of the world – I've only ever been to England and Wales and now Scotland – but there are certainly some beautiful places here. Nottingham, however is certainly not one of them, although it seemed like there was at least more going on than there had been at the coast. I hope you're not reading this having your heart set on going to University in Nottingham but the reality is that Nottingham is a pretty grim place. I don't know why, when they build some towns they don't make more of an effort to make them nice, why they can't just tear down some of the disgusting old buildings that clearly nobody wants to be in anymore and put in a park or something, anything just to brighten the place up a little. Maybe if they did it would just become a place for homeless people and drug addicts. Perhaps the cost of the buildings outweighs the benefits of having nice spaces or perhaps people just don't want them. I don't know. Maybe I'm just being unfair. Maybe it's not that bad. All I know is for every nice place there is an equally depressing one waiting not too far away.

I arrived there pretty late on December 23rd, too late to head to Paul's garage and so decided to park up and sleep in the back of the Campervan for the first time. I'd bought some supplies along the way and it was actually pretty nice being sat outdoors eating a sandwich and drinking some coffee that I'd made myself, despite the drabness of the surroundings. At least the sky looked nice.

As I sat there I started thinking about the last time I had seen Paul. It had been in our GCSE year and I was sixteen. Mum was long gone and dad and I were barely speaking any more. I don't even know if he knew it was my GCSE year. He'd never been to a parents evening and never looked at a report card. I'd gotten pretty good at signing his name and my grades were OK. We hadn't even celebrated a birthday since my mum left, I doubt he even knew how old I was. I put up a tree each year at Christmas, but there were no presents, no carols. Nothing. Most days he would simply come home and eat the dinner I made for him and then go and sit in front of the television or go to the snooker club with his work friends, whichever he was in the mood for. I'd spend the evening first fixing up my cuts and bruises and then studying for my exams, determined that I would get the grades I needed to get me out of that place for good. Sometimes Jack and I would sit and talk or do homework together but mostly I wanted to get studying and get my results. Jack was understanding and he wasn't around as much. We were still good friends, great friends in fact. But he said he had his own studying to do anyway, although we both knew he didn't really need to study. Plus he had a girl then. The only time dad and I ever really talked was when I needed something – books or new clothes, which therefore required some money. I had a paper round at that point but that wasn't enough to pay for all the things I needed. He gave me what I wanted and enough to do our weekly food shop, but that was pretty much all we ever talked about.

I had been taking beatings from Paul on a fairly regular basis over the five years of secondary school. The days of the week varied, as did the time and the place, but it typically happened a couple of times a week on average. He had moved on from simply walloping me when I was walking past and they had turned more into grapples, him wanting to choke me and rub my face in the dirt. I think he really just wanted to humiliate me in the way that, somehow, he thought I had humiliated him all those years ago back in art class.

I had, however, come up with a plan. In hindsight, a stupid plan. In hindsight a plan that had come out of a mixture of desperation and studying too much and thinking I was cleverer that I really was. A few years earlier I had had a brief brush with religion but it hadn't lasted and now I was in a place where my faith in God had turned into hatred for all of the things He had done to me during my life. Instead I had started reading about pacifists. It appealed to me, I guess. Stories of other people who had struggled with things like me and had overcome them without turning to violence, which was as little an option for them as it had been for me. People like Martin Luther King and Ghandi. They intrigued me, the way they held up their inner strength despite everything that the world seemed to throw at them. The fact that they never seemed to swerve from their path regardless of what happened. It was inspiring and the naïve part of me latched on to it. This was something I could do. This could help me out. The fact that they practiced and preached peaceful means also struck a chord with me since there was no way in reality I would ever have actually been able to beat Paul in a straight fight. Having read a great deal about them I decided one day that I would follow their example. I would put up no resistance to Paul whatsoever and I would tell him that I loved him and that I forgave him. Simple and stupid and naïve.

The first part of the plan might have worked. Had I never struggled again then he might have gotten bored of beating me up and gone in search of someone else although, given he had been doing it for five years straight and that we were near the end of our school careers in any case, it was doubtful. It probably would have just made me an easier target.

I was in hospital for three weeks and in bed at home for another two. I had a cracked skull, three cracked ribs, a broken nose, two broken fingers, two black eyes and a hell of a lot of bruises, cuts and scrapes. It would have been worse had it not been for the other "brothers" and two teachers pulling him off me in the end, although they took their time. I don't remember much of it and I don't remember much of the first week in hospital. Paul was expelled from school and I didn't see him again until a few days ago. The police came but I said I didn't want to get him in trouble. I don't know why. My father came to visit me twice in hospital. Once when I first went in and once to sign off on some medication that needed his approval since I wasn't old enough to do it myself. He waited in the car when it was time for me to be discharged.

Jack was there every day. Right by my side. I don't think he ever left.

I'd like to give you some kind of miracle Hollywood ending to that story. Ideally it would be that my mother turned up to take care of me and to nurse me back to health over the summer, only to leave me again when I was better and didn't need her anymore. But that didn't happen. Couldn't have happened in fact since, as it turned out, she was already dead by then. Although I didn't know that at the time.

I think I should probably take another break for a while.

We've arrived at our destination Huck and they were right, it is beautiful up here. It might be the middle of winter here but there is still so much colour – colours you don't see anywhere else. The deep purples, greens and reds of the hills as they roll away from you against the white peaks of the mountains in the distance. The sky, for today at least, is a beautiful light blue whilst the sea is more the grey of the mountains, white peaks flitting on the waves. Its poetic.

We pulled up outside of the cottage about an hour ago and it's just perfect, like something straight out of a story. It sits facing out to sea, painted a deep blue with four white windows and a chimney stack pouring out a grey trail of smoke from the fire that was lit and waiting for us. It's perfect. As we pulled up outside of the house you were already unbuckling your seatbelt and getting ready to pile out. You and your mother went and did the tour of the house while I carried out the bags and locked up the Campervan. It's probably the last trip that I will do in her. I'll let you and your mum take the van back home and I'll get the train back home to see Jack. My last stop.

As I was walking up the steps with the bags you came bounding back down them towards me.

"It's awesome," you smiled at me.

"Oh yeah?" I asked.

"Yeah," you said, "it's got two big bedrooms and a cupboard full of game and a TV and DVD player and two fireplaces so mum says we can make a fire every day and maybe cook marshmallows. There's one already burning and it's so hot!"

"Wow," I said, "that sure sounds like there's a lot to do in a few days." You nodded and the huge grin hung there on your face. I could feel it spreading across mine too.

"Oh and mum says do you want a cup of coffee?" You asked, suddenly remembering what you'd been sent out for. I nodded back at you. "Do you want me to carry one of the bags for you Michael?" You asked. I picked the lightest one and held it out for you. You picked it up with both hands and walked by my side up to the door, struggling a little but not letting on.

"Good man," I said as you dragged the bag over the doorstep and into the tiny hallway.

And now here I am sat by the fire drinking the coffee your mother made for me. I was going to continue where I'd left off but your mother just asked if I'd got to the bit where she and I met yet. I think she thinks I'm going faster than I am, but then I thought the same about our trip in general, so maybe I'm in the right place after all. Either way, she's got me thinking about that now so I might as well tell you what happened.

We met, of all places, on a cricket pitch in North Yorkshire. How I came to be in North Yorkshire is an entirely different story and one that I promise I will get to at some point, but the short version is that I had taken a job working as the assistant to the groundskeeper at a couple of sports pitches in and around the town your mum lived and the cricket club was one of them. I usually spent a couple of mornings there a week either mowing the grass, rolling the pitch or doing some odd jobs around the pavilion or anything else the boss had in store for me. It was pretty peaceful work to be honest and not particularly difficult. The pay wasn't exactly going to allow me to retire early and head off to my luxury yacht in the Caribbean but then if I was doing this kind of work for the rest of my life I wouldn't have minded.

One particular Thursday morning I was at the club with the head groundskeeper when the local cricket Captain, who happened to be your grandfather, turns up worried about the state of the pitch for their enormous local derby on the weekend. This was the match of all matches, the big run in of the year. Richmond versus Lower Ebbsworth. Highlight Reel material if ever there was such a thing. He spent about an hour running around poking holes into the wicket, testing the run of the balls on the outer field and checking whether or not he could see his reflection in the beer taps in the clubhouse. The local derby wasn't so much about the quality of the cricket that was to be played on the field as it was about the quality of ground and the post-game drinking. Both teams were shockingly bad and propped up a league they couldn't be relegated from because there wasn't one below it. To add insult to injury The Cap (as your grandfather was affectionately known) and his team were by far the worse of the two sides. Neither team had a player under the age of about 40 because all the local kids refused to play for them and you determined whether you were a batsman or a bowler by having a go at both and doing the one you were least bad at. Most of the team were fielders, and then only just.

The Cap as it turned out had a major problem on his hands. His wicket keeper had broken his arm trying to mend some tiles on his roof. Apparently his hammer had slid down the roof and he'd tried to grab it a little too ambitiously – some sort of Indiana Jones move, as the Cap put it – and had fallen off. He was lucky he lived in a bungalow. The wicket keeper also happened to be his "best" batsman and actually probably still would have been the best if he'd played with his injury, but that wasn't going to happen.

He was trying to convince the head grounds man to play on the basis that he himself had once been the wicketkeeper for the team, but my boss kept reminding him that had been thirty years ago and he wasn't entirely sure he was still up for the job. He was barely up for keeping score. The main reason they had an assistant greens keeper was because my boss was too old to move most of the equipment. He did however, suggest that I might like to give it a go.

Highly reluctantly, and after a huge amount of cajoling, I agreed that I would try on the basis that The Cap didn't expect anything from me and wouldn't blame me if we lost.

"Lose!?" exclaimed The Cap. "My boy, how could I blame you if we lose? We always bloody lose!"

He and I then spent the rest of the day going round the ground fixing up various bits and pieces to make sure the ground was looking extra special for Saturday whilst he also explained to me the finer points of cricket and the rivalry with the next village. He also told me what I would need to focus on in my position as wicketkeeper which, as I've already explained, was pretty much guessing how far wide the deliveries would be and diving as best as I could to try and stop them. It sounded like being a goal keeper in a penalty shootout. I asked him if it really made sense for me to keep wicket and he admitted this probably wasn't the best position for a novice but that everyone else already knew their positions and trying to teach two people a new role was inevitably going to be harder than teaching one. Plus I was young and everyone else was liable to break a hip or worse.

On Friday I was relieved of my caretaking duties so that I could concentrate solely on practicing keeping wicket and a bit of batting practice. That's how much the game mattered. I later found out your grandfather had taken the week off work entirely to prepare for this game although, to be fair, he didn't do all that much work anyway. His business pretty much took care of itself by then. In the evening I was invited to the pavilion for the pre-match talk with the team and a couple of drinks, although I kept to orange juice. At around eight The Cap announced that dinner, in the form of eleven portions of fish and chips, was being brought in by his wife and daughter. And that, Huck, is the moment that my life changed forever. And yours began I guess. Well, had a chance of beginning anyway.

The two of them walked in unannounced while the pre-match build up was still going on and, for a bunch of forty plus years olds, the team were getting quite rowdy particularly given the biggest match of the season was the next day. The Cap was just wrapping up his final points of a quite elegant, if not entirely motivational, speech.

"…and of course," he said, "as home team we will be naming a man of the match whatever the result and since it's the big game of the season despite being on the losing side the man will receive free drinks all night courtesy of the club."

This was followed by a big round of cheers from the rest of the team and some light hearted back slapping and calls of "that'll be my round paid for then" and more laughter. I was a little confused by that final statement though.

"Man of the match gets free drinks if we lose?" I asked and everyone nodded at me. "What does the man of the match get if we win?" I asked.

Everyone immediately stopped talking and laughing and stared at me. Admittedly, other than a shy grunt of hello when I was initially introduced, I don't think I had spoken until that point and so it's possible that they had all assumed I was either mute or stupid or something, but I get the impression it was more that it was something nobody had ever considered before.

"I mean," I tried to clarify, clearing my throat as I did, "what would the man of the match of the winning team usually get?" The team continued to look at each other, dumbfounded until a voice from behind me answered.

"That man would get to take me out for dinner."

I turned around and there she was. The woman who would become the love of my life. Your mother. People say that love at first sight doesn't exist Huck, but I think those people just haven't experienced it. Perhaps it only happens to a very privileged few, which based on the maths would make sense, but it happened to me. I had never seen someone that had a genuine glow around them, someone that seemed to emit light from every inch of their skin. Her hair was long then, well below her shoulder blades, not short like it is now, and the colour rich, thick honey that reflected the radiance that came from her skin. Her eyes were the same bright blue they still are today and her smile was so wide and her lips so inviting I would have been swallowed up by her in an instant. But it was her skin that I have always loved the most, so soft and warm to the touch and so vibrant. She just seems too alive, your mother. Do you know what I mean, Huck? I know this must sound strange to you kiddo, me talking about your mum like this, but I want you to know how very much I loved her from the moment we met.

I don't think she had realised that there was someone in the team her own age and so when I turned round to look at her she let out a little gasp of surprise and blushed. The team laughed amidst calls of "Well I'd better bring my A game then Rebecca" and "maybe I should stick to the waters for the rest of the night." Your mum walked back to the kitchen to plate up the food with your grandmother and as she did so flashed a shy smile in my direction. For the first time in my life I wanted to win something, I wanted to be the best at something.

The following morning I did two things I had never done before. Number one I did some stretching and number two I went for a run. Not a very long run but enough to get me out of breath. I figured that I ought to be limbered up for the game, especially given my position involved me rolling around on the floor a fair bit. After that, and a healthy breakfast of porridge and orange juice from my landlady, I donned my borrowed whites and headed down to the cricket ground.

Now some notes on the rules of the game as were played at that club. Each side was limited to twenty overs each which, based on the quality of the game, was more than enough. The game took a while. In addition, in order to keep the game from going on longer than a test match, wides were not given as additional balls but we were instead given additional runs, as well as any the team made off the bowl. Given the horrendous quality of the bowling, and therefore the difficulty for the wicketkeeper to actually stop the ball from going behind, this actually meant there was a huge number of points to be scored off of bad bowling and bad wicket keeping, something that hadn't been explained to me at all until ten minutes before the coin toss. Suddenly my position seemed remarkably more important and difficult.

We lost the toss and the opposition, who really did look equally as terrible as our own team during the warm up, decided that they would field first and let us do our best with the bat. Apparently they always did this in the hope that they would get us out for less than a hundred and then they could rack up our score quickly, predominantly based our terrible bowling, and the game would be over. That would then leave more time for drinking and ridiculing our team. However, this plan didn't work out for them this time around as our team put up a stubborn defence and managed to hold out until the last ball. Based on my pre-match warm up I was sent in to bat at number seven scoring a grand total of nine runs before being caught out, which was actually the third highest total behind the "star" batsman, who scored eleven, and extras, who top scored with an almighty eighty four. We scored a simply sensational one hundred and fourteen from our innings, which was apparently "not half bad that."

And so came our moment in the sunshine, literally since it was a glorious day and our efforts on the pitch more than matched it. I padded up and we went for a few warms up on the pitch, the team practicing their throwing in and me my catching. A couple of the guys practiced their bowling on the outfield, which gave me a sense of just how wide they really were capable of bowling, and so much of the warm up was spent with me running across the outfield collecting the ball. I had a sense that this really could be over all too quickly after all.

Eventually we took our places for the game and I prepared to face my first ball thrown in anger. Except that it wasn't, it was a real half-hearted effort that barely made it down the wicket but which the batsman also barely managed to connect with and it trickled to our nearest fielder about fifteen feet away from me. In the battle of David versus, well, David nobody was winning.

The second ball wasn't much better, the third however was an absolute monster and it went a long way wide. I made a half attempt at a dive and missed it, landing in a heap on the floor, the ball running most of the way to the boundary before it stopped dead. I lifted my head up in shame and as

I looked around your mother caught my eye. She was jumping up out of her seat, arms waving and shouting "Go and get it Michael, come on!"

"She knows my name," I thought. "And she's rooting for me. Fuck this!"

And I got up Huck, and I ran. I ran like I'd never run before. I scrambled as quickly as I could over to the ball, a quick spin on my heel and threw it back it with a nice clean loop. We stopped them for three, plus the extra. Not half bad that. From then on there was no stopping me. I dived, jumped, rolled and generally threw myself at the ground. I stumped out two and I caught an edge, which was more of a fluke than anything else, but still. Their top scorer was still extras with a grand total of forty four, a club record low, and we won. We actually won. When the last ball was delivered the team erupted in celebration and I was hoisted on their shoulders like a god. They carried me back to the clubhouse where your mother was stood by the bar beaming from ear to ear.

"Your prizes I believe," The Cap said and your mother kissed me on the cheek. I think I turned redder than I've ever been, but I was so happy I didn't even care.

"But I don't drink," I apologised.

"Well then," your mother said, "you can sit here and talk with me while the others drink for you."

And we did. We sat and I drank orange juice and lemonade while your mother drank wine and we talked about all the stupidest things in the world we could think of whilst people I barely knew came to congratulate me, slap me on the back, offer to buy me drinks and tell me how wonderfully I played and would I be back again the next week. I've never felt more important in my life Huck, and it had nothing to do with the cricket.

The following night I took your mother for dinner and then to the cinema. I won't bore you any more with the romance, but at the end of the night we kissed and the rest, as they say, is history.

Your mother is smiling as she sits there and I write this. That beautiful, radiant smile that never fades. I love her so much.

You'd be surprised from the way I've described it but sleeping in the back

86

of the Campervan was actually pretty comfortable. The problem was the curtains. They were pretty thin and didn't really cover the windows, which meant the light came in early. Because of that I woke up on Christmas Eve early and decided that I would drive into town, get some coffee and some breakfast and think a little bit more about what I was going to say to Paul. Assuming I saw him. I didn't really know what to expect from him. What do you say to someone that you haven't seen since you were sixteen? To someone who had spent five years making your life a living hell? I hadn't seen him since I was in the hospital and he had been made to come in and look at what he had done. The nurse had said he had been apologetic. Had genuinely looked sorry. Jack didn't agree. I couldn't see. What do you say to the person who did that?

I sat in a greasy spoon café for a couple of hours. It was a far cry from the old ladies tea shop by the coast with the silver pot and matching milk jug. A long way even from a Starbucks. In this place a polystyrene cup was plumped down in front of me full of a swirling black mess that had apparently at some point been coffee. It almost looked alive. The food though, fatty and slightly burned as it was, actually tasted pretty good. That was the only good thing about the place. I looked round at the other customers, not that there were many. Most people were only half awake. All were unshaven and in dirty clothes. I wondered how I looked compared to them. The same, I thought. The owner of the café had done as little as he could to get into the Christmas spirit and his efforts amounted to a small plug in, pre-decorated, plastic Christmas tree in the corner of the place and a faded red Santa hat he was currently wearing, which came with a thick black line of grease where the white fur had presumably once been around the front. Thinking about my own life, as I had been over the past few days, had led me to wondering about other people as well. How do you become the chef in a place like this? Presumably he was also the owner. Why else would he work here? Was it something handed down from his dad? Had he at one time wanted to be a real chef or had he just fallen into this? Did he make good money from it? Enough to support a family? He had a picture on the wall of a woman about his age and two teenage kids. Was that them? I wanted to ask him all these questions but I didn't. I just sat and drank my coffee and ate my breakfast and talked to no-one.

Alone.

I've been alone a lot in my life. From the time that I left your mother to the time I left Ealing I spent most of my evenings, and all of my nights, alone. That's a long time to be completely by yourself. That's a lot of time to spend inside your own head. I thought about what your mother might have done once I had left, what her immediate reaction to me not coming home was. Whether she thought I was ever coming back. I wondered what the birth was like, whether you had been born safe and sound. I had gone into a library once just after a drop off and the librarian had helped me search old copies of local newspapers to see if I could find a mention of you and your mother but I couldn't. There was no mention of me leaving. No scandal. I wondered what you looked like, whether you had any of my features, what your first day at school had been like, when you had learned to walk, to talk, what your first words had been. I thought about you endlessly Huck and when I wasn't thinking about you I was thinking about your mother. I missed you, both of you. Sometimes it gave me headaches to think of you both and I had to stop.

I thought about writing to your mother a number of times. Trying to explain the things that, as it turned out a few days ago, I could only say to her face. And even then not properly. I would write maybe three or four paragraphs and then find I was either too inarticulate to say what I wanted to or that it hurt so much I couldn't write any more. Maybe I tried to write too well. Maybe I tried to find too many excuses. Maybe I was being too honest. I think that's what's good for me about this trip – I don't have the time to read this back. I just have to let my brain flow onto the paper and leave it at that.

Once I did write a whole letter. I got as far as the post box with the letter I'd written and was on the verge of posting it, my hand in the slot in the post box. The envelope was addressed, sealed and stamped. I almost pushed it inside, but I couldn't. I pulled it out at the last moment and tore open the envelope to give it one last read. It was like it had been written by someone else. It didn't come across the way I wanted it to at all and so I ripped it up, determined to start again and put my true feelings and thoughts down. I didn't. I couldn't. I wish I could have written sooner Huck, I really do. I'm sorry I left it so long to come and see you. Too late. Always too late.

But I did make it in the end Huck, and perhaps it's better late than never, as they say. I guess you'll be the judge of that.

And so I had made it as far as the greasy spoon in Nottingham and eventually, after two hours of wasting time I finally decided to drive to Paul's garage and get it over and done with. So I paid up and went back out to the Campervan, started it up and put the address into the Sat Nav. It only took me about fifteen minutes to get there. I pulled up across the street from the bright yellow sign that clearly identified the place as belonging to Paul. "Burrows Garage" was painted in thick black letters across the front of the entire building. Suddenly it was real.

Underneath the metal rollers that shielded the entrance to the garage from the outside world were slowly lifting, signaling the place was shortly going to be open for business. There were no cars parked outside though and didn't look like there were any in the garage waiting to be worked on either. It wasn't a surprise I guess. It was Christmas Eve after all. Most people who are going to travel to see family have probably already gone and I doubt others that were staying at home were likely to book their car in for a service on Christmas Eve unless they really had to. I'm surprised he had bothered opening at all. In hindsight, I suppose, I'm glad he did.

As I sat there, waiting for the place to finally open so that I could go in, I started thinking about all the things he had done to me and I thought about changing my mind. Last minute nerves. Perhaps I didn't want to see him after all. I mean, it had been sixteen years. Yes he'd bullied me for five of my teenage years but there were hundreds of kids that had been bullied at school like I had. Thousands I bet. Now I thought about it I wondered if there were any kids that hadn't been bullied when they were younger. Paul was probably bullied himself when he was small, was probably how he learned how to fight. What was the point, after all this time, of me going and speaking to a guy who had hated me for some unknown reason? I put my hand on the key and almost turned it to start up the engine and drive off.

And then the door to the office at the side of the garage jerked open and someone stepped out backwards holding a large A-frame sign that advertised MOTs while you wait for £40, including a free clean inside and out. It was unmistakably Paul. His build was a little thicker, his hair receding slightly at the temples and a little lighter than it had been, permanent stubble on his jaw, but it was most definitely him and I knew in that instant that I had to go and talk to him. There was no going back. It was now or never, as they say, and it couldn't be never. This was my first step. As he fixed up the sign I climbed out of the cab of the Campervan and crossed the street towards him.

"Excuse me," I called across the road. Paul looked up from the sign, flashed a quick smile and started talking as he turned his attention back to securing the fastenings that stopped the frame from collapsing in the wind.

"Sorry mate," he said, cheerfully, "but I can't fix that kind of thing. We only do cars. My lift isn't great and I'm not sure we've got the headspace to get it up there anyway. Plus I wouldn't have the parts. There's a place on the outskirt of town that fixes that kind of thing. Might not be open today but I can give you the number if you'd like?"

"No it runs fine," I replied. "I…er…. Paul?" I finally managed to stammer. He turned his head again to look at me, still kneeling on the floor and the smile disappeared from his face to be replaced by nothing. A looking of emptiness. He just knelt there, staring at me and saying nothing.

"I don't know if you'll remember me," I said, "but we used to go to school together."

"Sure," he replied, still not moving. "I remember you."

"Oh, ok" I said. "My name's Michael. Michael Brighton."

"I know who you are," he said, sterner this time. He still didn't move from where he was kneeling on the floor but his eyes returned to the fixings on the sign. I nodded and looked down at the floor. I'd come all this way, built it so far up in my head and now I couldn't think of what I wanted to say. I looked at the garage behind him.

"So, you run this place now?" I asked. Paul clicked the last of the fastening in to place, stood up and turned to look at the sign above the door, as if he wasn't sure if he really did own it, and then turned back to me. He still didn't look at me though, just at a random spot on my shirt.

"Yeah I do."

The two of us stood and said nothing for a couple of minutes. Me looking at his face and him just staring at my chest and fiddling with his hands. He was nervous. I'd never seen him nervous before and it made me more uncomfortable than if he had been angry or jokey. I was about to make my excuses and leave when he started talking.

"What are you doing here Michael?" he said, still fixated on the middle of my chest.

"I came here to apologise," I said. He lifted his gaze from my chest, a look of confusion crossing his face. "For when we were at school. I came to apologise for that. I know that it was a long time ago and you've probably forgotten about it all but, well, I just wanted to say sorry. That's all."

He tried to say something but didn't seem to be able to get the words out other than a laboured "erm". He opened and closed his mouth a couple of times before cocking his head, screwing up his eyes slightly tighter and finally saying "Sorry, what?"

I cleared my throat, and spoke more confidently this time.

"I'm sorry," I said. "I don't know how much of it you remember. About how it started I mean. But when we were in year seven, you and I sat next to each other in art class and I said something to you that I think offended you. I'm not sure what it was that made you so mad at me or maybe you thought I said something that I didn't. Maybe it doesn't matter. But either way I just wanted to come here and say that I'm sorry for whatever I said that hurt you and for everything that happened after."

That was it. That was all I had wanted to say and I would quite happily have left at that moment. I had apologised for whatever I had done all those years ago. It was the first apology of many I needed to do but it was done all the same. I could have just walked away and moved onto my mum. But he stopped all that.

"I don't understand," he said, his head still at an angle as he stared at me in apparent disbelief. "You've come all the way here, after not seeing each other for sixteen years in order to apologise to me for something you said in art class when we were kids?"

"Yes," I confirmed. "Well, no, not exactly. I mean, I know that what I said led to lots of trouble between us and in the end that led to you getting expelled from school and even though I don't fully understand what happened between us or what it was that I did to make you hate me such much but I just wanted to say that I'm sorry and I never meant to hurt you. I didn't mean for you to get expelled from school. I didn't mean for anything bad to happen to you. If your life isn't what you wanted it to be and that's my fault, I'm sorry"

I felt a sudden rush of relief at having finally said all of it. For a long time I had worried about what had happened to Paul, worrying that it had been my fault that he had been kicked out of school and now, seeing him running his own business and doing OK for himself despite what had happen. And having apologised I suddenly felt a lot better for it. It felt good. Yeah, OK, his life probably wasn't exactly what he had planned it to be but he was doing alright for himself. What I had done to him can't have had that big an impact after all. He was one off my list. If the rest of them were going to be that simple, then maybe I could get through what I wanted to do after all.

What I had said didn't seem to have the same effect on Paul though. He'd turned a slightly pale colour and appeared to be having trouble keeping his legs underneath him. I was about to ask if he was alright when he took a slight tumble forward and nearly fell flat on his face. If I hadn't been there he would have hit the ground hard. I grabbed him before he fell and put his arm over my shoulder. I could feel him shaking beside me.

"Paul, are you Ok?" I asked. He nodded before taking a sharp intake of breath and moistening his lips.

"Yeah, I'm sorry," he said. "I guess… I'm just a bit surprised to see you after all this time is all. And. And I don't understand" He turned his head to look back at me and a slight nervous smile returned to his mouth. "Do you want to come in for, I don't know, a cup of tea or something?"

"Not tea," I said, smiling, "but coffee would be good." And we walked back into the office, Paul now recovered and walking under his own steam.

The great weather didn't last very long Huck. There was a storm tonight and you and I watched it together. It was a big one. We sat and watched it roll in to begin with – big, black ominous clouds looming in the distance, far out to sea slowly getting closer and closer. You liked it to begin with Huck, enjoyed watching the lighting flicker across the sky and then counting the seconds before the thunder hit. You giggled every times a flash of lighting made you jump. Excited and nervous at the same time.

The three of us sat there on the bench outside of the cottage, me sipping coffee, you and your mother both with cups of hot chocolate. It was only early evening but the clouds and the time of year made it feel late. The few cars that drove past had their headlights on and I could count the houses further up the coast by the orange dots on the cliff edge.

"How far away is it?" you had asked.

"You can count," I'd said. "One mile for every second between the lighting and the thunder."

You had looked up at me, a puzzled look on your face. Not sure if I was telling the truth or not.

"For real?" you asked.

"For real," I replied.

We watched the sky, waiting for another flash. Suddenly another bolt lit up the sky and you started your counting. One Mississippi, two Mississippi, three Mississippi, four Mississippi, five Mississippi. Still far away.

"Five miles?" you asked. I nodded and you smiled, relaxed back into the bench again and took another sip of your hot chocolate. Five miles is a long way. Half way across the world to a kid.

We carried on watching. I could feel the storm getting closer without having to count. The wind started to pick up, that sudden rush of cold wind that precedes a storm, not your usual coastal breeze, different somehow. Ominous. Another flash across the sky. Four Mississippi this time.

"It's getting closer," you laughed. A little nervous laugh, excited and worried all at the same time, and you squished closer to me, not wanting to seem scared but I could feel you pressed closer to me. I wanted to put my arm around you but wasn't sure how you'd react. I looked over at your mother but she was still looking out to sea, watching for more lightning. I felt the first smatterings of rain on the back of my hand, cool and fresh. Suddenly another bolt of lightning and you almost flew out of your seat.

"Three Mississippi!"

"Do you want to go inside?" I asked but you shook your head. You were enjoying yourself even if you were a little scared.

"Does anyone want another drink?" you mother asked.

"No thanks," you yelled, not taking your eyes off the horizon for a second. I shook my head and your mum smiled at me and ruffled my hair. I always loved it when your mum used to ruffle my hair. My mum used to sit by my bed when I was a kid and run her fingers through my hair and tell me stories about Jack until I fell asleep and it always made me feel so safe. I turned my gaze back to the storm as she went inside.

"How close do you think it will get?" you asked. You'd regained your confidence by then.

"I don't know," I said, "but it's coming this way."

No sooner had I said it than a huge bolt of lightning lit up the sky, instantly followed by a booming clap of thunder. It made me jump out of my seat like you had before and you threw your hands over your ears and buried your head in my chest. For a second I didn't know what to do and then instinct took over. I wrapped my arms around you and held you tight against me. I held you as tight as I could. It felt so good, holding you, making you feel safe. All I'd ever wanted to do was to make you feel safe Huck.

Your mum came running back out of the cottage.

"Did you see that?" She stopped in the doorway as she saw us. I brought my fingers up to my lips and she didn't say anything else. She just stood there looking at the two of us.

"Can we go inside?" you asked from inside the folds of my jumper.

"Sure Huck," I said, "It's getting a bit too cold for me out here anyway." You unfurled yourself from me and walked back inside past your mother. I picked up the mugs and followed you in past her.

"You're good with him," she said as I walked past, still looking out at the storm clouds.

"I like the storm" I said, "my mum and I used to watch the storms come in."

We did. My mum loved watching the rain from her bedroom window. When it started raining she would call me up and we would kneel on the edge of her bed with our elbows on the window sill and watch the rain tumble from the broken gutter into the garden and stare through the streaks across the window. When the lightning came we would hold our breath until the thunder came and count to see how far away it was. It was never close.

I remember once we were sat watching, her with a glass of wine and me orange juice in a matching glass. She was drunk. I was nine. One of the street lights came on.

"Mum," I asked, "why is it so dark when it rains?"

She didn't turn her head, just answered without thinking.

"Because they're swimming in the sky."

I didn't know what she meant. Not then.

Well Huck, all I can say is that you either have the tactical mind of a young General or else you are very lucky since you wiped the floor with both your mum and I at Uno. We played about fifteen hands and I don't think I won a single one of them, not even close. We'll put it down to beginner's luck I think.

The weather got a lot worse before it got better and so we've had to spend most of today locked up in the house. I did a quick trip down to the shops to get us some supplies, which was lucky as they were about to close for the rest of the day. I don't think they get many customers other than the regulars. Plus I think they just wanted to get home and make sure their houses weren't leaking and just to be safe and warm. It's a good job we got here yesterday otherwise we might have gotten washed away on the road or have had to park up in the middle of nowhere while it passed, which wouldn't have been fun. Instead at least we were safe and warm in the cottage.

We talked while we played cards, mainly you asking questions until I couldn't answer them anymore.

"Is this your house, Michael?" you asked.

"No Huck," I said, "we're just borrowing it for a few days while we're up here. Pick up two please Huck."

"How long are we going to be up here for?" You asked, picking up a couple of cards and not managing to hide how pleased you were with what you had.

"Just a few days," I said, waiting for your mother to play her card. She laid down another pick up two card, my penalty this time, and I picked them up still looking at you, waiting for your next question.

"Oh," you said, staring at your cards. You laid down a miss-a-turn card and looked up at me. "Where are we going to go after this?"

"Your mum and you are going to go home," I said, laying down a green four. You laid down a green three straight away and called out Uno. "And I have to go somewhere else." Your mum looked across at me and tried to force her mouth into a smile that wasn't really a smile at all. She laid down another miss-a-go card.

"Oh," you said again. You looked at the card in your hand and laid it down – a pick up four. "I win," you said but there wasn't any conviction in it.

"I have a present for you though Huck," I said, trying to smile at you. "Something for you to take with you when you go home." You looked back at me and gave me the same smile that your mother had just given me.

"What is it?" You asked although I don't think you really wanted to know.

"It's not for now," I said and you looked back at the cards.

"Can we play again?" you asked and your mother nodded. You grabbed the cards up and tried to shuffle them.

I do have a present for you. Two in fact Huck. This letter is one of them and the rest of the money, the money I took from Natalie, is also for you. I want to say this now so that I can get it out of the way. I know that the money doesn't in any way make up for me not being around when you were growing up. I know that it doesn't replace having a father, having something stable in your life, not that I would have been capable of being either of those things. I'm giving it to you because it's that only thing I have to give you that will ever be of any use. I don't care what you want to do with it. If you don't want it, that's fine. If you want to give it away to a charity or someone more deserving, that's OK. Hell, if you want to hunt down Natalie and give it back to her then you can do whatever you want with it. I just want to know that I gave you the best opportunity that I could, that's all. And believe me, if I could use money to buy being a better father then I'd mortgage out my future and spend forever paying it back.

Not that it would be worth much now.

I'm sorry Huck. I really am.

So back to me and Paul. We sat in the small room at the back of the garage that served as both the office and the break room, the two of us hunched on two sofas that had seen better days on either side of a small coffee table. We sipped instant coffee from our mugs. For a long time neither of us said anything and then it broke into small talk. We talked about the weather, the drive I made to get here, how the Campervan handled and so on. Nothing interesting. Nothing I wanted to talk about. Then I asked how he had ended up in Nottingham.

"That's a pretty boring story," he said, but he told it to me anyway.

After he had left school his father had reluctantly agreed to pay for a private tutor to get him through his GCSE's, which weren't that far away, and Paul would then start working for his uncle at his garage in town. Somehow he had managed to get through his exams and, while he mustered some fairly terrible results, he did pass most of them just about. He had never been the brightest student, but what he had always lacked in academic ability he more than made up for with his talent with his hands and he had really enjoyed working for his uncle.

However, something had happened which meant that he had to stop working for his uncle after a couple of years. He wouldn't say what it was but clearly it was something he had done. I got the impression it wasn't anything bad, but something that had either caused extreme embarrassment or awkwardness, or potentially both. I assume that this was the "trouble" his friend Matt had told me about over Facebook but I didn't think that it was anything bad from the way Paul skirted around the subject. It certainly didn't seem like the sort of trouble that he used to get in at school. Either way he had left his Uncle's business and decided to get away from home and he picked Nottingham for no other reason that he had heard it could be a fun place to live. This was when he was eighteen. He'd taken a job working in another garage in town and then after a couple of years had managed to get enough experience and put aside enough savings to go out on his own. He'd never really met anyone he wanted to settle down with, didn't really see his parents any more but saw his sister occasionally and that was about all there was to it. I didn't pry into any more detail about the "incident" that had led to him leaving his Uncle's garage and didn't ask about the name change either.

He was right. It wasn't the most interesting story in the world.

The story took maybe half an hour to tell me with all the details added in and then we sat there again, not really talking about anything. I was on the verge of thinking about leaving when the phone rang and he stood up to answer it. It was a brief conversation of "uh-huh"s and "ok"s from Paul before finishing with a "well why don't you let me know." He hung up and stood looking at the phone for a second and not talking, scratching his chin before turning back to me.

"That was my only booking for the day and they just cancelled," he said. "How about we shut up the place and we go to the pub for an early lunch and a Christmas drink?" That knocked me back for a second.

"Oh, I really ought to be getting back on the road," I said, not really sure if I wanted to go to the pub with Paul or not. He seemed to have changed a lot since the last time I had seen him all those years ago, but ultimately he was still the same person who had almost left me in a coma. And I had done what I'd come to do.

"Don't be silly," he said. "It's Christmas Eve for Christ sake. Do you have somewhere you need to be for Christmas?"

I shook my head. I hadn't really thought about Christmas. It hadn't really registered with me. I was just going to make my way to the next place on my list over the next couple of days and do what I needed to do.

"Well then," he carried on, "why not come and have a few drinks with me – my shout. I'm meant to be meeting a few people in town later for the usual Christmas Eve thing. You can always crash at mine if you haven't got anywhere better to be?"

Was this really the same guy? It had been a long time I suppose and he made a good point. I didn't have anywhere better to be straight away and actually the thought of spending Christmas Eve with some friends, even if they weren't mine, seemed like a nice idea. Definitely better that sitting alone in the Campervan. I hadn't spent Christmas Eve with anyone that I would consider a friend since I had left your mother. Plus we were grown-ups. I couldn't imagine that he still wanted to beat me up. It didn't seem likely that he was luring me back to his place just to punch me in the gut when I least suspected it. I didn't think so anyway. I decided I would stay, for the evening at least, and see how it went.

"I don't really drink though," I said.

"Well that's even better because I do," Paul smiled, standing up and throwing me some keys. "You can drive us home later and we can pick your wagon up in the morning. You can park it inside the garage if you want?"

And so that's how I ended up spending Christmas Eve at the pub with the bully who spent five years beating me up at school and who was responsible for the only reason I ever had to be in hospital since my birth. And you know what Huck? It was wonderful. I guess people really can change. The two of us drove in to town and spent the first couple of hours just talking about the things we remembered from school – teachers we hated, funny things that happened to other kids, the scandals of teenage love affairs and all the rest of it. The same conversation I'd had with Matt over Facebook only this was a two way thing. This was real. Later we were joined one by one by his friends who all welcomed me into the group with open arms. He had a good bunch of friends, Paul did, and none of them anything like the "band of brothers" from our school days. They were nice, normal, friendly people who laughed and joked about normal things. They were all our age – mainly men with their wives and girlfriends. Some had kids, some had manual jobs like Paul, others worked in offices. All of them were normal, happy people. And they were all incredibly kind to me. Paul introduced them to me as his long lost friend from his school days and I felt like I really was. I would have fitted in with that group I think. They could have been my friends too. A shame that I found them so late, a shame that Paul did too.

People drifted off throughout the evening and eventually at midnight, having said Merry Christmas to each of his three remaining friends at least twice, we walked back to the car and I drove back to his house under some rather dodgy, mostly drunk, instructions from Paul. I'm sure it took us at least twice as long to drive back as it should have done and I'm fairly convinced we drove past the pub at least a couple of times. However, Paul was in good spirits and I was enjoying being in his company.

When we go back to his house he showed me to the spare room and gave me an extra blanket and a spare toothbrush. He said goodnight and he wandered off to his own room to leave me to dream, for a little while at least.

I lay in my bed at Paul's house thinking about everything that had taken place that day. It had been a good day. I had expected Paul to apologise too, but he hadn't. That didn't matter though. I had said what I had wanted to say to him and that was the point. That's what I had come for. Anything else would have been a bonus. I knew that whatever happened to me after that I had at least partly rid myself of the guilt that had followed me around ever since that day when I was sixteen years old. And we had been friends, Paul and I, for a day at least. In the end we had been friends. It made me think that perhaps if things had been different we could have been friends when we were younger too. That I wouldn't have always been such an outcast at school and that maybe I was just a victim of bad luck. I wish I hadn't said what I'd said to him all those years ago.

His friends had all liked me too. They had all welcomed me into their little group and, whilst most of them had been a little drunk by the end of the evening, I think the goodbyes and the handshakes and backslaps were sincere and the "it would be good to see you again mate's" were genuine. Paul, again although drunk, had seemed happy on the drive home and actually surprisingly chatty. I don't think at school, after that first term, I had ever really heard him talk other than to scream obscenities at me and tell me what a piece of shit I was. Even though he had been a little drunk he was surprisingly well spoken and articulate. I think that if things had been different all those years ago then he and I would have been genuine friends. How different my life would have been then, hey Huck? Perhaps I would have been a happier kid without it all and perhaps some of it would have rubbed off on my mum and my father. Perhaps we could have been a happy little family. Perhaps your mother and you and I could have too.

Perhaps.

I lay there thinking about it and my eyes grew weary with sleep. I could feel them getting heavy and I rolled onto my side to let it take me. For the first time in a long time I was looking forward to it, thinking that I might actually dream of something pleasant.

I didn't though. Something still wasn't right. I was back there on the boat with Jack, watching the dark fish swimming all around me. One of the fish came closer to the surface this time and I saw it's great bulging, black eyes. And in that eye I saw a reflected face, but it wasn't mine. Not me, Huck.

I've always hated being ill, Huck. I used to get ill quite a lot when I was a kid. Not to the point where I had to be taken into hospital or anything like that because I don't think there wasn't actually anything really wrong with me. I guess I was just one of those kids that you would call sickly, or at least had the appearance of being sickly. It worried my mum a lot. She used to absolutely despair over it and would rush me off to the doctors at a moment's notice, barging in and complaining that I had a fever or that I looked the wrong colour or whatever it would be. Inevitably it would turn out to be nothing, nothing that a day of rest wouldn't fix anyway. I think most of the time I was probably just overtired like a lot of kids are.

Anyway, I hated going to the doctors. I always felt like everyone was looking at me and wondering what was up with me. Kids in the doctors surgery are always a bit apprehensive because they either understand that if you're at the doctors then there must be something wrong with you – even though they are there for exactly the same reason - and don't want to come near you, or because their parents keep trying to get them to stay away from you because they suspect you might be contagious. I always felt like a bit of an outcast sat there waiting to be seen. And that only added to the amount I felt like an outcast anyway.

Our family doctor was Dr Singh and he was not a nice man. People always seem to remember their family doctor with fondness and think why can't the doctor be like that anymore? Well not for me. He would constantly prod and poke me and took every word that my mother said at face value, presumably more worried that he was going to miss something than he was about having any kind of bedside manner or treating any of his patients properly. I spent hours in that surgery having my temperature taken, my reflexes tested, my ears and throat examined. Had I ever actually managed to get a job with NASA at least my medical record would have been clean. They would have had about a thousand samples to rely on. The nurses clearly knew the guy was incompetent and, being as he was at least 75 years old, past it. They tutted and rolled their eyes at every test he wanted carried out, at every request for a blood sample to be taken but they did them anyway. He and my mother riled each other up I think.

Inevitably the cure was the same; paracetamol and a day of bed rest. And bed rest was exactly what I got unfortunately. Whilst most kids aged seven or eight were grateful for a day off school I absolutely hated them. Other kids would get to lie on the sofa all day, watching TV and eating ice cream. I get paracetamol three times a day and blackout curtains. The only good thing about my mother leaving was that my school attendance suddenly sky rocketed, and presumably the average waiting time at the doctors halved. That was the only good thing though kiddo and it wasn't worth it.

I don't blame my mum. If anything she was just looking out for me, she just wanted me to be OK and to be happy.

My mum also used to spend a lot of time in her room with two paracetamol and the blackout curtains shut although, I later learned, that that was for a very different reason altogether. A sickness, yes, but a very different kind of sickness to the ones I supposedly had. A much worse one. Maybe, with the constant trips to the doctor she was just trying to fix me in a way she couldn't fix herself. Trying to make sure I wouldn't ever be sick in the same way she was. It was strange – our doctor never asked how she was. Never mentioned the bruises and the scars. I guess he couldn't see the patient stood right in front of him.

It left me with a simple contempt for doctors after that Huck. Most things that you thought were wrong with you were just tiredness or something else you could fix yourself and going to the doctor wasn't going to make any difference to you. All you would end up doing is going to bed and taking some paracetamol. Slight coughs, colds, sore throat – all of it could realistically be sorted with some paracetamol and some rest. Headaches, repeat headaches, those headaches that go on for a couples of days where you can't really stand the light and you actually need those blackout curtains. All can be solved with paracetamol and some rest.

That's what I thought anyway Huck. Maybe that one wasn't my fault after all.

When I woke up this morning it was still dark out – the sun comes up pretty late this far north in the winter. It was still only about seven in the morning but the curtains over the windows in the front room don't cover the windows completely. I guess they weren't made for having people sleep in there. Everything was quiet in the house – you and your mum were still both asleep in your rooms upstairs.

I put on some warm clothes and headed outside to stretch my legs. Even with three layers and a coat on it was still bitterly cold outside and the wind froze my hands together so I could only just open them. I closed the door gently so as to not wake you up but I didn't lock the door. I figured nobody did around here.

I pulled the collar up on my coat and headed towards the village a mile or so up and round the coast. It didn't take me long to get there but when I did I was glad to be out of the cold and the wind. The door of the shop opened with a tinkle of the old fashioned bell that rang overhead. There was nobody else in the shop but me. I took a basket and looked around. The shop was pretty basic – just long wooden shelves with bits and pieces laid out in rows. There wasn't much choice, not like the supermarkets in London, but there was pretty much everything anyone would have needed, even if there was only one type of anything. I filled up the basket with as much as I could and headed over to the counter. The old guy on the till looked at me and nodded.

"Morning," he said in a light Scottish accent. I nodded back at him.

"Morning," I repeated. He started to run things through the register, typing everything in by hand.

"Are you up here for the week?" he asked. I nodded again. "You and the family eh?" he carried on. "It's a nice place to be spending Hogmanay with a young family." I didn't know where to look. He kept scanning.

"Boy or girl?" he asked.

"I'm sorry," I said. As soon as the words left my mouth I understood what he has asked.

"Do you have a son or a daughter?" he said, smiling back at me.

"Oh," I said, embarrassed, "a son. Huck." The old man nodded and turned around. He pulled a packet from a pile on the shelf behind him and filled it up with sweets from the jars. He twisted the top of the packet and dropped them in to one of the bags with the rest of the shopping.

"On me," he said and rang up the register. He held out his hand while I fished the money out for him and he handed me back my change.

"If you're here for Hogmanay," he said, "everyone around here goes to the Hotel. It isn't much to look at but its good fun and there's music and beer all night." I nodded at him and smiled. As I walked back to the house it wasn't so cold anymore and I half walked and half skipped back. When I got home you and your mum were up and your mum was putting on some coffee. You turned and smiled as I walked in the kitchen door.

"We're making breakfast," you beamed, "and I'm on toast duty."

I smiled down at you and your mother turned from the stove. I held out the bags of shopping for her to see.

"I got provisions," I said. "Should be enough to last us a few days at least."

"Well look at you," she said, "providing for us." I looked down at the floor when she said that.

"Oh no," she said, "I didn't mean it like that."

I knew she hadn't. But I also knew what it meant to me.

And so now, full of energy from eggs, toast and tea as I am it's time to get the rest of this written down before we have to leave the cottage. So onwards and upwards.

I woke with a start in Paul's spare room. I have always been a light sleeper on account of having to look after my mother so much as a child and the sound of creaking doors was one of those things that always alerted me to the fact that my mum might need me, either to help her into bed or, worse, if she was getting out of bed to stop her potentially falling down the stairs. That had happened a couple of times, Huck, as had genuinely walking in to doors, despite the looks that the people she told sometimes gave her.

I was laying on my side facing the wall and for a moment I just lay there, not moving. I could see the light on the wall next to me clearly signalling that it was my door that had creaked open. I could hear someone breathing in the door way but no movement. I stayed still and said nothing. I could tell it was him, who else could it have been? Paul stood in the door way for what seemed like an hour but, in reality, was probably only a minute of two before he closed the door and went back to bed. I lay awake for maybe thirty minutes before I eventually fell back to sleep.

When I woke up I was surprised to see that it was actually pretty late in the morning. Well, 9:15, but that was late for me anyway and it took me a while to realise that it was also Christmas day. My door was almost closed but I could hear a whistling and a sizzling coming from down stairs together with the unmistakable smell of a fry up and I couldn't work out which one of them it was that had woken me up – the cheerful tune or the smell of frying bacon. Either way I was glad for both so I got up and made my way down.

Paul's house wasn't particularly big, a two bedroom terrace, but it was light and something about it made it feel homely. The place was tidy, something I hadn't expected either of him or of a mechanic, which is probably an unfair stereotype. I had expected that he would live in some sort of bachelor pad, all black chrome and glass, but it wasn't like that at all. I wondered if perhaps there had been a woman in his life up until some point in the recent past that had actually done all of the work for him but I didn't ask. He had said there hadn't and I believed him. I walked in to the kitchen where Paul was stood over the hob, spatula in one hand and a mug of tea in the other, wearing one of those aprons that made it look like you had the body of an Adonis.

He turned to me as I walked in and flashed a shy smile, nodding his head towards the breakfast table. There were two places set out and a cracker at each place setting. A steaming black mug of coffee sat in one of the places and next to it was a small parcel wrapped in red and green wrapping paper and a name tag on it that clearly said "Michael".

"Merry Christmas," Paul said. "Take a seat and breakfast will be ready in a second."

"Merry Christmas to you too," I replied, sitting down and picking up the present, turning it over in my hand. "What's this?" I asked.

"Oh," Paul said, keeping his back to me as he started plating up breakfast. "It's for you. Something I thought you would like. Seemed rude to invite you over for Christmas and not to give you a present." He laughed as he said it but he sounded nervous.

I squeezed the package in my hand, trying to work out what was inside but all I could make out was that it was a long, flat box. The kind of box that an old pen would have come in or a woman's necklace. I looked up at Paul and he was looking down at the parcel in my hand, his lips moving as if he was worried. I tore open the paper and saw that it was in fact a jewellery case, long and dark red with a velvet cover. I hesitated and then, slowly, I opened it and saw something I had thought had been lost a long, long time ago.

Once, after PE, I had been getting changed and ready to get in the showers. We'd been playing football and despite not really being involved in the game I was wet and muddy from the winter rain. I was stripped down to my boxers and, as usual, waiting for as many of the other boys to finish showering before I went in. Paul had not been playing due to the usual excuse of having forgotten his kit or some fake illness, one of the two, something that happened frequently for him and the brothers. Usually they were forced to sit and watch from the side-lines, other times they were made to pick up litter from the playground which inevitably really meant going for a smoke. I guess the teachers knew. The skivers never came back with a bag full of rubbish. But it got them out of having to play, which was what they really wanted. They always had to come back to get their stuff though and that meant they were always in the changing rooms at the end of every lesson. I stood by my bag, waiting for the last few boys to return from the showers when suddenly I felt an enormous hand land on my shoulder. I turned around and Paul was beaming right into my face. I could smell the smoke on his breath.

"Alright fucknuts," he said, breathing on me as he did so.

I pulled back away from him towards the benches and my bag. I decided then that I wouldn't bother with a shower. Despite how sweaty I was it was best just to get out of there. If I stank and my classmates added that to the list of things they hated me for then so be it. Most of them didn't come close enough to me to smell me anyway. I tried to turn around sort my things about but Paul's grasp on my shoulder was too strong and he swung me back so I was facing him again.

"Whoa, whoa whoa mate," he said. "You can't go yet, you need to get yourself all cleaned off. Let me give you a hand." And with that he pushed past me and dove a hand into my bag. This was the kind of thing that I had to put up with every week, Huck. This highly intellectual sense of humour that the rest of the brothers, and most of my classmates to be fair, seemed to find hilarious. The greatest comedian they had ever seen.

"Please Paul," I said with no real conviction. I knew that nothing I said was going to stop him. He pulled out my jumper, held it up, sniffed it and threw it into the showers.

"This is a bit smelly mate, think you probably need to give that a wash." This was met with echoes of laughter around the changing rooms. Everyone either watched or laughed or stood and did nothing. Nobody helped me. He turned back to my bag and pulled out my shirt. That too was inspected in the same manner and thrown in after the jumper, as was my tie. They sat there in a heap in the showers, soaking up everyone else's filthy water. He pulled my trousers out of the bag next and went through the same routine but when he put them to his nose to fake smell them something fell out of the pocket and landed with a metallic tinkle on the ground. Both of us looked down at it and as I bent down to try and grab it he covered it with his foot, dragged it away and picked it up. He open his hand and held my mother's necklace in front of him. It was a simple thing, a small gold St Christopher on a plain simple chain. My mother's name and date of birth were etched on to the back of the pendant, a present from her god parents on the day of her christening. She had worn it every day despite not really being a believer in anything. Had worn it for good luck more than anything else. Not that it had worked of course. When she had left she had given it to my aunt to give to me. It didn't work for that either I guess. But it was all I had to remember her by. Everything else was gone.

"What's this," he snorted. "Have you stolen this off some girl?" I made a feeble attempt to grab it back from him but he easily pulled it out of my reach. "You been wearing this?" he added. "Practicing for being a cross dresser on the weekends?" This drew another round of laughs from the changing room and I could feel all of their eyes on me.

"It's my mothers," I said. "Please just give it back Paul."

"Nah," Paul laughed, "I think she probably would have wanted me to have it, don't you?" And with that he balled the necklace up, stuck it in his pocket, looked back at me with a self-satisfied grin and punched me in the stomach, hard. I doubled over in pain and couldn't move for about thirty seconds. By the time I had gathered my clothes, wet and sopping as they were, shoved them into my bag and looked around he was long gone. I didn't stay in school the rest of that day. I ran home in my PE kit, locked myself in my room and cried until I slept. My dad wasn't happy when he got home that there was no dinner waiting for him, but I think it's one of the few times I truly didn't care. He tried to come into my room. Shouted through the door for a while but I didn't respond. I had nothing to say anymore. Eventually he sloped off and out of the house.

And now here it was sat in front of me again. My mother's necklace. The last thing she had ever given me. I pulled it out of the case and held it up in front of my face, letting the pendant spin on the chain in front of me. I just let it hang there for a few moments so that I could see it was really hers. It looked just as I had remembered it, except that it had been polished and shined now more than I think it had ever done. The same picture, the same inscription. It had to be the same one. I didn't understand.

"You told me you'd thrown this in the river," I said, not taking my eyes off it for fear it would change and no longer be the same necklace, just a cheap copy. "I asked you then next day if I could have it back and you told me you'd thrown it in the river."

He hung his head in shame, the smile gone from his face now.

"I know," he said. "I don't know why I said that, but I'd kept it. I wanted it."

I stared at him, the blood beginning to boil inside of me. For one of the few times in my life I felt angry and it felt like it was going to boil over. Anger is a feeling I rarely have. You have to understand Huck, most people feel angry a lot, when things don't go their way, when something happens that shouldn't have happened to them. When other people make life difficult for them or when life simply throws them something unfair. For me that has always been difficult to grasp. Things don't go my way, don't happen the way I want them to, because of me. Because of things I've done wrong. But this wasn't my fault. This was something someone had done to me through no fault of my own. He had done it just to be mean. To play a trick on me. He'd invited me back into his life, into his home for God's sake, just to play this one cruel trick on me. It was sickening. Sickening and low. What was next? A quick punch to the stomach? A little stomp on the head. I'd misjudged him. Really, really misjudged him. And now I was going to pay for it.

"Why were you so mean to me Paul?" I stared at him and he continued to look at the floor, his shoulders shrugged.

"You were mean to me for five years, Paul. Every fucking day. You and your friends bullied me and belittled me every day for five years and all I did was ask about a fucking drawing. What did I do wrong?" He carried on staring at the floor, barely moving, barely breathing. I was so confused and I could feel the anger building in me and I didn't want it to stop. I had never felt like this before. Was this how my father felt his whole life?

"What did I do Paul? I continued, desperate and raging. "I want to know Paul I really do because I don't understand it. I must have done something pretty offensive to you for you to want to do that to me, surely. What was it?"

"I don't know," was the simple reply but I didn't believe him. I stood up now, stood up and walked out of the kitchen. He followed me into the hall and as he did so I turned back around and stared him in the eyes. It was my turn to be up in his face now, my turn to be the aggressor and in that moment I liked it. I loved it. It felt good, Huck. After all those years of being the victim I began to understand how good being angry could be. How good being mean could be. How powerful my father must have felt all those times. I wanted to hit him, Huck, hit him square in his fucking mouth.

"What Paul, what the fuck did I do that warranted you beating me up twice a week for five years, huh? What the fuck did I do that warranted you putting me in hospital and nearly killing me?" I stared him in his expressionless face and he continued to stare at my chest, saying nothing. I turned around and started up the stairs to get my things so I could leave.

"You can't even say it Paul can you? Can't even say why you fucking hated me so much." I called over my shoulder.

"I didn't hate you," he suddenly shouted back and then mumbled something under his breath. I turned around half way up the stairs.

"What did you say?" I shouted back down. I didn't want to waste any more of my time on this shit, didn't have time for him to be meek and pathetic. I had to get my stuff and get out of there before my anger boiled over any more and I did something he would regret. Or something I would. Or both. Something my father would have been proud of.

"I said I loved you," he replied. He said it as calm as you like. "You didn't do anything wrong, you were simply you, and I loved you. And…." he trailed off.

And then all of a sudden it all made sense again. He hadn't done anything wrong. The world hadn't dealt me an unfair hand. It was simply me. The story of my life. It was my fault after all, just as I had always thought. How could I have doubted for a moment that it was any other reason than that? I was me and he had fallen in love with me for some unknown reason and he couldn't live with that. Couldn't live with liking someone as awful and pathetic as me. Knowing, or at least thinking, you might be gay at that age would have been hard enough. Imagine adding to that someone like him loving someone like me. A nobody like me. The school alpha male in love with the school loser. No wonder he wanted to punch me every day. As the realisation dawned on me the anger left my body again and any feeling of power or pride left with it. I sat on the stairs and looked at him as he continued to look at my chest. Neither of us said anything for a very long time.

I wonder how you'll fair with the ladies Huck. A little too early to tell at this stage although you seem to be able to charm even the most cynical of service station check out girls into giving you a smile. Don't be a heartbreaker Huck, that's all I can say. At least, not in a big way.

I was never very good with women, as you can probably imagine. Your mother was the first real relationship that I ever had and I suppose that went well for a while, until I messed things up. Girls at school were not really an option. There were girls I liked of course but my reputation, as well as my awkwardness, proceeded me there and so nothing really happened until I went to University. I was a different person there, for a while at least, and I saw it as a bit of a fresh start. The opportunity not to be the loser I had always been at school. The chance to make new friends and be seen as an equal. But it didn't last long. I had a few friends in the early months, people who didn't know anyone else I suppose. Other people who were home sick and lost without their usual friends and so buddied up with the first people that spoke to them until they made some real friends. I also met a girl that I liked – one of our group of friends. We saw each other for a few weeks and then I told her I loved her. It was too soon I suppose, freaked her out and we broke up shortly afterwards and most of my "friends" suddenly seemed to prefer her to me.

I didn't last very long at University after that. It's a hard place to be when you aren't confident, when you don't really have anything interesting to add to any conversation. When you aren't much fun. And like I said, you tend to make your friends in the first couple of weeks and when those people desert you in favour of the more fun half of you, it can make the place even more lonely. I spent a lot of time in the library or in my room reading, studying some of the time, but mainly just reading and thinking. After about three months I decided I'd had enough of it and then realised I didn't really know what to do. I didn't want to go home, not that I had one at that point, and I didn't want to stay there. That's when I started looking for jobs and saw the ad for the groundskeeper. It was an easy decision and nobody from University missed me. My tutor didn't even try to convince me to stay and by that time my love interest and her friends would barely even acknowledge me. I was already an outcast and so I decided to swim for land rather than carry on drifting in the ocean.

Jack on the other hand was what can only be described as an absolute ladies man. God's gift. Girls literally swooned when he walked past them, particularly once word about the big fight at school got around. He was easily the most popular kid in his school and had the pick of basically any girl he wanted, including those as many as two years above him.

But he didn't abuse his position. He too had a crush. It was a girl in his year who he adored and doted on constantly. He had probably hundreds of other offers from girls but he never batted so much as an eyelid at any of them, intent on being instead with the love of his life – Katy Walters. It was incredible how similar the two girls were that we had fallen for – Katy and my girl at university – both slim, brunette, just a little shorter than we were, deep brown eyes, a light dusting of freckles across their cheeks. Both lovely.

Jack however had far more success than I ever did with my crush. They spent many a happy hour in class or after school talking, walking around, joking, and playfully jostling one another. After six weeks or so they started holdings hands and a month or so later their first real kiss, by the river, watching the swans glide past. They were fourteen when they first got together and they lived the dream – childhood sweethearts who would go on to marry, have wonderful children, live in a beautiful old Edwardian house on the outskirts of town. Katy went on to become a lawyer, which meant they were able to live a very comfortable lifestyle despite Jack's fairly low income as a fireman. Even when Katy had gone off to University they didn't have any problems. He managed to find the perfect balance between allowing her to live her own life there and maintaining their love for one another. All the time at University really did was make them realise how much they truly loved one another and meant they blossomed into the people they were always meant to become, neither living in the others shadow.

Jack has a wonderful life. I am envious of him, sometimes a little too much. But I am here Huck, and he isn't. He doesn't have you for a son and I am grateful for that. The only thing in my life I am truly thankful for.

We carried on staring at each other for a long time, Paul and I, neither of us saying anything, until he finally broke the ice.

"Will you stay," he said, still not looking up at me. "Just for the day. It would be nice to spend Christmas with someone rather than on my own again and I've bought more than enough food for two anyway."

I hesitated. This wasn't really part of my plan after all and I didn't know, after his revelation, what he really wanted.

"You don't have to," he said. "I just thought it might be nice. But if you have to be somewhere its ok. You could always pick up your van tomorrow morning and then go wherever you're going."

I didn't have to be anywhere and he was right, spending Christmas Day with someone would be nice. I didn't know what was going to happen on the rest of my journey, even if I was going to be able to find any of the rest of you for sure. And I sensed that, for whatever reason, he needed me to stay just then. Anyway, this was my fault now – the way he was, the turmoil he seemed to be in. Whatever had happened since we were kids I was surely at least partly to blame. I made up my mind then.

"OK," I said looking up at him. His gaze finally lifted off my chest and onto my face. He flashed a smile at me and seemed more at peace with himself.

"Thanks Michael," he said.

We spent the day together, the two of us and for the most part talked about something and nothing. He was a good cook and knew exactly what to do with the turkey to get it ready and I have to say he made probably the best Yorkshire puddings I have ever tasted in my life. We pulled crackers, told each other terrible jokes. We watched the queen's speech, something I've never done before in my life and made fun of her voice. Then we spent another hour trying to imitate other famous people as best we could, literally rolling around on the floor, our sides on the verge of splitting from laughing so much. He did a great Boris Johnson, I could do a passable Ian McKellan.

And the more we joked and laughed that more Paul relaxed into himself. The more he told me things that were less something and nothing and more personal – about his sister and what she was doing with her life, about his parents and how much it hurt him that he didn't see his mother anymore, the fact that he didn't see any of his school friends anymore and how that bothered him.

"They didn't know," he said eventually.

"Didn't know what?" I asked, sitting up on the floor after a particularly side aching bout of laughter brought upon by his Boris Johnson Prime Minister acceptance speech.

"That I liked you," he said, first looking at the floor before glancing up at me to check that it was OK to carry on that conversation. I looked back at him and nodded that he should keep going. I didn't know what he was going to say, but I wanted to hear it anyway.

"Go on," I said. And he did.

He told me that he had always known that there was something different about him, since he was about ten. That he had always enjoyed being around boys but not in quite the same way that other boys did. That kiss chase hadn't been quite as exciting to him as it had been to the other kids. At that age he didn't really know what it meant but by the time he got to secondary school he had a pretty good idea. He had tried not to think about it, to suppress it and bury it deep down as most kids that age probably would have. But he couldn't help it.

He said that he knew as soon as he had first seen me at school that he liked me. There was just something about me, he said, something that made him want to be close to me and yet at the same time he was scared of me. Scared of the way he was feeling about me I guess. Scared of what it might lead to. He said he had chosen to sit next to me in art class in a moment of madness buoyed on by wanting to be who he really was and then had immediately regretted it. But there wasn't a chance to change afterwards. As in all our classes the seat someone chose on the first day was theirs for the rest of the year, unless the teacher decided they'd had enough of the two of you sitting together.

His dad had known, or sensed at least that there was something different about him and his father wasn't exactly the sort of man who wanted his son to grow up to be a fag. Paul used that word, fag, when he talked about his dad's reaction and clearly hated the sound of it. Said it through gritted teeth. I got the impression his dad had used that word around him, perhaps to him, too many times. Once is too many times I suppose, if it's aimed at you by your own father. I know how much a simple insult can hurt when it comes from your old man.

"He used to tell me I needed to take a long hard look in the mirror at the man I wanted to be," Paul said. And it all made sense. "That's what you did, Michael, you called me out about the same thing I was thinking about. What my dad was thinking anyway. And something inside me just snapped. You saying it to me, like you knew my secret, it just broke something inside of me. I figured the best way to keep you out of my mind was to hate you." I carried on staring at him, and nodding. Still smiling a little and trying to let him know it was OK. It wasn't his fault. I wanted him to let it all out.

"The more I hit you, the more times, the worse it got," he continued. "The more I did it the more I hated myself for it, the more I knew what it really all meant. And then one day, despite everything I did to you, you told me you loved me. I don't know why you said that. I couldn't understand it. I don't even know what happened really after that other than that time I really snapped. I mean, really, really snapped. I was out of control."

I flinched when I thought about that day. He wasn't looking at me at that point, I think he was lost in his own shame, and he didn't see my reaction. I told him to carry on.

He told me about how that evening he had realised what he had done, that he had been terrified he was going to be arrested for assault, but more so he had been worried about me. The police had come round and, as he understood it, it had been touch and go as to whether or not he would be cautioned and possibly taken to the station. He had been relieved of course when he hadn't. My father decided he didn't want to press charges. He didn't want the hassle. Said it was probably six of one and half a dozen of the other. I wasn't even asked. Paul said that had been a turning point for him, he said, a genuine life changing moment. A revelation. He studied for his exams, was allowed to sit them at a different school and had done "alright" with his grades, but had been distracted worrying about me. I think that was a bit of an excuse but I didn't interrupt. He'd heard things here and there from his friends about how I was doing, them bragging to him about how much he had messed me up, him trying to pretend he was glad but secretly hoping I was ok.

As I've already said after he got his results he took a job with his uncle at the garage and had genuinely enjoyed it. He'd never really been one for school frustrated by having to learn things that he didn't enjoy and never thought would be useful to him – frustrated in the way lots of young men are I suppose for exactly the same reasons. Being in the garage and working with his hands had allowed him to do something different, had given him focus and a sense of achieving something tangible after a day of work, mending things, making things work. He had a purpose but he was still troubled – couldn't admit to anyone what he really wanted to, couldn't admit who he really was.

And then, as I've already said, something changed. The difference was that the garage took on another apprentice, a young 18 year old lad that Paul immediately took a liking to and whom, apparently, also took a liking to him. Or so Paul thought. They worked together a lot, went to the pub after clocking off, and stayed late doing overtime together. And it was on one of these occasions that Paul had made his move and found out that he had judged things spectacularly badly. The other guy had reacted badly and told Paul's uncle, who wasn't impressed. Faced with a choice of either firing his gay nephew or the straight new kid he'd decided to stick by his principles and Paul had to leave. On the same day his dad, having heard about the incident almost immediately, kicked him out of his house rather than live with the shame for another day. He moved in with his older sister for a couple of weeks before he picked a random town off the map and decided to move there for a fresh start.

"Changed my surname as well," Paul said. "Partly because I wanted a fresh start, and fewer people to be able to find me, and partly because I didn't want to be associated with those people any more. Except my sister of course, she's always been great with me. But then she's not a Francis anymore anyway."

He took a sip from his tea and sniffed, maintaining his composure.

"It was hard moving here, not knowing anyone," he said and I thought back to my first week at University. I felt for him then. "But I got a job pretty quickly and things settled down as well – made some friends. Not my usual sort of friends – I guess I'd grown up a bit by then. Very different from the brothers." He snorted the last word – clearly he didn't think very much of them anymore.

"I've still never really told anyone though," he continued. "I mean, there have been people here and there but never anything serious. I guess I've just never really been comfortable with that part of me."

I didn't say anything the whole time that he was talking, just looked at him and nodded every now and again, letting him say whatever he wanted to. To be honest I didn't really know what to say. It's strange, you go through your entire life fixated on your own problems, especially as a kid. Maybe if I had spent a bit more time thinking about what was going on with him I could have helped him.

"Anyway," he finished. "That's my story. I'm not sure it really excuses any of the things I did to you, but it's all I have I guess. Life was hard for me as a kid."

You have no idea, I thought. But I didn't say it. I just smiled and nodded at him, and then I heard myself saying something I hadn't expected to say.

"I forgive you."

He didn't really show it but a small change in the way he sat said that meant something to him. At least, I like to think it did. He simply nodded and turned back towards the television and I watched him as a single tear rolled down his cheek. He wiped it away on his arm and went back to his tea. The two of us sat in silence again, but now the silence was comfortable. We spent the rest of the day watching old Christmas movies. We ate turkey and stuffing sandwiches for supper and then, at about midnight, we went to bed.

I lay there again, staring at the ceiling and thinking about the day. Thinking about how cruel people can be and how different both our lives might had been if the world was a different place. We were similar, Paul and I. Both still under the influence of an all-powerful father who didn't understand us. A father who chose not to understand us. Both with our own dark fish swimming in our dreams. It didn't matter though. Too late to change anything. Too late now.

After about fifteen minutes I heard my door creak again and this time I rolled over and smiled at Paul standing in my door way. He smiled back at me and walked over to the bed. I budged across to make room for him and he climbed in next to me, a double bed but slightly too small for the two of us. We lay there, side by side in the darkness until eventually we both drifted off to sleep. In the middle of the night I woke up and found myself laying on my side, Paul's hand draped over me. I left it there.

In the morning he was gone, downstairs, whistling and cooking again. I got dressed and went down. Another cup of coffee waiting for me, another cooked breakfast.

"Something to set you up for the road," he smiled. "You never did tell me where you were going."

"No, I didn't," I replied, thinking about the next leg of my journey. "I'm going to see my mum."

He smiled and chewed his breakfast. He didn't know. Couldn't have done. We ate and joked again – him doing more Boris, me laughing. I sensed that he didn't want me to go and, to be honest, I could have stayed a few more days but I knew I was only delaying what I really needed to do, and dragging it out would only make it more difficult when the time came. Plus I had a timetable of sorts. Eventually I packed my bag and he drove me back to his garage and to the Campervan. I stood outside the van, ready to go.

"Well," I said, "I guess this is goodbye."

He looked me in the face, a warm smile on his.

"Don't be a stranger," he said. I didn't have the heart to tell him. He threw his arms around me and I hugged him back. As he squeezed me he whispered in my ear. "Thanks Michael, you don't know what a difference this is going to make to me."

And with that he turned and walked back his car. He opened the door as I climbed into the cab of the Campervan. The engine turned over and as I drove away he stood, half in and half out of his car, waving me off. He looked the happiest I had seen him the whole time we had been together, probably the happiest I had ever seen him. I hope some small part of that was down to me.

I spent most of the morning writing Huck, writing and thinking about you to be honest. After a couple of hours your mum thought it would be a good idea if we went for a walk and got some fresh air. It was still drizzling a little but not as bad as it had been the day before and you seemed a little fidgety from spending all day cooped up in the house playing board games with your mum and watching TV. As soon as your mum mentioned the idea of the beach you were off like a shot, digging out your wellies from upstairs and scrambling into you rain mac.

The walk down to the beach wasn't more than a few hundred meters but it was down an overgrown track that ran across a steep field of green and red and purple heather. I wanted to go first to make sure the path was OK but your mum insisted on leading the way. She always did. And so we walked down to the beach, the three of us, with you in the middle and me behind watching you plod down the hill. As soon as we reached the beach you ran off at full pelt towards the sea, your mum calling after you not to go deeper than half way up your wellies and to be careful of the waves. You started walking up the beach in the sea, splashing as you went, stopping every now and again to look into the water or wave at us. We tracked you, walking side by side on the sand, neither of us saying anything until suddenly she spoke, still looking at the sand beneath her boots.

"He likes you," she said. I didn't say anything, I knew what was coming.

"He likes you," she repeated, "and in a few days you're going to leave us. Going to leave us again and we're never going to see you and that will be that. And he is going to be heartbroken and it's going to be worse than ever because before he never had a dad to lose until now and…" She didn't finish. She turned instead and watched you splashing in the sea. You saw her looking at you, she waved and you waved back. I waved too.

"We shouldn't have come here with you," she said, still smiling and waving at you. "We should have stayed at home and let you drive away from us." She looked back at me, tears were in the corners of her eyes. I wanted to reach out and wipe them away but I couldn't. Instead she turned, walked away from me and down the beach towards you.

"You should have come sooner," she called over her shoulder, "but you didn't even think. Didn't think about him at all did you Michael."

But I had thought about you Huck. I'd thought about you most of all during my trip, thought about how you'd spent your Christmas, what you'd unwrapped, what the Cap had bought you. I wanted to see you then Huck, had wanted to drive to see you as soon as I could but you weren't next on the list. And I had to stick to the list. Had to do it in the right order and my mum was next because it was easier.

I said that my mum hadn't written to me when I was in hospital, and that was true, she hadn't. She had written to me before then but I wouldn't get the letter for another five years, a long time after she was already gone. It took a long time before I found out what had actually happened to her.

It turned out, unsurprisingly I guess that my mum had been thinking about leaving for a while. Over the years the pain of living with my father had built up a deep hatred and confusion inside her and she had decided she needed to get away from both of us – me and my dad. Why she had wanted to go without me I'll never fully understand but she had made up her mind that would be the best thing she could do. She thought she was a bad influence on me. That she couldn't control herself and her drinking and that eventually she would do something to hurt me. She wouldn't have. Would never have, Huck. Deep down in my heart I know that. It was just him and the pain he caused her. But she didn't understand that. She thought that being around her and my father would be worse for me in the long term and that the centre of that problem was her. That somehow, if she wasn't there, he would be better. That we would be better. Better without her. How could she think that?

She decided that she would go somewhere that neither of us could find her. Somewhere my father could never track her down. She was scared of him, of course she was. Scared that he would go looking for her to take out all the pain and embarrassment her leaving had caused him, which it did. Scared that he would drag her back to look after me and him. Scared that he would find and hurt her and she would forever be in a cycle that I and my father we caught in, circling around her.

She didn't even tell aunt Sarah where she was going. She just wanted a clean break. A new life. One that didn't involve either of us. How she had settled on Wales I never found out. The man who told me all this said she just turned up one day at his hotel and asked if they had any jobs going. She wasn't well, he said, and she looked upset and in trouble. He said he was wary about whether or not to offer her anything – they weren't used to having people just turn up like that, especially someone who was hurt the way she was. He didn't want any trouble and it wouldn't look good to customers to have someone with two black eyes working there. But she had begged him. Said she needed somewhere to stay, even if it was only for a short while. She'd promised that her past was her past, that nobody would be coming to look for her there and, in any case, she wasn't even entirely sure where he was. The car was gone. I don't know where. How she had got to the village the man didn't know.

The man took a chance on her.

The town she had settled on was called Trawsfnydd – I have no idea how you pronounce it. I'm guessing that's part of the reason she didn't know where she was. He did tell me how to pronounce it in his covering letter but I couldn't then and I can't now. You can look it up if you want to see it, but it doesn't really matter. It was a very small town, nestled in the Snowdonia national park. Quiet outside of tourist season and not particularly busy in it. The town sat on a lake of the same name and she had loved it, so he told me. She had loved to sit and look out over the lake, or go hiking round it. That's what he said. Loved being outside in the sun.

She was true to her word and hadn't been any trouble at all. She gave up the drink almost immediately. It turned out she didn't need it at all when she wasn't around me and my father and her bruises and scars healed quickly. She was a hard worker too. She had started off working with the only other maid in the hotel, which was small – only twenty rooms - and the one maid the owner had working for him was about 60 and grateful for the help. She taught my mum how to make the beds properly, the sheets tight and close to the mattress, how to arrange the flowers in the windows to make them look the most inviting, the order in which to clean the rooms so that the ones that caught the midday light were ready first for the early arrivals and the later ones to catch the afternoon sun. By the time the scars on my mum's face were healed she was a seasoned professional.

David, that was the name of the owner, took a liking to her. How could he not? How could he not fall in love with my mother? It wasn't long before the short chit-chats after her shift between boss and employee took longer and longer and turned into long evening talks. Talks turned into even longer conversations, which turned into dinner by candlelight. He had told me all of this in a letter he sent to me in my first term at University, when he had finally tracked me down.

Eventually the two of them had become more than just good friends and she helped him with every aspect of running the hotel. She had told him everything apparently – about me, about my father, about why she had run away and he understood. Why she had not gone back for me when things had gotten better. He understood. I couldn't. It's not what he would have done, he said to me, but he understood why she hadn't. She told him about her drinking and how she no longer wanted to be that person and he promised to support her, even stopping drinking himself. He sounded like a good man and I think he made her happy.

The drink though had taken its toll on her and she fell ill a couple of years after she had arrived there. "In my life all too briefly", was how David put it, but grateful for the time he had. I don't know what it was that was wrong with her in all honesty. David had said it in his letter but I had read it numbly and hadn't kept hold of it. I had just noted down the address of the town and the name of the churchyard her grave was in. It was only her letter that I had really been interested in.

She had died not long after she had been diagnosed – died painlessly, he told me, but I don't know if he was just saying that to make me feel better. She had been buried in the graveyard in the town, facing towards the lake. She had written to me he said, on the day she died, in the hope that I would come and visit her before she went, not knowing how little time she had left. She was too late. She died before she could send it. She had never given him our address and it had taken him the three years until I was at University to track me down – my school eventually, albeit reluctantly, telling him where I was. It was lucky that he had persisted – a couple of months later and I'd have been gone from there too and nobody would have been able to track me down. Or perhaps a couple of months too early. I could have happily have lived the rest of my life thinking my mum was alive somewhere. Alive and happy. Couldn't I? Could I have gone without saying goodbye to her? I don't know.

When I had received the letter, I hadn't known what it was. I'd opened his letter and read everything, her letter held unopened in my other hand. It took me three weeks to open her letter. I eventually opened it, alone in my room at three in the morning, two days before I told my University sweetheart I loved her and my world collapsed completely. Not the best of weeks for me Huck, not the best at all.

This is, word for word, what her letter said:

My Dearest Michael,

I'm sick Michael, really sick. I know that I don't deserve it but it would mean everything to me if you would come and see me, just once more, before I go. Please.

I miss you Michael. I'm sorry it's taken so long. I thought about you every day.

Love,

Mum

And that was it. After four long years of not seeing my mother that was all that she wrote to me. Four, miserable years living with my abusive, ignorant fuck of a father and my mother, the woman who was meant to protect me, the woman whom I had spent so many years looking after, had written me two lines. 52 words. That's all she could muster. That's how much I meant to my mother. She had written to me once in the four years that she had been gone and it was to tell me that she was leaving me for good. Forever. Couldn't find her or follow her this time however much I wanted to. Asking me to go and see her so that she could die in peace and with a clean conscience.

I was angry, Huck. For a long, long time I was angry. But, over the last few months I have come to realise how she felt, come to reflect how similar her story is to my own. But at the time of reading the letter I couldn't reconcile it in my head. Couldn't understand why she would make that choice.

I hope I'm making the right choice with you, Huck.

Jack. I'll be home soon, Jack.

Travelling from Nottingham to deepest Wales was exhausting but I had actually decided to do it in one go, rather than taking my time. The way that things had gone with Paul had left me feeling good about what I was doing but the nearer the journey took me to Wales the more nervous I became. I wasn't sure exactly what I was nervous about, after all I knew what was waiting for me. A headstone, some dirt, maybe some flowers if David still visited. Nothing more than that. And yet seeing it all would be difficult. Knowing that she was really gone. Seeing it for the first time with my own eyes. And, whilst I understood now, the letter still hurt me.

I had toyed with the idea of phoning the hotel ahead to see if they had any rooms but I decided to leave it to fate. If there was a room I would stay there and if there wasn't I would sleep in the Campervan. Either way I knew where I was headed.

It took me about 5 hours to get there with my top speed of 50 and a couple of breaks on the way to keep my mind on the road and to keep me awake. But the roads were clear and the scenery when I got into Wales was spectacular so the journey wasn't all bad From the brief glances I took out of the side window while I was driving I could understand why my mum had wanted to come here. She had always loved the rawness of Cornwall and Devon, despite my dad's hatred of the roads, and this was similar. Sometimes we would spend hours just walking across fields to nowhere, my mum and I. I don't know what my dad did when we were on those trips. Sat and read the paper I suppose. Enjoyed us not being there. Did he sit and watch other families, wishing he could be with them instead of us. I don't know. I don't know that any family would have been good enough for him. Or maybe every family that wasn't us would have been just perfect.

The lake at Trawsfnydd really was beautiful. It stretched out across the landscape and mirrored the cool blue sky perfectly, the ripples made by the few boats out sailing hardly making a scratch. There were a few amateur fishermen I could see out on the lake and stretched along the shore, no doubt enjoying their Christmas presents or happy just to be out of the house and away from their families for a couple of hours. I'd never been fishing, except in my dreams. My dad used to go when he was a kid and had enjoyed it, or so my mum used to tell me, but my dad never wanted to take me out. Jack and I never went, Jack didn't want to. He didn't like being near the water very much.

I drove along the side of the lake for a while before I finally arrived in the town. I say town but the reality was it was just one main high street with a few shops, a couple of pubs and the hotel. It was pretty though, nestled as it was by the side of the lake. The houses were all dark stone with slate roofs, most of them had been there for a long time by the looks of them – weather-beaten. I could see why my mum liked it here. She would have fitted in.

The church was off at one end of the village and I thought about going straight there but decided against it. I wasn't quite ready to see her yet. Anyway, curiosity had gotten the better of me and I wanted to see if David still owned the hotel. And maybe to meet him. I wanted to know what he was like – the man who made my mum happy when I couldn't. I knew my dad couldn't, I knew why he couldn't. I wanted to see why I couldn't. I wanted to know what the difference was. To know what was wrong with me or what was right with him.

I parked up outside the hotel, Trawsfnydd Arms as it was called, locked up and left all of my stuff inside. This didn't seem like the sort of town where you had to be careful about locking up your belongings. It seemed like the sort of place most people still didn't lock their doors before going to bed at night.

Inside the hotel the décor was old but not gaudy – comfortable I guess you would say, and fitting for the place it was in. There was an old, dark wood front desk with a little brass bell on the top that said "press me" in English and then something underneath in Welsh that I guess meant the same thing. I did what it asked. While I was waiting I turned to look round the rest of the entrance hall. It was small with lots of pictures on the wall. All different shapes and sizes of frames squashed into every conceivable space on the wall. Smiling faces of all different kinds beamed out at me, all stood outside the hotel. I scanned them all over and suddenly saw a face I recognised. I moved closer to look at it in more detail when a thick Welsh accent boomed out behind me and I span round to meet it.

"We don't like strangers here," it said.

"Uh, wha-what?" I stammered. The man in front of me was big. I mean really big. And not just tall, he was huge. Enormous forearms folded across his chest with big, thick dark hair covering them. He was heavy, but not fat, just a huge solid mass of a man. He looked like he could have wrestled the bear and given the beast a run for its money. He was clean shaven but his jawline was dark anyway, the early signs of the evening poking through and the hair on his head was a similar darkness to that of his arms with a few flecks of grey. His face was stern, his eyes narrowed and focused on me. He looked exactly the way I imagine a lumberjack to look, minus the ridiculous outfit.

"I said," replied the man, "we don't like strangers here. Which is why we insist everyone who stays here gets their picture on the wall, so they're part of the family." As soon as he said this, a greeting I'm sure he had delivered a hundred times so believable was the disapproving look he carried off, he broke into a smile and opened his arms in a manner that suggested he was about to hug me to death. I'm certainly not the size of a bear – I think he would have killed me.

"Oh," I said, laughing nervously "I thought you were being serious." I turned back to the wall and stared at the picture of my mother. She was smiling, a big, wide smile. The sort of exaggerated, cheesy smile that you only pulled for stupid photographs but something about it still says that you're actually really happy, otherwise you wouldn't be able to muster it. She looked well too. No bags under her eyes, no fresh scars, no bruises. Just happy. I pointed at the wall vaguely.

"Do you remember any of them?" I asked.

"Some," he said. "Of course some more than others. Some come back again and again. Others are only here for a couple of days so it's hard to remember them properly." He was stood next to me now, looking at the same pictures I was.

"Any you remember in particular?" I asked. He turned to look at me and the smile dropped from his face.

"Maybe," he said. "Depends on who wants to know I guess." I pointed at the picture of my mother.

"Do you remember her?" I asked, never taking my eyes off the picture. He looked at the picture briefly and then back at me. He stared at me for a few moments before he spoke again.

"Yes," he said. "I remember her well."

"Tell me about her," I said.

"She was beautiful," he said. "The most beautiful woman I've ever known." I nodded as he said it and he turned to look at me as I carried on staring at a picture of a mother I didn't know. A happy one.

"I thought you'd never come," he said.

"Me either," I replied. He put his arm around my shoulder and the moment he did all doubt in my mind disappeared. I knew why she was happy here, why she could be herself here when she couldn't with me and my dad. She was safe here. I started to cry and as I did so he pulled me into his chest and I sobbed and sobbed as if the world were ending. For me I guess it already had.

My mum, Angie as she was before she was my mum and I suppose afterwards, hadn't had the greatest start in life. Her dad had never wanted to have children and she had therefore come as somewhat of a surprise. Nobody was ever sure whether she was partly planned, on her mother's side, or whether it was a genuine accident but the fact is she was born unwanted by at least one of her parents. Her father was a man set in his ways – he had his work, he had his friends at the social club and he had rugby and he had no intention of giving up any of those for this intruder. Even if it was his flesh and blood.

Angie therefore spent most of her time with her mother, who loved her dearly but struggled to maintain the balance in her own life whilst also being effectively a single mother. She did everything for Angie – taught her to read, ride a bike, ferried her to and from after school clubs and so on and so on. As a result Angie's mum was constantly exhausted and Angie, being the main cause of this fatigue, usually also got the brunt of it. That left a strain on Angie and her mum's relationship that neither of them ever really got over.

To make matters worse, four years later there was another accident and Sarah was born. For Angie things probably couldn't have gotten much worse, except they did because her father suddenly, and for no apparent reason, took a huge shine to his second daughter. Perhaps he was suddenly at the age when he was ready for children, perhaps all his friends at the social club were at the age where they were also "in the club". Whatever the cause of the change of heart nobody seemed to know or understand, but suddenly he wanted everything to do with Sarah. Still nothing, however, to do with Angie. It seemed that whatever had sparked this unusual interest in his second child had not been enough to ignite even any kind of passion toward his first born. She was a write off. He wasn't mean to Angie, not in the slightest, he simply didn't pay any attention to her.

The result of that was that my mother didn't just feel unwanted, she simply felt like she wasn't good enough for her father and, as Sarah demanded an equal amount of attention from their mother, became more and more frustrated at her seeming worthlessness. That her sister was simply the version of herself that everyone else had wanted. When, therefore, at sixteen my mum had met my dad, the first real boyfriend she had ever had, she was determined to make it work and use it as her way out of her parents' house as quickly as possible.

My mum and dad met at a disco in town on a Friday night. He was a couple of years older than her and, whilst he wasn't the best looking man at the club, she would tell me, not the greatest dancer and not the smoothest talker she liked him anyway. Plus he liked her and he was serious about her going out. About going steady. He was serious, that was what she liked about him the most. Not that he was fun, not that he was good looking, not that he was romantic. He was practical. He was prepared to be in a relationship with her, wasn't looking to mess her around and she interpreted that to mean that he would probably want to marry her as soon as he was able and she could get the hell out of her parents' house and have her freedom. Not the most romantic of stories hey Huck? And as for getting her freedom, well, how wrong could she have been?

I don't know when he started hitting her. Whether it was before I was born or after – we never talked about it, obviously. I was old enough to have to deal with the aftermath of it all but not old enough to understand it all. She always used to tell me stories about how nice it was when they started going out and after they were married and the stories always ended when "then you came along."

They were happy. They went on dates, not extravagant ones, but he took her out. They laughed together and apparently they had fun. Then I came along. It was pretty obvious to me what the cause of the fighting and the bickering was.

I don't think I can remember being at home when they didn't have some sort of fight almost every day even if it was only to throw some cross words at one another. They would either be fighting, or at least dad would be in a terrible mood with her, or they simply wouldn't be talking to one another at all. The best you could ever really hope for was that mum was in a good mood and that dad was resenting it and therefore didn't talk to anyone at all. He didn't hit her that often. I've made it sound like he beat her every day, which he didn't. But once is too often. Once a month maybe. Maybe more. Is that a lot? I got beaten twice a week by Paul and I was just a kid. But my mother didn't deserve it.

I worried Huck, worried for a long time that it was in me. That that ability to treat another human being in that way would have found its way into me. Maybe it did. I guess we'll never know. I hope it's not in you Huck, I really do. And I never hit her, Huck, believe me when I say that. I never hit your mother. I wouldn't let myself get there.

I am back in the boat. Jack and I and the blackness and the dark fish. And I am watching Jack now, no longer looking at the dark fish and I realise what is happening. I see now that Jack is sat with his net at his feet and he is holding the fish in his hands and he is breathing on them. Breathing on them deep and full breaths. And I think that he is catching them and putting them in his net, but he isn't.

David and I sat at the long table in the restaurant, which was the only table there, and talked for most of the evening and mostly about my mother. He told me virtually everything that had happened to her since she had come to live in the hotel and I told him everything I could remember about her from my childhood. It was strange talking to someone who loved her as much as I did.

He said it wasn't all plain sailing, of course. She had wanted to give up drinking and that's something that is never easy, especially when you've left your only child with the man that drove you to it in the first place. He said he never could understand why she had left me.

"I would have looked after you, protected you and him," he had said to her.

"I know you would have, David," she had said to him. "But who would protect Michael?"

When he told me that his face dropped. I asked what he thought she meant by that but he said he didn't know.

She never relapsed though, at least that's what he said. Apparently they had to drive a long way to find some Alcoholics Anonymous meetings but he drove her every week, waited for her outside, drank glasses of milk with her to celebrate every new week that she was sober, sat with her in the dark when it all got too much, held her as she cried.

He didn't talk about him and her very much. I guess because he probably thought it would have been strange for me to hear, but I think it would have been nice. You could tell from the way he talked about her that he had been very fond of her, even if it had been for only a short time.

Her illness as I've already said was a sudden and short affair. He didn't say much more than he already had and it clearly pained him to talk about it. Short, sharp sentences, big pauses in between. I changed the subject.

"Do you know why she didn't write sooner?" I asked. It was the only thing I really wanted to know.

"She tried," he said, wiping a tear from his great cheek. "Tried lots of times actually, but I don't think she could ever find the words It's hard, wanting to tell someone you love why you can't be with them." I nodded. And suddenly the world made sense again. After all those years wondering why she wrote so little I finally understood. We were the same, my mum and I. He couldn't know how much I knew what that was like.

"A few times she told me she was going to write to you," He said. "She wrote you a really long letter and never did send it, shoved it in a box she kept in our – her – room. Then when she got really sick she wrote the short one I sent to you."

"What happened to it?" I asked. "The longer one I mean. What happened to that?"

David stood up and walked out of the room. A moment later he returned carrying a small white envelope, stamped and addressed in my mother's handwriting, just as he had said. It sat on the table between us, I dared not open it. I stared at it for a long time before I spoke again.

"Why didn't you send it?" I asked. "When you sent the other letter to me, when you finally found me, why didn't you send it then?"

David sighed and looked down at his hands. His huge, bear like hands.

"I thought you might come looking for her," he said. "I thought if you had this letter you'd get the answers you needed and you'd never come here. And I. I wanted to meet you Michael. She talked about you so often. I'm sorry. I didn't have the right."

It didn't matter anymore.

"It's ok," I replied. I understood. I picked up the envelope. It was thick and heavy. I held it up to my face and smelt it – it still had her scent on it. My mother wrote letters to her sister all the time and she always scented them with her perfume and that's what I could smell now. Faint but still there. I could feel my mother all around me.

I opened the letter carefully and pulled out a thick wodge of paper. My mother, who couldn't think how to say what she needed to say to me had written 17 pages. Her scrawling handwriting crammed into every corner of every page, front and back. Smudges ran across the pages where tears had fallen as she was writing and she'd tried to brush them away.

I won't repeat what she said Huck. There were many things in that letter that you don't need to know, some that I still don't understand and some that were just for me and her. But there is a part I want you to hear Huck, because it says so wonderfully everything that I have always wanted to say to you and have never been able to find the words for.

"After everything that has happened Michael, all of the terrible things that have happened to me, after all the people that have hurt me and used me, it would have been so easy for me to give up, would have been so much easier to leave this all behind and be gone from this world. You're the reason Michael, the reason I'm still here. You give me hope."

Love your mum Huck, love her with all your heart, because she loves you so much. We both do.

All this miserable talk about mothers hey Huck, and here your wonderful mum is making us both supper. Still looking after me even after all of this. Or maybe she's just looking after you and I happen to be there. Either way I don't know but it's been wonderful spending time with her these last few days. Spending time with you too Huck.

But I'm getting ahead of myself. I haven't left Wales yet and after that it's not long until I'm reunited with her and I see you for the first time in my life. So let's power through and get there, hey Huck?

After I finished reading the letter, and finished wiping the tears from my face, David and I carried on talking. This time about where our paths had led us after my mother had left our respective lives. His life continued much as it seemed to before he had met her, but with an extra twinge of hope for having met her and a dollop of sadness for having lost her again. I told him as much about my life as I wanted to – told him a little about you and your mother and simply told him it hadn't worked out, told him about travelling around and my various jobs, told him about living in London for a while, but not what I was doing.

"So why now?" he asked. "What made you come looking for your mum right now?"

Good question. A really good question, and one I didn't feel like answering just then.

"It's time," I said, and nothing more. He could tell I was holding something back but he didn't pry. He was a good man, Huck.

"Well," he said, standing up. "There's a room upstairs for you, on the house, and breakfast for when you get up in the morning. You're welcome to stay as long as you want but I sense you're probably going to be leaving again tomorrow."

I nodded, I was going tomorrow. Needed to get on my way. The room he gave me was big and warm, despite the wind howling outside, the bed soft with thick blankets. I fell into it and was asleep before I can even remember trying. It had been an exhausting day, but a good one, from start to finish. I couldn't remember the last time I had ever thought that about my life.

I woke up late again, around nine, and simply lay there in my bed for a while, enjoying the warmth of the room despite it being the middle of winter. I tried to imagine my mum having laid in a similar bed after she arrived and how good it must have felt for her to be safe and sound in such comfort. After a while I got up and went down to breakfast. There were two couples sat at the long table. I joined them and happily made small talk whilst we ate and David kept a never ending supply of food going until we all had to admit defeat. He smiled, he enjoyed looking after people I think.

"You'll be the death of us," joked one of the other patrons. I laughed a little harder than the rest. A private joke just for me.

After breakfast I went back to my room, took out the necklace that Paul had returned to me and, after some directions from David, I walked down the road to the churchyard. It was small but pretty, the headstones arranged in a higgledy-piggledy fashion of different shapes and sizes, brand new stones next to ones that had been there for centuries. I wandered through them until I found my mothers in the corner.

Her headstone was small and simple, a plain white marble with a simple inscriptions – Angela Elizabeth Smith, her maiden name, aged 40, beloved mother and friend, we miss you. I couldn't have said it better myself and I smiled when I saw it.

I sat down cross legged in front of the grave and did nothing. I had thought for a long time about what I would say when I got there and when I did, I realised nothing complicated needed to be said. No big long speech. My mother knew that I missed her, knew that I loved her. There was only one thing I needed to say and then nothing else.

"I'm sorry," I whispered, my head pressed against her stone. "Sorry that I couldn't save you from him. Sorry that between us we drove you away. I wish it had been him mum, I really do. But I'm grateful for the time we had together. I love you."

After that I just sat there, closed my eyes and thought about her. After an hour or so I got up, put her necklace on the headstone and walked back to the hotel.

"Where are you off to now then?" David asked as I climbed into the cab of the Campervan.

"I have to make up for some lost time," I replied. He nodded wisely, although he couldn't have understood.

"Well," he said, "I hope to see you again soon Michael."

"I hope so too," I said, leaning out of the cab to shake his hand, in what was only a half lie. I hoped that I would see him again. Knew that I wouldn't. And with that I drove out of town, heading out of Wales to look for you kiddo.

We're well over half way through my story now Huck. Paul and my mum down, you and your mum, my dad and Jack to go. Jack doesn't count, I guess, because that's who I'm going to see when I've left you and your mum behind and so that part of the story will have to wait. So, counting you and your mum as one, we're two behind and two in front. But before I get to that there is something I need to tell you. You'll find out soon enough anyway and actually, when you're reading this you'll know anyway. It's important you know so that you can understand what is to come. So that you can make sense of what will happen. I don't know what your mum will or won't have told you. So I'll tell you myself.

I'm sick. Not just sick, but really sick. It has a name, something very specific and Latin sounding, but all the fancy names boil down to the same thing.

I'm writing this to you now, going on this journey because I'm dying. I have a tumour on my brain and there's nothing anyone can do about it. I've known about it for about six months now and, when he, the doctor or consultant or whatever he was, told me about six months ago, he told me I had at most a year to live, which at best gives me six months from now. When I got the message for my last delivery working for Natalie I had just been to the doctor so that we could have another "discussion" about what my options were. I know what my options are Huck. The options are death. Nothing else. I can die sooner or I can die later and there are a few things they can do to probably make the later more likely, but either way it's still going to happen.

It was hard to take – knowing that I was going to die. To begin with anyway, before I made my peace with it. I spent about the first month or so in complete denial. I decided that they were talking nonsense and didn't know what was what. Then I saw the scans for myself, the doctor pointing out what was wrong, asking me about the headaches I'd had, and asking me about lots of things. The more questions he asked the more I nodded, the more he already knew I was going to say yes anyway. I don't know why he bothered asking the questions.

After that I kind of resigned myself to the fact it was going to happen. I came to accept it very quickly, apparently. Most people go through various phases they told me; denial, blame etc. etc. It seems I skipped all of those and went straight from denial to acceptance. Nobody to blame I guess. My body, my fault.

I took the medication they offered me, the simple stuff anyway. The stuff that wouldn't make me ill but at the same time wouldn't extend my life any longer. I didn't need my life extending by much. They told me I had a year to go and there were only a handful of things I still needed to do in such a short space of time, why would I need more than a year?

It's not hereditary Huck. At least that's what they told me anyway. They don't know how it happened to me, just one of those things I guess. They don't think its genetic. You might have a higher chance of getting one I suppose, but those chances are pretty slim anyway. You should get yourself checked out though. Another thing to add to the list of things you have to thank me for.

I decided, once I'd accepted it, that I would do this trip. That I would make my list and go and see the people that I really needed to see before I went. That I would try and make peace with the world and the people I had wronged and that maybe I would get some forgiveness. That didn't matter so much though, I wasn't expecting people to forgive me. I just wanted to be able to say my piece and maybe try and do a little good.

It's strange to think that by the time you read this it will have already played out. The end will have come and gone and the world will be no more and no less without me in it. I wish we could have spent more time together Huck, I really do. I'm sorry it took so long for me to come and find you. I'm sorry it took this. But I guess there could never have been any other way.

I wish your mother and I had the chance to get married. We had talked about it a couple of times and I'd even bought her an engagement ring but the right time to ask her never came up and then, well, then I was gone.

Jack's wedding on the other hand was an absolute hoot! He got married on New Year's Eve, a typical Jack thing to have done, and of course his mum and dad put on a sensational party. Despite the time of year the weather was perfect – a bright, crisp winter's morning with not a cloud in the sky and gentle frost on the ground. They erected a huge marquee at their house which filled out almost the entire back garden. The trees were filled with fairy lights and the dance floor had been set up among them in the centre of the marquee – an idea of Jack's sister, Sophie.

Both Jack and I looked dapper in our matching top hat and tails – dark grey, long jackets with those fancy striped trousers that go with them. Morning suits I think they are called. Our waistcoats were a lighter grey with piping down them and we wore purple cravats, Jack's a slightly different colour from mine and the other groomsmen to differentiate himself.

As good as we looked however, Katy looked absolutely stunning. I mean, everyone looks beautiful on their wedding day Huck but Katy was something else. Women gasped and men could hardly keep their mouths shut as she walked down the aisle. Jack took her arm as she arrived at the altar and the two of them just beamed at one another. I stood by his side, just happy to be a part of the whole thing.

The ceremony itself went off without a hitch. The hymns were boomed out by all present, Jack leading from the front and even managing to out sing the vicar. Once it was finished we filed out of the church, me with a bridesmaid on each arm and Jack with the new Mrs Lawrence who ran through a snowstorm of confetti to the silver Rolls Royce waiting for them.

The reception was amazing. I haven't been to many parties in my life Huck, in fact his was the only wedding I ever went to, but this was the party of all parties. Champagne flowed all night, smiling faces everywhere, music, dancing, Auld Langsyne at new year, fireworks and I even managed to get through my speech without making a fool of myself.

Best of all Jack was there and he was happy and in love. And I was his best man and I couldn't have been happier for him.

I wanted that for your mother and I Huck, I wanted all of that. What was I so afraid of?

Finding you wasn't quite as easy as finding Paul. Your mum wasn't on Facebook, nowhere to be seen. I expected that you and your mum still lived not far from The Cap and so I decided I would call him up and find out. I didn't want him to know it was me trying to find out since, as nice as he had always been to me, I very much doubted he would have given me the time of day based on the manner and timing of my fall from grace. So that ruled out just driving up there and knocking on his door. The alternative then was to give him a call and ask about your mum, without letting him know it was me. The conversation was awkward but, in the end, fruitful.

"Hi, is that Mr Waters?" I asked when he eventually answered the phone with his usual Hello-ello.

"Yes it is," The Cap replied. Hearing his voice dried my throat almost instantly. "Who's this?"

"I'm a friend of Rebecca's from way back," I said.

"Oh, who's that then?" came the reply.

"Just an old friend," I said. "Look, I was wondering if she still lived in the area."

"Uh, yes she does." Stony silence after he stopped talking.

"Oh, so she still lives in Richmond then?"

"Sorry, who is this?" He was getting suspicious.

"I told you," I said, "we used to go to school together. I doubt you'd remember me."

"Try me," came the reply.

"So she is still in town then?" I ignored his question. I could have used a fake name, don't know why I didn't. Mind you, the school she went to was pretty small, he probably did remember everyone in her year. The Cap was a sharp one.

"Look, son, I don't really want to give out my daughters address to a stranger over the phone. Maybe I could get her to give you call?" That wasn't going to work, she'd know it was me, would recognise my voice in a heartbeat.

"I understand I said, I'm traveling though, so no fixed number I'm afraid." He sniffed at this and tried to say something about a mobile before I cut him off again. "Are you still playing cricket at the club?"

"I am actually," this changed the mood of the call and suddenly he was chipper again. "Still doing terribly though my girls still enjoy watching." Bingo. He was still laughing to himself when I put the phone down. My girls was how he referred to his wife and Rebecca, which meant she still went to watch him. Which meant you and your mum still lived in Richmond, or close by anyway.

Trawsfynydd to Richmond is about a 4 hour drive as the Porsche flies but not as the Campervan does. More coffee, more service station food. Seriously kiddo, if it hadn't been for the fact I was dying from a tumour this journey would have taken a few years off my life. Sorry, that's probably in poor taste.

I eventually got there late on the Thursday evening and decided that I would park up just outside of town before driving in to town in the morning. This one definitely needed time and a seven hour drive, as it turned out to be, wasn't enough time to think. It was a cloudless night so I built myself a little fire just outside the door of the Campervan, wrapped myself in a blanket and drank coffee while I looked up at the stars.

Your mum and I had gone camping once, not long after we had started dating, in the woods a couple of miles outside of town. Despite the short distance we'd driven your mum insisted on bringing just about every piece of camping equipment we could possibly need. I thought we were just going to rough it for one night – a tent, a kettle and maybe a throw away BBQ. We ended up walking from the car with two enormous backpacks full of stuff – blow up mattresses, a camping stove, a port-a-potty, two lanterns, and a first aid kit. I had to go back to the car for a second run just to make sure we had everything. Seriously Huck, we could have lasted two weeks in the Amazon the way we were kitted out.

Still, it was the perfect night. Just the two of us, the skies dark above us with just the stars for company. We toasted marshmallows on sticks like a million young lovers before us and watched the sun set. Then we lay there and talked for hours. Your mum telling me about her life growing up, how ashamed she was of some of the boys she had liked, the wonder of her first kiss, of being in love and being heartbroken. I sat and listened to it all, thinking how incredible it must have been to be loved by her. And then she rolled over and kissed me and told me that's how she felt about me. She loved me, Huck. For a time your mum loved me and I was never happier than at the moment.

As I sat outside the Campervan I looked up at the stars, the same stars that your mother had told me she loved me under so long ago. I was happy again.

In the morning I got up, washed in the sink as best I could, shaved and made myself look as generally presentable as I could manage given the limitations of both my own physical appearance and the amenities provided by the Campervan. It has served me well over the past few days but it certainly isn't a luxury mode of transport. Then I drove in to town.

I figured that I would go and look for your mum in all the places I would most likely have found her when we were together. First off I went to the place we lived in together briefly, but judging by the woman stood outside with her kids either your mother gained about 5 stone and turned black or she didn't live there anymore. I guessed the second and drove off.

I considered driving round to The Cap's house but that was a no go. If he saw me he'd lock your mum up and not let her come see me no matter how much she wanted to, which was probably very little. That or he'd chase after me with a cricket bat and neither of those seemed like a good idea. I could probably have taken him, given how old he was, but still. Not a good idea. I tried driving by a couple of other places your mum used to hang out, including the cricket club, before I parked up in town. I figured I would walk around and that maybe I would bump into her and, if I didn't, I'd grab some coffee instead and think about my next steps.

I spent maybe an hour walking up and down the same couple of streets, wandering into each of the shops, browsing around as though I were genuinely looking for something but really just checking out each and every person to see if they were someone I knew. I ended up randomly following the same woman into three different shops and I think she thought I was stalking her when I followed her into the sewing shop. I quickly realised what I was doing and walked straight out, back the way I had come.

I started to realise then that this might actually be more difficult that I had envisaged and I decided to get myself a coffee instead. So I again found myself sat in a quaint, old world coffee shop, just me, a china mug and a silver coffee pot looking out the window as the world wandered past and I watched it go on by without me.

After about fifteen minutes a little boy skipped past and stopped in front of the shop, hands on his hips, looking back up the street, waiting impatiently for someone who was supposed to be following him. He looked so funny, like a comic actor playing the part of a moody old man. I smiled watching him and the kid turned around to look at me grinning at him through the plate glass window. He smiled back. I stuck my tongue out a little and he stuck his out too and laughed. Suddenly a woman's arm appeared, grabbed the kid by the shoulder, shouting a stern word in his ear as she did so. Then she looked up to see who had been encouraging her boy to act like such a monkey.

I stared your mother in the face.

Huck, before I tell you what happened next I should probably tell you what happened the night I left. And try and explain why.

That night in the hotel with your mother wasn't the start of it, although it was the first time I had seen them since I had been with her. The first time they had come back to me. And I know, now , that it wasn't your mother who brought them. And I know that it wasn't her who made me start to lash out. And it wasn't them who made me think the things I did. It wasn't you either Huck, you have to know that. It was them. And me. And him.

There were a couple of times she said things, of course. Things that I didn't like. Things that made me angry or hurt or ashamed. She would make jokes at my expense sometimes and they hurt and made me feel small. She would say the sorts of things that my father used to say, without meaning them, only as a joke. Things she couldn't have known he had said and meant. But still. They hurt me and they let them in. She couldn't have known he used to say those exact thing but… I don't know. And sometimes she would drink. Not much, not like my mother and she was in control. But sometimes when she was drunk she made jokes. The truth comes out when you're drunk, that's what my dad always used to say and I worried it was true. Maybe that was what your mother really thought of me. When I look back at it now I know they weren't true, were meant as harmless jokes, probably signs of how comfortable she was around me. It wasn't what she said that made me leave though Huck.

Sometimes I could feel them. Could feel them in me and they sounded like him, sneering at me the way he used to laugh at me in real life. I could hear him sniping away at me in my mind.

"She doesn't want you Michael. She doesn't love you," they, he, would say. "She says those things because they're true Michael. She thinks you're just as fucking worthless as I do. You can't make her happy Michael, how the fuck could you? What's fucking wrong with you?"

Most of the time I could suppress them. Push them back inside of me where they belonged. Where they waited, swimming in my stomach until the next time. I could tell them to shut up and to leave me alone. Tell them she loved me. Tell them that I knew she did. But they were stronger than me Huck. He was stronger than me and no matter how much I shouted at them, how much I screamed at them, they would shout at me, louder than I could scream back at them. There were too many of them. Your mother said she loved you Michael, and look what fucking good that did you.

Most times I could walk it off. I could bury it deep inside of me and then let it out when I was alone. I would drive out to where we had gone camping and just walk to the spot where she had first told me she loved me, and by the time I got there everything was fine. I knew deep down that she loved me Huck, I really did, just as I always knew that my mum loved me.

But then that night, the night with the bath tub, I couldn't bear it anymore. When I saw them, swimming in that water, around her, snaking their filthy way around her body, touching her skin and waiting. Waiting for you to come out. I couldn't let them.

Two weeks later, when she told everyone she was pregnant and everyone was so happy for her and she was so full of life I knew I had to go. How could I have stayed Huck? How could I have hung around you and her with that bubbling inside of me? My dad had loved my mum before I came along. They had been happy. He'd never hit her before that, never as much as a cross word and yet here I was, getting angry with her before I even knew that you were coming along. What was I going to be like when you were there? I could barely cope as it was and when she was tired from looking after a baby all day, when she was stressed from you not taking a bottle or crying all night or teething or soiling yourself when she had just changed you. What would I be like then Huck?

My father was a monster Huck. And it made the dark fish come to my mother. And I had them both inside of me. I had the dark fish inside of me and they wanted to destroy me. And they wanted to destroy your mother and they wanted to destroy you. Your mother was nothing but love kiddo, nothing but love and joy and happiness. Her family loved her, her friends loved her and I knew that you would love her. I was a poison, a ticking fucking time bomb just waiting to explode and ruin everything. I couldn't let that happen to you Huck, I wouldn't let her end up like my mother and I wouldn't let you end up like me.

I did it for you Huck, for you and for her. I know that it probably doesn't seem like that to you right now and it doesn't make up for me not being there. I hope one day you come to understand me, Huck. I hope they aren't in you Huck. I hope he isn't in you. I hope I'm not in there.

If they are inside you Huck, if you see them, do what I did. It isn't fair any other way.

Your mum and I stared at each other for what seemed like a lifetime, but in reality it was a matter of seconds. I think she just wanted to make sure that it really was me in front of her. But she knew. She knew as soon as she laid eyes on me. She grabbed you by the arm and started marching you down the street. I tried to speak and realised she wouldn't have been able to hear me through the window anyway. Instead I threw my money on the table, grabbed my coat and ran out into the street.

You and your mum were already half way down the road, her trying to walk a pace that retained her dignity but clearly said don't you dare fucking talk to me. That's not an easy thing to do when you have a seven year old kid in tow who doesn't understand what's going on. Between tugs to keep you moving at her pace you kept looking back to see what you were running away from.

I tried to keep up just by walking as fast as the two of you were and found I couldn't keep up. Your mum had always been a fast walker. I guess you've probably developed it from having to match her stride for stride all the time. I started into a jog that turned into a run as the adrenaline got the better of me. I grabbed her by the shoulder but she shrugged me off and carried on up the street. I called after her but she didn't turn around. You turned your head again to look at me, curious to see who the weirdo following you was, but only briefly. She squeezed your hand tighter and you obediently looked back.

I again trotted up behind her and called out her name but she didn't so much as flinch so I ran ahead and stood in the middle of the pavement, my arms stretched out at my side.

"Rebecca," I pleaded, "I need to talk to you."

Your mum didn't stop, just ploughed through one of my arms and dragged you through with her. I turned around to watch the two of you march up the hill.

"Rebecca, please," I yelled up the street, no longer caring if I was making a scene, "I'm sick."

Your mum turned round then, marching back down the road to me and leaving you standing where you were. She came right up to my face, I could smell her perfume engulfing me. She always wore a little too much.

"You're right," she hissed at me, "you are sick. You'd have to be sick to do what you did to me. To him." She half yelled that last part, pointing at you as you stood staring at us, scratching the back of one of your legs with the foot of the other. With that she turned back up the road and grabbed your hand again. I didn't know what else to do.

"I'm dying Rebecca."

She stopped then, just staring up the street for a few moments. Then she knelt by you and whispered something in your ear and pressed some money into your hand. She smiled at you, as though she were sending you on some fun adventure that you were sure to enjoy. But you didn't move, just stood there looking down the street at me. She kissed you on the forehead and pushed you away, towards some unknown destination. You started walking ahead but your head was still craned back, still looking at me. She marched back down the street to me but this time spoke in a hushed whisper.

"What kind of messed up thing is that to be shouting in the street? You'd better not be lying to me Michael," she said.

"I'm not," I replied. I stared her right in the eyes, wanting her to see inside me, to see that I wasn't making it up. We stood like that for a few seconds before she looked away first and I knew I had won the battle, for now anyway. She looked up the street to where you were meant to be going, but you hadn't gotten very far. She let out a long deep sigh and called you back.

"Let's get a coffee," she said.

A few minutes later we were sat back inside the same coffee shop, at the same window, watching the same people walk back and forth. Your mum had a tea, white one sugar, as she always did and I a black coffee. You were sat at the counter with a chocolate milkshake talking to the woman who ran the place, a woman who was clearly fond of you. You seemed to have forgotten the episode outside, content with your shake as if nothing had happened. It was like old times, she and I sat there watching the world go by. Except this time there was no love between us, at least, not from her to me. And except that you were there Huck.

I couldn't take my eyes off you. Kept flicking them back from you to the window to her and back to you. There were so many things I wanted to know and so little she wanted to say.

How are you? Fine. How is he? Fine. He's seven now right? Yes. Off school for Christmas, right? Yes. Going back soon? Soon. Does he do well at school? OK. I bet The Cap loves him? He does. Did you ever tell him about me?

"What do you want Michael?" She asked. "You say you're sick and you're dying and whatever but what do you actually want?" I took a sip of my coffee and stared at you.

"Not what you think," I said. "I'm not here to try and make things right, not here to try and spend my last few months with him."

"Then why are you here?" she asked.

141

"To say that I'm sorry and to try and partly make up for things in the only way I can, to maybe repair a little of the damage that I did."

"And how will you do that?"

"I have some money," I said. She snorted at that.

"You want to buy forgiveness," she said, "It doesn't work Michael. We don't need your money". She never raised her voice, just said it in a very matter of fact way. It hurt more like that.

"I don't expect forgiveness," I said, "just to make as much amends as I can."

"Amends, Michael?" She snapped. "You want to make amends? Amends for what? For the fact that you walked out on me the moment you found out I was pregnant? The fact that you embarrassed me in front of the whole town for getting knocked up by some pathetic run away like every other cheap slag in town? For the fact that I had to go through labour without the father there? For the fact that every time anyone says ooooh I bet he's the apple of his daddy's eye that I just have to stare at the ground blankly and hope they shut up? Or for the fact that your son had to grow up without a dad? Is going to have to grow up knowing that his dad didn't love him enough to stick around? Huh? Which one Michael?"

"I left because I loved him," I whispered but she didn't hear me.

"What?" She said. "What was that Michael?"

"I said I left because having a dad like me is worse than having no dad at all." She rolled her eyes.

"Don't give me that cowardly crap," she said. "You left because you didn't want to be a dad, left because you got scared at the thought of having a kid and you weren't ready for it. It's fine Michael, loads of men do it every year and I'm sure they all have their excuses."

"It's not an excuse," I said.

"Well," she said, finishing her tea, "either way it doesn't really matter to us. So you can say what you wanted to say and then you can go, wherever it is you want to go after this." She stood up as she said it, ready to leave, looking down at me. I didn't move, didn't look up at her. It wasn't right.

"Well, come on, out with it" she said, hands on her hips.

"Can I at least give you a ride home first," I said. I needed more time Huck. Now it was here I needed more time to think about what I wanted to say. She tutted and called you over and led you out of the shop. I threw my money down again and followed her back out into the street. We walked silently down to the Campervan.

"Cool," you shouted as we neared it and ran over to inspect it. "Is this yours mister?"

"Huck!" she called and you came running back to her. We climbed up into the cab and drove off up the hill, your mum in the middle, keeping you away from me. The town isn't large and it didn't take us long to get back to your new house. It looked nice, a small middle terrace. I parked on the curb outside and turned the engine off. Your mum gave you the key, told you to go and wait inside and then turned back to me.

"Well?" She said. "What have you got to say?"

What a question. What did I have to say? I love you Rebecca. I've never stopped loving you, never been able to think about anything else other than how much I love you and how much I would have loved Huck? How much it hurt being apart from you every single day. How some nights I would just sit for hours on end staring at the wall, thinking about you. How many times I wrote, how I could never find the words to tell you how I felt because I don't think the words exist. How much I hate myself for leaving you, for leaving him. How I feel like what happened to me is my fault, that karma you always banged on about for being the monster that I am? For the monster that lives inside of me? For not standing up to him?

I said none of those things.

"I'm sorry," I said. Not easy, is it? I heard my mum whisper somewhere inside my head.

"And?" she asked. "Anything else?" Yes, Rebecca. Everything.

"Just this," I replied, pulling Natalie's tin out from under the seat and handing it to her. She didn't open it, just held it in both her hands and looked at me for a few second before climbing out of the car and slamming the door shut. I started the engine and drove off down the street.

Jack of course has an abundance of children. The kind of man he is was always destined to have a large family and they started almost as soon as they got married.

First off a boy, Daniel, who must have been born around the same time you were. He was barely any trouble when he came out and was born smack on his due date. He arrived a perfect healthy pink, started sleeping through the night almost immediately and took to his food like a duck to water. Or a duck to fish, or whatever it is they eat. All in all he was a joy to be around, just like his dad.

Second were identical twin girls – Amelia and Bethany – gorgeous little things they are and arrived not long after Daniel. I guess they would be about five now. Their mother dresses them in matching outfits somehow without making them look like the creepy girls from The Shining. Jack dotes on them of course, they're his two angels.

Finally came Dominic, who's now about two and already walking and talking. Clearly the most mischievous one of them all, taking after his dad in that respect.

And Kate is now pregnant with a fifth. I don't know how she does it. She's a partner at the law firm she works at, the youngest partner they've ever had, and she's managed to fit in squeezing four kids out of her and is home for dinner every night. The perfect mother. It's a miracle if ever I saw one. Jack had switched so that he only had to work during the day, and very rarely in the evenings if they really need him to. And they have a wonderful nanny during the day who pretty much must have modelled herself on Mary Poppins.

Jack was of course the perfect dad. Spent as much of his time with his kids as he could but always left just enough time for him and Kate to be together. He was fun to be around as a kid and I guess he never grew out of it. The Peter Pan of dads.

From what I gather your mum had a slightly tougher time. On our trip to Thurso I made your mum tell me everything that had happened from the moment I left her to the moment I met her back in the street in Richmond. I know she can be private at times kiddo and doesn't particularly like telling stories. So I thought I'd better write it all down just in case she never gets round to telling you. Plus, I kind of want to run it all through in my head again.

You were born on the 8th of September at 11:50pm. You weighed less than 6 pounds, which even I know is small for a baby and you took 36 hours to come out. They nearly had to give your mum a caesarean. After you were born apparently you were so tiny they thought you weren't going to make it. Your mum stopped eating after I left and she didn't gain as much weight in the first few months as she should have done. Your grandparents were great though kid. The Cap took over and insisted that your mum move back in with them and wouldn't take no for an answer. Once she got in the house he pretty much watched over her night and day, making sure she was eating right, sleeping right and taking care of everything else. He's a wonderful man your granddad Huck, the best man I know.

Still, it was touch and go apparently but you made it Huck. You're a fighter and don't let anyone tell you any different.

You were in hospital for five days before they let you come home and a few weeks after you did, when you were fit and ready for it, they had a big party to celebrate at the cricket club. Your mum said you were spoilt rotten – presents from everyone on the team, hugs and kisses from all the players and all their wives. It was like you had eleven sets of grandparents and about as many aunts and uncles. The best day the club had ever seen The Cap said, best day of his life.

You were christened in Richmond and again pretty much the whole town turned out to see you and then the Cap threw another huge party at the cricket club. Second best day there apparently. I think your grandfather dotes on you a little.

After your initial troubles it was plain sailing according to your mum. You gained weight quickly, learned to walk when you should have, learned to talk right on time. Your granddad is convinced that your first word was "Cap" but your mum thinks it was just a noise, maybe even a sneeze. She thinks your first word was really "tick-tock". I guess not everything can be meaningful!

Your mum says your first day at playschool was the most difficult of your young life for her – watching you go off by yourself and having to leave you for a whole three hours. She cried, you didn't. You seemed happy enough just to meet some new people and wonder off without her. Don't get too independent Huck, your mother will always need someone to look after and you're all she has. The first day of school was apparently a breeze by all accounts – I guess she was more prepared for it. Still cried though. She says she has pictures of that. I guess I'll never see them.

Do you remember being in your first year Christmas assembly? You played exactly the same role I did – head King who got to walk in front of the others and point out the star. You stole the show with your wonderful method acting, according to The Cap. He believed you were a real king on your way to Bethlehem, bowed down at your feet after the performance and everything.

I wish I could have been there to see that Huck. There's so many things I've missed, so many things I'll never get to see. First steps, first swim, your first girlfriend, first time you get you heartbroken and need someone to help you mend it, the first time you get drunk and try and sneak home, your wedding, grandchildren. Your mum tells it all so beautifully, and her eyes light up whenever she speaks about you, it's just like I was there.

Except I wasn't. And I won't be.

That was it Huck, that was all the interaction your mum and I were to have after all these years of being apart. I was going to drive away down the road and she was going to go back into her house, give you an enormous hug and then you would go back to your lives. All I had wanted to do was to say I was sorry and to give you what I could. I don't deserve what else I got.

What I got was maybe two hundred yards down the road before I looked in the side mirror and saw your mum stood in the middle of the road waving her arms over her head. I slammed on the breaks and swerved the Campervan to the side of the road. I sat for a second. She hasn't had enough, I thought, she wants to bawl me out a little more before she sends me off on my way. Maybe hit me. Probably hit me. I deserved it. Still, I climbed out of the door and started walking back down the road. Your mum was running straight at me by that point and, if I'm honest, I was a little scared what was going to happen when she reached me.

When she did she stood panting for a second, hands on her knees as she caught her breath, looking up at me with an uncertain expression.

"You're really dying?" she asked. I nodded and managed a half smile to say it was true. "And you really just came all this way to tell me you were sorry and then to walk straight back out of my life again?" I nodded again. Your

146

mum laughed in disbelief.

"And then what?" she asked.

"I'm going to see my dad," I said, "and then to see Jack."

"And after that?" I shrugged my shoulders. I didn't want to play my hand then Huck, I wasn't ready for that.

"Jeez Michael," she laughed again. "I should slap you. Wait here," she said pointing directly at the spot I was standing on and she turned and ran back to the house. I didn't move, did exactly as I was told. Five minutes later your mum walked back out of the house, you in tow still in your duffel coat, she carrying a bag with her. She thrust the bag into my arms.

"What's this?" I asked.

"If you think you can just waltz back into my life, tell me what you just told me and then expect to disappear you've got another think coming." She looked down at you. "Huck, this is Michael, Michael this is Huck." I nodded down at you and you stuck out a hand for me to shake. I had to juggle the bag around so I could put out a hand in reply. You shook it – nice firm hand shake for a seven year old kid. Well done Huck.

Your mum opened the side door to the Campervan and you jumped up first this time. I threw your mums bag into the back and climbed up into the driver's side, you sat next to me this time and your mum by the window.

"Where are we going?" you said squinting up at me.

"Good question," I replied as I put the Campervan into first gear and pulled away.

Mum and I went on a car ride once, just the two of us. My father had gone to work and I was dressed in my school clothes ready to walk to school when she came down and told me to change.

"We're going on a trip," she said and she looked happy.

We drove for hours and we sang and we played games and we stopped on the way and she bought me a huge milkshake and let me drink it in the car as we drove. We were in the car for what seemed like hours until we finally pulled up at the coast, near to where we had gone camping the summer before. The day they had a fight and my mother and I had walked off. We walked the same path. We came again to the same cliff edge. It was cloudy but not dark and my mother held my hand and we looked out over the sea.

"What do you see?" she asked me.

"Where?" I said, looking out into the water.

"In the waves," she said, pointing out to sea. "Do you see them?"

I looked into the sea but I couldn't see anything. She pointed again

"There," she said, excitedly, "there! The dark fish. Can't you see them, Michael?"

I didn't know what she was pointing at then. I couldn't see them. But I didn't want to disappoint her. She seemed so excited. So I lied.

"Yes, mum," I said. "I can see them!"

She turned and looked at me and nodded her head, smiling. She was happy now. And with that she tightened her grip on my hand and she stepped forward, over the edge and I pulled her back and we fell in a heap on the grass and a man with a dog came and made sure we were OK and we drove home.

Six weeks later we drove together again and that was the last time I saw my mother.

I thought I'd better write a short note about what happened to my dad after I left for University so that you can understand the rest of the story. I say a short note for two reasons. Firstly, what happened to him is not really that important to me and my life, the damage was done well before I left. Secondly, after I went to University he and I stopped talking and, apart from the occasional text in the first couple of years after university, I had very little contact with him and even that at times was too much. It's incredible how much a simple text message can hurt you. Words and nothing more. Perhaps that was what hurt, the fact it was only words.

Anyway, doesn't matter now.

So, not long after I left for university the company he worked for decided to move up north to Halifax, as I think I've already said. He was therefore left with a choice of either taking early retirement and staying in Witney, our home, the house and the town I spent all of my youth in, or moving up to Yorkshire. Given his life by that point pretty much revolved around being at work and his friends at the social club, most of whom would be moving with their own jobs anyway, he decided to go too.

So he sold up the family home. I wasn't consulted – I don't know where I was supposed to live when I came back from University in the holidays, not that it mattered as it turned out. He bought a one bedroom flat in the centre of town. Again, I wasn't consulted on the new purchase and it was clear indication that I wasn't welcome to stay during the holidays. One bedroom. One person. Definitely not a family home. That was a big part of the decision to sever all of my ties with him to be honest. I never even told him I had left University. He didn't ask. I can't imagine he gave much of a shit to be honest.

And so that was his life. Working, socialising with people from his work and generally not giving a dam about anything else, including me. As far as I knew that was how he had spent the rest of his day's right up until the moment I left your house to go and see him. He had no idea that Rebecca existed, no idea that you existed and, for all he was aware, I could well have been dead. What a nice little family reunion it was going to make for when we arrived. I don't know if he knew about mum. I doubt very much that he cared.

Still, I hadn't planned on visiting for long. Just long enough to say what I had to say and go.

Richmond to Halifax isn't far, only an hour and a half and a pretty simple route, but I definitely wanted to engineer some space between having just found you both again and seeing my dad for three reasons:

1.   I wanted to spend some time getting to know you;

2.   I wanted to spend some more time talking to your mum. I couldn't decide if she was genuinely being nice to me, was still in shock, or was waiting for the right moment to explode and kill me. Her initial flash of

anger aside, she seemed to have taken my sudden reappearance very well;

3.   I wanted to spend some time thinking about what I was going to say to my dad when I saw him. Just like with you and your mother I'd thought for a long time about all the things I wanted to say to him and I wanted to get it just right.

We passed a sign on the A1 for York – it wasn't far off our path.

"York's nice," I said, looking over at your mum. A little shrug of her shoulders suggested to the average passer-by that she could take it or leave it, but I knew it meant she liked it. She had always liked York, had wanted us to move there when I got a "proper job" to support the family. I looked down at you. "They have a Viking centre." Your eyes lit up and you turned your head to look at me.

"With actual Vikings?" You asked, excited and yet still suspicious in case it turned out to be a trick.

"With actual Vikings," I confirmed. Your head then swung back round to you mum.

"Can we?" you asked. She sighed, but a sigh I again knew meant she wanted to, she just wanted to play it a little coolly.

"I guess we could take a little trip," she said. You bounced up and down and, after about another mile, I flicked the indicator to turn off into the city. We followed the signs until we arrived at the Yorvik Viking Centre, you sat bolt upright calling out directions at every turn – right here, next left and so on. I'd barely parked the Campervan and turned off the engine before you were scrambling over your mother to get out the van and racing across the car park, your mother having to call after you to make sure you didn't run in front of a car.

"He's certainly got a lot of energy," I said. Your mum smiled.

"He does," she replied, "but I don't know where he gets it from."

We walked silently across the car park, shoulder to shoulder, until we reached the ticket office. It was already two in the afternoon, but still plenty of time for us to see most of the sights.

"Two adults and a child please," I said through the ticket office window.

"Cheaper if you get a family ticket even if you don't use the extra child one," the twenty something behind the window replied, smiling at me. A family ticket. That sounded nice. I hadn't been in a family for a long time. Not sure I ever had. I bought the ticket and put it in my pocket.

Your mum and I walked round the exhibits, talking to one another while you raced round them. Every now and again you would grab your mum to show her one of them and our conversation would trail off, soon to be picked up again once you found something more interesting to take your imagination.

"So how have you been, Rebecca?" I asked.

"Oh I can't complain, apart from the runaway fiancé," she let out a little smile when she said this, letting me know she still meant it, that it still hurt. "Actually things have been OK. Huck's doing well at school and I have a job I can do from home when he's there. He has friends and so do I. The house is small but it's nice and it suits us just fine."

"How about the Cap?" I said, looking at the remnants of a long boat laid out before us.

"Daddy's good," she said. She never called him The Cap, always daddy. "They are both well actually. They were so, so good to us the first couple of years. We really needed them and they didn't let us down." They didn't let us down. You did.

"Are you seeing anyone?" I asked. She scowled.

"Not sure that's any of your business." I backtracked.

"I just mean it would be good for him to have a father figure." I said.

"Yeah, it would," came the reply, still staring at the boat, "shame you didn't think that seven years ago." Ok, I deserved that, but this wasn't really going to plan. Not really sure I had a plan, no idea where this was really going.

She sighed.

"The truth is I don't really have the time, or the inclination. I don't want him to get hurt by someone else who just ends up leaving us again." I nodded. I hadn't just ruined your chances of having me as a father, the man who should be your father, I'd ruined the chance of you ever having a dad.

"Plus we're alright just the two of us, aren't we Huck," she called over at you and you turned around beaming. She waved at you. "What about you anyway Michael, anyone special in your life?" There have only been three special people in my life, I thought, and for the last few years I haven't been with any of them. You made it four Huck.

"No," was my reply. "Nobody at all."

"Well at least you didn't leave us for another woman, Michael. At least I can say that for you." I think that was meant to be a joke but neither of us laughed.

We wandered round the rest of the exhibits, you continuing to race on ahead of us, me and your mum continuing to make small talk about what had happened in our lives since we had parted. Nothing interesting, nothing warm. The kind of conversations you have with someone you barely know when you get stuck together in the queue in the supermarket. It wasn't what I wanted. We went to the gift shop and I bought you a Viking helmet, a bouncy ball and a post card. You wanted to send something to your granddad. I think you thought you were on holiday.

"What now then?" your mum asked as we left.

"I'm hungry," was your reply and you looked up at both of us.

"Pizza hut?" I suggested. Your eyes lit up, but a frown crossed your mum's face. I quickly followed it up, "Pizza Express?" That was the better answer and seemed to please everyone. We drove into town and walked through the high street until we found a Zizzi – not a Pizza Express, but basically the same thing.

You and I both had a pepperoni pizza, thin base and a diet coke, your mum had a chicken tortellini. Our first meal together as a family, to go with our family ticket to the Viking Centre and our family trip. Our family. I wish. We sat there and I made nervous jokes about the pizzas, making a smiley face with my pepperoni pieces which you copied with yours until your mum told us both to stop playing with our food. The kind of telling off that says I find it funny, but if I laugh I'm not being a good mother. We ate cheesecake for desert and you and I ate half of your mothers because she couldn't possibly finish it all. I paid. It was how it should have been. How it should have always been.

We walked out of the restaurant and back towards the car. When we got to the main road your mum yelled "hands" for you to cross road. You stuck out both, one for your mum and one for me. I looked down at your hand and then up at your mum. She nodded and I took it. Your hand in mine. It felt so small. I could have cried.

We only ever fought once, Jack and I. Only once that I can remember anyway.

It was the first summer after I had met your mother and she and I were living together in the small two up, two down that we were renting. We'd had a fantastic time together – it had been a glorious summer – hot with blues skies virtually every day. When we weren't working we'd spent time walking in the woods, just the two of us. It was after one of these walks that he turned up at our house unannounced. Your mum was in the kitchen, fixing us something for dinner, when there was a knock at the door. She didn't hear it so I so answered it. When I opened the door Jack was stood there, beaming at me, arms wide open. I hadn't seen him for months.

"Hey buddy," he said, "long time no see!"

"Uh, hey," I replied. I had no idea how he even knew where we lived. "What… what are you doing here?" I glanced back in the house to see if your mum had heard him.

"I thought I'd come see you old chap, just to say hey," he replied, still beaming at me. I stepped out of the house, closing the door behind me.

"Seriously Jack, what are you doing here? You can't just turn up unannounced like this!" Jack's expression didn't change, he just carried on smiling right back at me.

"Stop joking around Michael," he said, reaching a hand out onto my shoulder. "I've come to save you from domestication. I thought we could take the Porsche out for a spin." He pointed his free hand back at the car Kate had bought for him. I brushed his hand off my shoulder.

"Seriously Jack," I said, "you can't just turn up unannounced. You should have called first. You're going to have to go. I'm sorry."

"Are you kidding me?!" Jack replied, the smile replaced with a look of confusion and hurt. "I've come all this way mate. I thought we could have some fun."

"I've gotta go," I said, turning back to go in the house. "I'm sorry Jack."

"You owe me," Jack replied, pointing at me as I closed the door on him. "You owe me big time."

"I know," I said as I closed the door. "I know I do."

I didn't see him again for a long time. Not until after I left your mum.

We're getting closer Huck, closer to him. Now that we're nearly there I don't know if I want this trip to end, not the way it's going to anyway. But I have to. I'm just being a coward. It's the right thing to do Huck, I need to make things right.

We drove the Campervan to a service station outside of town, just off the A1. I had suggested getting some hotel rooms but you liked the idea of sleeping out in the van – an adventure you'd said. It didn't matter to me. It was warm enough inside and I just wanted to be near you both. We parked up and pulled down the bed in the back and you got into the pyjamas your mum had packed for you – the Ben 10 ones. It's funny how much smaller kids look in their pyjamas, much skinnier. Far more fragile. She tucked you in and climbed in next to you, the two of you talking softly. You whispered the events of the day, how much you enjoyed the Vikings. I heard your mother ask if you liked me, didn't hear your response but she laughed at whatever it was you said. I took that as a good sign.

After a while you dropped off to sleep and your mother climbed through to the front of the cab. I handed her a tea and we sat staring out into the darkness, the two of us lit up only by the street lights in the car park. The wind rocked the Campervan gently, just enough to keep it comfortable. It was your mother who eventually broke the silence.

"What's wrong with you Michael?" she asked, staring at the steam rising off her tea. "I mean how are you sick?"

"I have a brain tumour," I said, doing the same. "An inoperable one. Nothing they can do about it."

"Oh," she said quietly. "They can't do Chemo or anything like that?" I shook my head.

"No. It would give me some more time, but not much and most of that would be spent feeling like crap. Maybe an extra few months but, what am I going to do with that? I'm doing what I need to do right now."

Another "oh" and then a short silence, which she again broke.

"Does it hurt?" I shook my head again.

"No, not really. I get headaches, quite bad ones, but I just thought it was normal headaches. Maybe if it had hurt somewhere else or if they lasted a bit longer I might have gone to the doctor. But maybe not. You know how much I hate going to see the doctor." Another pause.

"Did anyone go to the doctor's appointments with you?" Shake of the head. "Was anyone with you when you found out?" Another shake. Another "oh". Another pause.

"Why did you leave Michael?" That question, again. Always that question. The question I asked myself a thousand time over, except I had always known the answer before. When I was sat next to her, when I could see you asleep on the bed, I was so sure I knew what the answer was. Then I think back to the night in the hotel, when I got angry and I remembered.

"It's too hard to explain," I said, not wanting to have to think about it anymore. She rests her hand on top of mine.

"Try me," she said. I sighed and I closed my eyes while I talked.

"Being with you is the only time in my life I've been happy," I said. "There were times when I was with just my mother, or with Jack, that I was happy for a short period, but it would always be interrupted, disturbed somehow by him. But with you there was never an end to it, Rebecca. Every day I woke up happy, I worked happy, I came home happy and I went to bed and dreamed about how happy I was. No monsters. Nothing. It was perfect, everything in my life was perfect. That was because of you Rebecca, nothing else. No other time in my life had I been that happy and the difference was that you were in it. Before I met you I was miserable and after I left I was miserable. It's not a coincidence.

"But there is something inside me Rebecca that doesn't want me to be happy, something that wants to push me away from the light and into the darkness. I could feel him inside me, feel him trying to claw his way out of me.

"Before I left I could contain him, and I knew that you were strong. You had some power that meant you could push him back inside. There were times when he poked his ugly head out of me, but you stopped him. Sent him back deep down inside of me.

"But when you told me, told me about Huck, I" I looked over to where you were sleeping. "He's so small," I said. "So small and so beautiful. So perfect. How could I have let him live with that? How could I have hung around knowing that monster was inside me, waiting for a chance to come out? Because it would have come out Rebecca, would have sneaked past you when you were tired from chasing after Huck all day and I was tired from a day at work and he would have ruined everything. Would have ruined his life like my father ruined mine. I couldn't let that happen Rebecca, I couldn't. I did it for him."

Tears were welling in my eyes when I said that and my hands were shaking. I could feel her grip on my hand tightening as I was talking and when I finished and looked up at her, tears were rolling down her cheeks.

"You're not him," she said, reaching over and putting her other hand on top of mine. "You're not him."

"But what if I am?" I said, the sickness rising in my stomach.

"You're not," she said, squeezing tighter, "I know you're not because I love you." And with that I let it all out. I buried my head in her shoulder and I cried and cried and cried.

OK Huck, we need something to lighten the mood. That bit wasn't exactly the most uplifting part of this letter and, without wanting to spoil it, the next part isn't exactly a barrel of laughs either. So I thought I would teach you some jokes. Every kid has to have some jokes up his sleeve. All of these came from Jack, who was a fantastic comic – used to have me and everyone else in stitches all the time. So here we go: I'll test these on your mother while she's driving.

An easy one to warm up - What's brown and sticky? Give up? A stick. Ba-dum. Yeah ok, that's a pretty old one and not so great. Your mum knew that one.

Second one coming up. Did you hear about the magic tractor? It went down the road and turned into a field. Get it? It's a play on words that one, it took your mother a while to get it. Perhaps by the time you tell her it after you read this she might have gotten it from the first time around.

Third one. What's worse than finding a maggot in your apple? Being shot. Yeah so that one only really works if you know the original, or if you don't find the whole thing a little tasteless and not really for children, which is apparently your mothers point of view.

OK, final one now kiddo. How does Robin know when it's time for his tea? Because Albert shouts "dinner, dinner, dinner, dinner Bat Man!"

That last one was Jack's favourite. He's a joker. Always smiling that kid.

He doesn't fish, Huck. He doesn't fish at all.

Your mother and I fell asleep in the front seat of the Campervan, although when I woke up she was back lying next to you in bed. The two of you looked so perfect snuggled up next to each other in bed, her with her arms around you. Protecting you, just like she always had. I went for a walk to the service station for a pee and to get some coffee – in that order. I got your mother her usual tea and some flavoured milk for you. When I walked back you were both up and sat in the cab.

"Are there showers in the services?" she asked. I nodded. We sat and drank our drinks before we walked back over to the services together. You and I went in adjoining stalls and I checked you were ok. We both came out smelling fresh and waited another fifteen minutes for your mother.

And then we were back on the road again, driving the last few miles to Halifax. We stopped a couple of miles outside the centre and asked a few people if they knew where the place my dad worked was and eventually found someone who gave us directions to an industrial estate just outside of town. It took us about ten minutes to get there and we pulled up at the back of the car park. It was mid-morning. If he was still there at all he was bound to be there now. The factory had never shut over Christmas in

Witney, good to see traditions didn't stop here.

"Do you want us to come with you?" Your mum asked. I shook my head.

"I didn't force you to meet him when we were together," I said. "No reason why I should inflict him on you now. I'll be back soon." She nodded.

"OK, good luck."

I climbed out of the cab and walked over to the reception. I rang the bell and they buzzed me in. Inside they had one of those old receptions that serves as just a window to the accounts office. I tapped on the translucent plastic and after a few minutes a middle aged woman slammed it open and stood staring at me like I'd just robbed the place.

"Yeah? Can I help?" she charmed me.

"I'm looking for someone called Christopher Brighton," I said. "I think he works here." She sniffed and turned round to look into the back of the office. "Is there anyone work here called Christopher Brighton?" She yelled it. A few murmurs, a few shakes of the head, then a cough and a beckon. "Scuse me," she said and slammed the door closed again. I was left staring at the white Perspex. After a couple of minutes the screen flew open again.

"He used to work here but he doesn't anymore," came the response.

"Oh," I replied, a little lost, "well, do you know where he is now?"

"Yeah," she said, "he's in Calderdale hospital just down the road. He's been there about six months. On the cancer ward apparently." She said it so matter of fact, as though it was the simplest thing in the world. My mouth dried up, I hadn't expected this. I took a step back and nearly sat down on the floor in the middle of the reception.

"You ok kid?" she shouted, leaning over the counter to make sure I hadn't slipped on something that might have been her fault. I mumbled something, nothing intelligent and pushed my way back outside. Fresh air. That was what I needed - fresh air.

I stood by the side of the entrance for a couple of minutes, just holding on to the wall and getting my breath back. He wasn't supposed to be ill, wasn't supposed to be suffering. He was supposed to be fighting fit, ready to take everything I had to say to him just like he should have done all those years ago. It wasn't fair, wasn't right. I must have looked pale when I came back to the van.

"What's wrong?" your mum asked.

"He's in hospital," I said. "The cancer ward apparently. Sounds serious."

"Oh," she replied. "Well, do you want to go and see him there?" Another great question. You guys are good at these. Do I? Yes, I do. I definitely do. Of course I do. I haven't come this far just to pass him over now.

"I think you'd better drive," I said, handing her the keys. It took your mum a while to get used to it, it takes a bit of brute strength to put the gears in place after all this time but she got used to it and we were soon trundling the few short miles to the hospital while I stared out of the window, watching but not really seeing the scenery go past.

When we arrived I jumped out of the cab to go and find out where he was from the reception, while you and your mum went and parked the Campervan. After a few minutes of searching up and down the register, finding two different people called Christopher Brighton and then working out which one was the right one, she eventually worked out where he was, by which time you and your mum had caught me up.

"Third floor, Ward E," I said and we made our way over to the lift.

I've only been in hospital a couple of times, Huck. Once after Paul hit me and a couple of times to get my tests done. It's funny how they all look the same though, Huck. Different towns, different locations, different lay outs, different designers you would assume and yet they're all essentially the same. I guess they have certain restrictions, especially the NHS ones. Always the same drab, slightly nauseating colours, the same smell, the same miserable atmosphere. I guess a hospital isn't ever going to be the happiest of places, except maybe on the maternity ward. Maybe it's not so unusual they're all the same.

We exited the lift and followed the signs down to Ward E. A gaggle of nurses were stood around the station, a little intimidating as I walked up to them. I had to clear my throat a couple of times before I could get their attention, but as soon as I did one of them turned around, beaming at me.

"Hi there," her voice bounced, "are you visiting someone today?"

"Yes," I said, clearing my throat again, trying to sound at least one tenth of happy as she was. "My dad is in here. Christopher Brighton?" She thought for a second.

"Oh yes of course," she said, "room 6. I think he's asleep at the moment though, do you want to go and see?" She looked past me at you and your mum, "Are you guys here to see granddad?" she chirped.

"No," I said, a little sterner than perhaps I should have done, I corrected myself and repeated it a little softer, "no, I don't think it would be great for them to see him just yet." The nurse nodded and pointed to some chairs that you and your mum could sit on. Your mum made the international sign of "do you want some coffee" and I nodded, she smiled back at me and held up five fingers to suggest she would be along soon.

The nurse led me down the hall and into a small sunlit room. The room was bare, not like you imagine a hospital room to be. No flowers, no get well soon cards, no balloons. Nothing. There, on the bed, was something that resembled my father. Older, of course, with thinning hair and more wrinkles across his face. The thing that struck me most was how much thinner he was. He looked smaller than I ever could have imagined him. Smaller and weaker. His eyes were closed, a respirator lurching away next to him, a thick tube coming out of the machine and into his throat.

"He's in a bad way?" I whispered to the nurse. She nodded.

"Been here for about six months," she said. "It's just a matter of time really." She paused, clearly wanting to say something but feeling it wasn't her place. Eventually she said it anyway. "You're the first visitor he's had. Shame really, seems like such a nice man."

"We were never that close," I said, not quite sure she had said what I thought she had.

"I thought his brother would have come," she said, "he talks about him all the time." I looked at her in surprise.

"He doesn't have a brother," I said.

"Oh," she said, shrugging her shoulders. "Maybe he means someone else. Anyway, I'll leave you to it." And with that she walked out, leaving me alone with the monster. Only he didn't look like a monster anymore. Not the monster I had feared anyway. I went and sat by the bed, hands in my lap, staring at him. Funny, he didn't look like someone who could have done what he did to my mother any more, didn't look like someone who could have brought so much misery on the two of us. Mind you, nor do I, I thought.

I stared at him for a long time, watching the respirator go up and down. I thought about how easy it would have been to stop it now. To have pulled the plug on the machine. Or to have slipped a pillow over his face. Anything to have given my mother a little taste of revenge. Not revenge, justice. I watched the respirator, presumably the only thing keeping him alive, going up and down, up and down.

I must have dozed off for a second just sat there because I suddenly opened my eyes and he was staring at me. I focused on him and when I realised I wasn't dreaming I sat bolt upright in my chair a little afraid all of a sudden. He chuckled to himself, a thick, grizzly laugh.

"Still afraid of your own shadow hey Michael?" He laughed again and tried to pull himself up in his bed. "So finally come to see me then," he said, "after all these years, thought you'd pay your old dad a visit huh? Bit late really."

"You could have called me?" I said.

"I didn't know where you were son," he replied, smiling. "I tried to get you at that University of yours."

"I left," I said, "it wasn't for me."

"No, it was never going to be for you was it Michael. All those clever people and you having to look after yourself, so far from home." He tried to pull himself up again and failed, so he tugged on the chord by the side of his bed instead. The nurse who had brought me through came back in, all smiles and lightness.

"Are you ok there Mr Brighton?" she said.

"Yes, yes," he replied, smiling right back at her. "Just trying to sit myself up. And I told you, call me Christopher, please?" He said it with such sincerity, such humbleness that I forgot who I was watching. The nurse grabbed one of his armpits and pointed me to the other to give him a hand. We hoisted him up and she fixed the pillow behind his head so that he was comfortable.

"Thank you son," he said, smiling at me. So fucking patronising.

"Right, I'll leave you boys alone," the nurse said, turning on her heels. "See you soon Christopher."

"Not if I see you first," my dad replied and the two exchanged over the top smiles. "They're great," he said, turning back to me and still smiling. I remained expressionless. How could he be like that with other people? How could he be so fucking happy and smug after the way he treated my mother? I continued saying nothing.

"So," he finally said, moistening his lips, "did you come all this way just to sit there and stare at me?"

"No," I said. I decided to lie. I didn't want him to know why I was really here. "I heard that you were dying and I decided to come and see you one more time before you went. Just to make sure you were really going."

He seemed shocked by that, shocked by a tiny dig at him in comparison to all the things he had done to me and my mother.

"Hey now," he said, "That's no way to speak to a dying man, let alone your own father."

"Maybe if you'd acted more like a father I'd be treating you more like one now," I snapped, finding my anger. I didn't care how old he was, how weak he was any more. This was my time, my chance to make up for what he had done to my mother. My chance to slay the monster once and for all.

"What, Michael? I was a good father to you. I never did you any wrong. I provided everything you wanted, put a roof over your head, food on the table. I tried to teach you how to be a man, Michael, tried to teach you how to provide for a family."

"Oh is that how you provide for your family, dad?" I said, my voice getting stronger. "You provide for your kid by smacking your wife around? Huh, is that the lesson you were trying to teach me dad?"

"Your mother was a drunk, Michael," he said, "She was a curse on our house."

"Oh that's right dad, blame mum, like you always did."

"Our house was a happy house kiddo, until she started drinking. We had a deal, I provided for the family and she looked after you and the house. Which one of us didn't live up to their end of the bargain, hey kid? Which one of us didn't do as they were meant to? Which one of us let the house go to shit? Which one of us brought up a bed wetter for a son who got the crap beaten out of him every day, huh? I was out there working my arse off every day and all I expected was to come home to some food and a clean house and a son I could be proud of. Was that so much to ask?"

"So your answer was to hit her?" I yelled. The nurse came back to the door way but I flashed her a look that said fuck off and she left again. "Did it ever occur to you to ask her why she drank, dad? To find out what made her so sad?"

"You know exactly why she was so fucking sad Michael." He stared at me, his eyes wide open. I did know. My fault. I looked back down at the floor. "Why are you really here?" he said.

"I came to tell you something," I said. "To tell you something that I should have said a long time ago but I was too afraid to ever say. And then I'm going to leave and you won't see me again." I stared at him and he said nothing. Here goes, I thought to myself.

"I'm sorry," I said. "I'm sorry I wasn't ever able to be the kind of kid you wanted me to be. Sorry that I wasn't strong enough, wasn't fast, wasn't smart enough, wasn't whatever the fuck it was you wanted me to be. I'm sorry I didn't like the things you liked, I'm sorry I was afraid of things, I'm sorry for being a kid. The thing is dad, as much as you wanted me to, I never wanted to be like you."

I stood up to leave, but he grabbed me by the cuff of my jacket and called out my name softly.

"Michael," he said, "I'm scared."

I looked down at him.

"So was I dad, so was I." I pulled myself free and as I turned towards the door you and your mum were stood there looking at us, your mum with a cup of coffee in one hand and your hand in her other. I walked towards them and picked you up as my dad continued to call out my name.

"Michael," he said, "Michael please come back."

"Come on," I said to your mum but she shushed me and walked over to my dad. She bent down by his side and whispered something into his ear. As she did he stopped talking and his eyes began to well up. As she carried on talking tears streamed down his face and he gasped for breath. She stood up, stony faced and walked back past.

"Come on," she said, and we left.

That was the last time I ever saw my dad.

When we got back to the car she climbed in the Campervan and put her hand on my thigh before she quickly pulled it off again, realising what she had done and embarrassed by it.

"Right then Mr, where are we off to now? Is that your list done?"

Another good question, I thought, but it's not time yet. I can't take you on the last step. I need more time.

"No," I said, "I can't go home yet."

"Well," your mum said, "what now then?"

And that's how we ended up here. The last stop before I have to head out on the final leg of my journey by myself. I said earlier that I didn't believe in the supernatural – ghosts and all of that kind of stuff. I had always believed in science and fact. But there had been one thing that had always made me wonder. I had seen the Northern Lights on television before and even though I understood how they worked it still seemed like magic to me. How could something so beautiful happen by pure chance.

I'd seen on the news a few years ago that the Northern lights had made their way down as far as Norwich. I'd thought you could only see them really far north, as somewhere like Norway or Finland, but after a bit of digging around I found out you could see them fairly regularly in Scotland, especially in the Highlands. Thurso it seemed, or round there anyway, was the best place for it.

That's what I told your mother I wanted to do, with the week or so before we could go and see Jack, we would go to Scotland, rent a cottage or something for a few days, see in the New Year and then head back down to see him. A family holiday. A proper family holiday and a wonderful way to see in the New Year. Together. Like we were meant to be.

We stopped at a café and did a little research and then booked a cottage over the phone. Then we made the long drive up there together, you me and your mum. The three of us talking the whole way up there just like I've already told you. On the way I made her tell me everything about you, and you listened, enjoying your own life story. We talked about my life, about my trip, about Paul and David and my mother. I told her parts of the story about Natalie, not everything, but enough so that she understood taking the money wasn't necessarily a bad thing. It wasn't as if she had exactly got it by fair means anyway.

I asked you things about yourself. Your favourite subject at school, your favourite colour, who your best friend was, which girls you liked, what your teachers were like, if your mum was nice to you. She laughed. You laughed. I was happy. It was like all the holiday journeys I'd never had as a child. I don't think you really understood who I was, but you seemed happy to tell everything to this man who had taken an interest in you. Like most kids I suppose you were just happy talking away.

And now here were are, the night before New Year's Eve, the three of us sat round the dinner table talking and eating. Laughing together and playing games. Just like every dinner time I've ever missed out on. At least I get this one Huck. In a couple of days I'm leaving to go and find Jack and I won't see you again after that. I can stay with you and have you watch me fade away Huck, I just can't. I'm sorry.

He wasn't fishing Huck. He wasn't putting the fish into the net at his feet. He was taking them out. Taking the fish out of his net and breathing his filthy stink into them and letting them out into the water.

I hate you, Jack.

This is going to be my last entry Huck. I can't write any more. This is too hard. I'll say what I have to say and then I'll be done.

It's New Years' Eve morning and we've spent the morning just the two of us on the beach, walking along and skimming stones together out into the waves. Jack was an amazing stone skimmer Huck, did I ever tell you that? He used to be able to skim them right across the corner of Ducklington Lake near our house – make them skim right onto the bank opposite. I think he did anyway, sometimes my memory of those times is a little hazy. Maybe it was me who used to skim them across or maybe it was another kid. I can't remember. It doesn't matter anymore.

I wanted to talk with just you Huck. I don't know if you'll remember the talk we had but I hope something stuck in there right in the back. We sat on the edge of the beach on an lump of wood that had floated in from the ocean and been dragged up the beach and watched a family walking down the beach close to the water edge. You stared at them as they went past and watched as they walked down into the distance. You looked down at your shoes and fiddled with the zip on your coat.

"What is it Huck?" I said, looking down at you.

"Mum says that you're my dad," you said, still looking at your laces and kicking at the sand.

"Oh," I said, "well, what else did she say?"

You shrugged your shoulders.

"She said that you were my dad but that you couldn't stay with us," you went on, your foot moving quicker now. "But she said that you weren't like other dads."

"Well," I said, "she's right. I can't stay with you. I wish I could Huck, but I can't."

"Why?" You looked right at me when you said that. Straight into my eyes and despite it all, despite everything that's happened to me I couldn't think of an answer to that. I tried to speak, tried to say something that would tell you what you needed to know and I couldn't. You looked back down.

"All I wanted was a dad," you said. "A dad who loved me and loved my mum." And you cried. And my heart shattered into a thousand pieces.

I can't stay Huck. I couldn't tell you then, couldn't put into simple words all of the reasons why I couldn't stay. It's too hard Huck, it's too difficult to explain. There just aren't the words. Aren't the words to explain the fear and the hatred and the love that boils away inside of me. And I'm so scared. So, so scared of what will happen if I say. I'm sorry Huck.

I love you.

Dear Huck,

We're on the road again Huck. I didn't think I'd be writing this but here we are, on the road again. Let me explain.

You and I walked back to the house and your mum was waiting for us. You ran to her and the two of you spent a few hours upstairs, quietly at first and then with more and more laughing and giggling until all seemed to be right with the world again. You came downstairs and we played board games in the afternoon before bath time – baths for all three of us apparently.

"We're going up to the hotel," your mum said. "I've made us a reservation for dinner and we'll stay for the band and fireworks." I nodded and smiled, it sounded like a good plan. "And then," she said, with a resigned smile on her face, "we'll see what the new year brings us."

I dressed up as best as I could – a pair of relatively new jeans and a shirt and jumper. I looked OK I guess, although as it turned out the locals weren't any better dressed for the evening. You were dressed in a similar way, looking by far smarter and more handsome than I'd seen you before. Something you definitely got from your mother's side. And then your mother came down, looking radiant in a long blue dress and her hair tied up. She looked beautiful. She stood behind you and put her arms around your shoulders. I couldn't speak.

"Well," she asked, "how do we look?" I smiled and she knew.

"You both look perfect," I said and you both smiled. "But won't you be cold?"

"It's only a few houses up the road," she said, "and anyway, I'm sure there is chivalrous man who will lend me his coat."

I smiled and wrapped my coat around her shoulders and we walked the short distance to the hotel. The evening was wonderful. The food was delicious, although I'm not sure you liked the haggis much by the look on your face when you first tried it. But you ate it anyway.

After dinner there was Scottish dancing with a real caleidgh band. You were in awe of them. You stood and watched them song after song until one of the local girls who was probably about twenty invited you to dance. You were shy at first but as more and more of the girls wanted to dance with the handsome Englishman you were soon swinging round and laughing out loud. After a while of watching I could stand it no more and I stood up, bowed to your mother and asked for her hand. She took it and we danced and danced and danced.

At midnight the hotel let off fireworks and we all stood outside and watched them, my arm round your mother and you in between us. You face lit up brighter than the sky itself.

When the fireworks were done and we'd had one last Whisky for the road, which by the way you tried and did not like at all, we walked back to the cottage. I carried you home and you were asleep before we got there. I lifted you up to bed and tucked you in while your mother took a bundle of blankets and hot chocolate outside and she and I lay there under the bundles, warm from the blankets and the drink and the hot chocolate and each other.

Afterwards we lay, wrapped together in the blankets, just holding one another contentedly. Suddenly the sky shimmered with green, before it burst with light. And there they were, the Northern Lights. Hers and my dreams projected onto the sky.

"Oh my god," she said, "it's beautiful."

I had never seen such a thing. All of the pictures I'd seen and the videos were nothing compared to this.

"It's like looking at the face of God," she whispered, interlocking her fingers with mine.

"I don't believe in God," I said.

"What do you believe in then Mr?" She said, rolling on her front and resting her chin on my chest.

"You," I said, smiling at her, "and Huck." She laughed.

"And the mighty Jack of course," she said. And all of a sudden it felt wrong. And I knew it was wrong and it was a lie. Everything I had ever told her, had ever told anyone else. It was all wrong and ugly somehow and I had to let it out. Had to get it out of me somehow. The smile faded from my face when she mentioned his name. She noticed and sat up.

"What is it?" she asked. I shook my head, I couldn't say it. "Tell me Michael. Why are you going to see Jack last? Why did you have to wait before you could go and see him? And why can't we come with you?"

And then I told her. The same story I'd told everyone I'd ever known, word for word, a thousand times before. Only this time I told the truth.

We were out walking Gnipper on Langel Common, a stretch of land that sat like an island in between the two forks of the river Windrush. It was January and, whilst the river was high from the winter rains and flowing quickly, the common hadn't flooded. We walked along side by side, stopping every now and again to retrieve the ball from Gnipper to throw it again, all the while chatting away at a thousand words a minute as we were prone to doing.

Jack picked up the ball. We'd been competitive about who could throw it the furthest and, as was typical, Jack could inevitably out-distance me without a huge amount of effort. We were making our way back to the bridge over the river towards my house.

"Bet you can't get it all the way over the bridge," I challenged. Jack turned and looked at me, the flickering of a smile that always meant the same thing.

"Betcha I can," he said. He turned to look at the bridge, looked down at the ball and tossed it up and down in his hand a couple of times, sizing it up. He spat on the ground, something we had just learned to do and threw it with all the might his young arm would allow. It looked good, initially at least, sailing through the air in a perfect arc. Gnipper took off after it as soon as it had left his hand. But Jack's aim was a little off, as was his confidence in his strength. The ball hit the bridge and bounced a giant loop before landing in the river below. Gnipper wasted no time in diving in to the water after it.

"Shit," Jack shouted. Another word we have recently added to our vocabulary and therefore used any time we could.

"Shit," I agreed. We ran over to the bridge and looked over the edge. Gnipper was gone. We ran to the other side and looked down and still saw nothing. I was panicking, no idea what to do, my eyes darting from one part of the grey water to another. Jack however, didn't wait. He clambered up onto the side of the bridge and plunged into the water. It was stupid and I knew it, but it was also the bravest thing I've ever seen.

Jack disappeared into the grey and the ripple he had made on entering was soon swallowed up by the pace of the river. I waited for him to come up. One Mississippi, two Mississippi.... when I got to ten I was worried. I left the bridge and went to the river side, running up and down the same stretch of ten yards repeatedly. He didn't appear. I started shouting his name, hoping he could hear me under the water but nothing happened. It must have been at least thirty Mississippi by this point and he wasn't out. I looked back towards the bridge, thinking maybe he was further that way, but nothing.

I got to twenty Mississippi and then thirty. Then forty. I stood and watched the water. I did nothing. Fifty. Sixty. Seventy. I stopped counting. I just stood and watched.

It was two days before they eventually dragged Jack's body out of the river. It was the firemen that eventually pulled him out. They never found Gnipper. Stopped looking for him I guess. I wanted to go and see Jack but they wouldn't let me. They said that he had been too badly hurt in the water and that I wouldn't want to see him. Bloated and ruined by the water I guess. I'm glad I never saw him like that.

"Just imagine him like he was," my mum said. And that's what I did. That's what I've always done.

"Why didn't you jump in," he said. "Why was it him?"

Your mum stared at me.

"I don't understand," she said. "I thought that Jack was still in Witney?"

"He is," I said.

"But I thought he was a fireman, he married that girl, the solicitor." I shook my head. None of it was true. "But your mother, you told me your mother used to tell you everything that Jack had done. She used to sit up at night and you'd talk about what you and he had done."

"We did," I said, "but none of it was true."

"But you went to his house, sat in his garden?"

"I sat in the garden," I said, "I wasn't allowed in the house. His father wouldn't see me. Couldn't. My mum would go, her mother and mine would sit in the house and drink but... they didn't want to see me. His brother and sister did, but not them."

Your mother sat and stared at me in disbelief. I didn't know what to say.

"I'm sorry I lied about him. He was all I ever wanted to be."

I see it now Huck. I see it all so clearly.

He is gone. Jack is dead. He's been dead for a long time.

I've known it deep down the whole time, of course I have. I was there. How couldn't I know it. But, even though I saw him, watched him dive into that water and waited for him until he never came up, I didn't want to believe it.

He was everything to me, Huck. You have to understand that. He was everything that I had ever wanted to be, everything I still want to be. He was some of it. He was none of it. Now I try to look back and remember which parts of it were real I can't. Of course none of it was him, I know that now. Which parts of it were someone else? Something read somewhere of another life? I don't know. The fireman story was real I think, read in a newspaper at University I think. The wedding made up I think, just an amalgamation of every wedding from every film I've ever seen.

He had a family, of course he did. A wonderful family. The Lawrence's. And they were wonderful, until that day down by the river. The day I was afraid. The day I lost our friendship. And then everything changed. His mother wasn't kind and light and all Julie Andrews any more. She drank with my mother, succumbed to the same fate as her. His father wasn't fun anymore, didn't love the world and everything in it. And neither of them would look at me, wouldn't let me in the house anymore. I don't think they blamed me, just reminded them of him I suppose.

Jack's brother and sister still spoke to me, still looked for their little brother in me I suppose, but I wasn't the same. I wasn't Jack. I tried to be. Tried to be like him for all their sakes. I wanted so desperately to be like him and to replace him for all of them but I couldn't do it. I wasn't enough. Never enough.

Dad was right. Why hadn't I jumped?

My mother got worse after that. Drank more than she had before and Mrs Lawrence spent more time at our house, the two of them drinking together and wallowing in pity together. I put my mother on a pedestal Huck, put her there for the whole world to see. The trouble is when I was afraid, when I let Jack die, I took that pedestal out from under her. I'm not saying that life before Jack died was great, not saying that my mum and dad were the perfect married couple and that it was only this great tragedy that tore them apart. I can't say that Huck, but I know deep down that things got a lot worse after it happened. Mum drank more because she was sad. She'd seen the last drop of hope for me disappear from the world I think.

And I was worse. I was happy when I was with him, Huck. I've only really been happy around three people in my life. My mum, Jack and your mum. And I ruined all three of those Huck, ruined them all. I can't be with my mum anymore Huck, not anymore. It's too late. Far, far too late to be with her. And I can't be with your mum either. I can't have you sit there and watch me die Huck, as much as I want to be with you and to spend the last few months I have on this Earth with you I can't. I don't want you to watch me slip away. Don't want you to love me and lose me all in a heartbeat.

And I can't watch you slip away from me Huck. That's the truth of it. Every minute that I spend with you I love you more and more and more and I can't. I can't.

He's the only one I have left Huck. The only one I can go to now.

Dad was right. I should have jumped. I wish I'd jumped.

I didn't mean that Huck. I'm glad I didn't. I'm glad I got to spend this time with you and with your mum. But I have to be with him. I have to go to him. I'm sorry.

I'm here now Huck. Back here where this all began. I'm calm and I know what I need to do.

The three of us have been driving for the last couple of days. I haven't written for a while. I've just been spending time talking to you and to your mum. I haven't told you why we are here, of course, and I haven't told your mum either. She knows that I need to be here, to go back to the place where it all happened and to see Jack. But I haven't told her why. We parked the Campervan in the centre of town and walked down to the river together, just the three of us. I said I needed some time alone and the two of you have gone back into town. I left the rest of my letter to you in the van, just these last pages to write.

It looks smaller than I remember, the river I mean. I guess it would. I never came back here you know, never came back since the day it happened. It was always going to be bigger in my head. We were just kids back then. Jack still is.

The water is high, grey and flowing fast, just like it was all those years ago. But even with how fast it's flowing it still doesn't look deep enough for someone as big as Jack to drown in it. Still looks big enough for someone as small as me though.

I've thought long and hard about this Huck, about whether or not it's the right thing to do. The first couple of days of the New Year we were all so happy. It felt so good to get everything off my chest and to just be me, you know? But that's just it. How can I be me and be happy with you and your mum knowing what is going to come. Knowing what I did. It's the right thing to do Huck. I know that now. I know that your mum will be sad and that she won't understand to begin with. I know that she will think we could have another six months together but in the end it will be easier this way. She will come to understand.

Huck, what we had these past few days has been so perfect, I don't want anything to spoil it. I don't want you to see me get sick, don't want you to get too attached and then have to lose me. Better to have never really had me in the first place. You'll forget all these days, of course you will. She won't, I know. Neither will I.

I've come here to be with Jack, for the last time. To do what I should have done all those years ago, but was never brave enough to do.

He was my best friend Huck, my best friend in the whole world and I should have done the right thing, I should have followed him. I should have been braver. I should have saved him. I will now.

I loved him, Huck, and I wanted to be him, but you know what, you can't live your life wanting to be someone else. You can't live your life pretending to be the person you're not. If you want to be that person Huck, you need to go out and be him, you need to do everything you need to do to be that person. All those years ago, I wanted to be the person who dived into the water to save my best friend and I didn't and for twenty three miserable years of my life all I've done is pretend I could be that person.

Today I will. Today I'm going to follow him Huck, not to save him, but to save me. To save me from them. It's the only way, Huck. I can't spend the rest of my life running from the dark fish Huck. I need to swim with them. Today I'm going to make you proud son.

I love you Huck. I love you and your mum. You will always mean the world to me, always be in my heart. Just promise me one thing Huck, promise me that you'll always be you. Because you're perfect Huck. My perfect boy.

I have to be brave Huck, have to do what I came here to do. Don't I? I've come all this way. Put right all the things I needed to with Paul, with my mum, my dad. Your mum. You. Now I just need to be brave and do what I should have done so long ago. All these years Huck, all these years I've had to live knowing that I let him down. Knowing that I wasn't good enough. Wasn't brave enough to follow him. Now I can put that right, kiddo, now I can follow him where I was meant to. Now I can be like him.

And yet, now that I'm here I don't know.

It's strange, the last few weeks I've felt different. As strange as it sound, even though I'm dying, I've felt so, so alive. From the moment I made the decision to do what I think I'm here to do. No, from the moment I made the decision to do what I am here to do, I've felt so alive.

And why is that, hey Huck? It's because of you. Because of you and you mum. Spending time with you, spending these last few days with you, has been the most wonderful time of my life. Does it have to end? Does it have to end right now? Why can't I have more? Why can't I be selfish and foolish and have more? Does it matter that I'm sick, Huck? Does it matter that you'll have to watch me get sicker and fade away from you? Is it worth it? Six months of me slowly drifting away from you? For what? For six months of the dad I was never able to be?

There are two types of brave in this world, Huck. And I don't know which one I am.

I owe you both and I don't know who I owe more.

I love you both, love you with all my heart. I will miss you both, always. I've missed Jack for so long, but he's not here anymore. Is he?

I have to be brave. For once, Huck, I have to be brave.

I know, Huck. Deep down I know which the right answer is. My mind is made up. I hope I'm making the right choice.

Forgive me,

Dad

Dear Jack,

I'm sorry. I'm sorry I couldn't be as brave as you.

There is nothing else to say but this.

I Love you,

Michael

Dear Dad,

It's funny, now that I come to write to you I don't know where to start either. So let me tell you where we are. It's a warm summer's day and we're sat here next to you, just the three of us. Me, mum and Jack. It's nice here, calm and peaceful. Just us and the sun and the rustling of the trees.

This is my first time writing to you and I'm not sure if I'll be quite as good at it as you were, but here goes anyway.

Mum gave me your letter on my 16th birthday, a few years later than I think you were expecting, but I think she got the timing just right. I'm not sure I would have understood it a few years ago. But I get it now.

Thank you so much for writing to me. I know it must have been hard but it's helped me a lot. I don't think I can forgive you, not yet, but I'm getting there I think. It really has helped me though. I spent a lot of my childhood struggling with who I was, watching the other kids grow up with both their parents and not really knowing much about my dad, other than that you died young. Mum talked about you a lot but I always felt like she was holding something back, something she didn't want me to know and now I guess I understand. It's good hearing it in your own words. When Jack is old enough I'll let him read it too. He deserve to know all this just as much as I do.

I remember you, you know. I remember that week in Scotland. Not all of it, just snippets here and there. I remember the fireworks though and walking on the beach. And I remember the man who seemed to love me and my mum very much.

After you died mum brought you back here to be buried, so that we could come and see you whenever we wanted. I think I must have known you had died but I never really pieced the two together, the man who appeared so suddenly and was with us for a while and then not around anymore. Us suddenly going to visit my dad's grave every week when we never had before. The grave of the man I had never met. Mum told me I would understand one day. I guess she was right. I don't remember the funeral. Mum says I was there and so was Jack, sort of, but I don't remember it.

The Cap doesn't play cricket any more. He's a little old for that but still coaching. I've started playing for the men's senior team and so have a couple of my friends. I think we have a genuine chance of winning the league this year. Well, granddad thinks we do anyway. I hope we can, it would be nice for him. I play wicketkeeper just like you dad, must be something inside that you've passed down to me. Jack is going to play for the firsts when he's old enough as well.

I thought I'd answer some of your questions, not all of them as I don't have time but just the ones I thought you would want to know. So here goes:

I don't drink coffee. It's disgusting.

We went to the coast and stayed in the B&B just like you asked me to. We used some of the money that you left for us to stay there and we met with Sarah and Chris and their son. It's strange, having an uncle the same age as me. I wish you could have met him, I think you would have loved him. And Sarah and Chris are so happy.

I'm saving the money for Uni and then probably as a deposit for my first house. Half of it is going to Jack so he can do the same thing. I think he deserves some too.

I don't know what I want to be when I grow up – I haven't even settled on what I want to do at University yet. One thing I promise though Dad, I'll be brave and do what my heart tells me to do, rather than what some grumpy old man tries to bully me into doing (that's a joke by the way).

Oh and mum swears she didn't change anything that you wrote, which I believe. I do know that she cut a part out though. One minute you and her are sat outside the cottage in Scotland under the blankets and the next you're wrapped in each other's arms and staring at the sky? Come on! She thinks I'm stupid.

I'm glad though. Glad that I don't know the details obviously and more glad that it happened. We wouldn't have Jack if it hadn't.

Anyway dad, I'm going to go now. We're going round to granddad and grandma's tonight for dinner. Gran cooks a great roast – but you already know that.

I'll keep writing though, if that's OK? It helps I think, makes it seem like you're still here.

I love you dad, now and always,

Huck

Ps The dark fish. The ones you saw. They're everywhere.

A NOTE ON THE TEXT

Firstly, this story, the characters in it and the events that unfold, are entirely fictional. I have no personal experience of any of the troubles that Michael or his family go through. It's just a story.

Secondly, this is my first experience of writing and publishing a novel. I massively appreciate you taking the time to read my book and, having done so, I'd equally hugely appreciate any feedback you might have that would help me improve this book in any re-writes or my future work.

Thirdly, a huge thank you to all those who have helped edit the early versions of this book. I couldn't have done it without you.

Thank you,

Mark Bishop

e: markedwardbishop2016@outlook.com

Facebook: www.facebook.com/DarkFishSwim/

27286645R00103

Printed in Poland
by Amazon Fulfillment
Poland Sp. z o.o., Wrocław